STRANDED

STRANDED

A SAMANTHA STARR THRILLER, BOOK 4

S. L. MENEAR

Book and cover design by eBook Prep
www.ebookprep.com

October, 2020
ISBN: 978-1-64457-217-7 (Large Print)

ePublishing Works!
644 Shrewsbury Commons Ave
Ste 249
Shrewsbury PA 17361
United States of America

www.epublishingworks.com
Phone: 866-846-5123

For Gal Pals: Cindy Weeks, Vicky Edwards, Barbi Leonard,
Tiesha Starkes, Sonia Díaz, Debbie Saari, and Patti Roth

ONE

Present Day, RAF Brize Norton Air Base - Oxfordshire, England

Three weeks ago, I almost destroyed the world. Destiny averted—at least for now.

I'm Samantha Starr, an American closely bonded with Great Britain. The Brits call me Sir Lady Samantha, but my friends call me Sam. My older twin brothers saddled me with the nickname Danger Magnet—a name I've been trying to ditch for years.

I earned my fourth stripe at the age of twenty-six, the only female pilot at elite Luxury International Airlines. Except for two small bombs that exploded on board during my first flight as captain last summer, the bad stuff tended to happen outside the B767. And it happened way too often—like three weeks ago in the Himalayas.

Hence my nickname.

Fears continued to haunt me about my destiny, which was tied to the ancient city of Atlantis, recently discovered underwater near Cuba.

For now, I kept my mind focused on flying the Bearcat. I turned and lined up with the runway at the RAF base in Oxfordshire. My final landing in the mighty beast was flawless, and I taxied to the parking ramp with a big smile on my face.

The deep rumble of the radial engine sputtered out as the propellers wound to a halt. My checkout in a rare two-seat WWII fighter from Duxford's Aviation Museum was complete. The tailwheel airplane sat at a nose-high angle on the pavement.

"That does it, Sir Lady Samantha. You're good to go," RAF Major Arthur Ferguson said in his sexy Scottish accent as he slid back the glass canopy.

I climbed out of the front tandem seat, stepped onto the wing walk, pulled out a rag, and lovingly wiped oil off the windshield and left side of the magnificent old airplane. Spitting oil and belching fire were part of the Bearcat's charm.

After I climbed down from the wing, I stowed the rag and shook the major's hand. "Please, call me Sam. The unique title your queen gave me should be reserved for special occasions."

"This *is* a special occasion. There hasn't been a woman pilot in this airplane since the WASPs in

World War Two." Tall and lean, with thick salt-and-pepper hair and an aristocratic bearing, the major unzipped his leather flight jacket.

The April weather was special too—unusually sunny with a few puffy clouds and balmy temperatures in the mid-sixties.

"Your VIP passenger should be here any minute. Then I'll lead you back with the museum's British bomber." He gestured at a big four-engine Avro Lancaster parked beside us. "It should be about a fifteen-minute flight to Duxford."

"I'm taking a passenger?" I scanned the ramp as I unzipped my leather flight jacket.

"An American actress, Carlene Jensen. She said she shared quite an adventure with you last fall." He pointed. "There she is."

"This Bearcat might not be big enough for her larger-than-life personality." I waved and braced for impact.

A curvy, five-foot-nothing blond bundle of dynamite in five-inch stiletto boots ran up and hugged me.

"Sam, how the hell are ya?" Carlene squealed in her high-pitched, slightly nasal Texas drawl.

"Things are finally getting back to normal." I smiled. "It's good to see you again."

"Hey, your eyes look different...still aqua," she moved closer to my face, "but now they're studded with deep blue and emerald green." She squinted. "Are you wearing colored contacts?"

"I wish it were contacts." I shook my head. "Some strange things were done to me in that Himalayan enclave." *Can't tell anyone what really happened there.*

"Huh, I don't understand how they changed the color, but I like it." She grinned. "I called our favorite copilot yesterday. Lance told me all about you and them triplet *goddesses*. Hard to believe."

"Harder to forget, but that's all over now, and I'll be back in the left seat of an airliner soon."

"Are you gonna help the Navy with that underwater city they found near Cuba?"

I shook my head. "They'll have to wait. I don't want to lose my airline job."

She glanced at the major and lowered her voice. "Any news about all the weird stuff we discovered together last fall?"

"Turns out everything we found was connected to the underwater city. Maybe you should make a movie about it."

"Is it really Atlantis?" she asked.

"Yep, definitely Atlantis. A bunch of pictures were posted on the Internet, so it's not a secret anymore. I can't wait to see it. Bet you never dreamed you'd be connected to a discovery like that." I grinned. "I know I sure didn't."

"Hot damn, girl!" She did a little happy dance. "How about helping me write a screenplay for the movie? It's sure to be a blockbuster."

"Sam should be in the movie with you," the

major broke in. "She's better looking than most movie stars—I mean, except you, of course." His face flushed from his minor faux pas.

To help him save face, I didn't acknowledge his compliment. "Sorry, Carlene, but I'm like a home-sick eagle. I need to get back to flying with the airline. And I'm sure there are plenty of experienced screenwriters who'd jump at a chance to work with a famous actress like you."

"Okay, but when the movie begins production, you have to play the airline pilot."

"Alrighty." I glanced at a serviceman as he finished topping off the Bearcat's fuel tanks. "On another subject, what brings you to merry old England?"

"I just wrapped up a bodice-rippin' medieval romance movie based on one of your mother's steamy Highlander novels." Carlene adjusted her ample bosom, displayed in a tight, low-cut red silk pullover under her unzipped leather jacket. "Good thing it's finished. Those big dresses would be hot as hell in the summer. 'Course, my dress was off more than it was on, but the dang corset smashed my titties and damn near suffocated me."

After a quick check of the airplane's fuel tanks, I turned to Carlene. "Why are you flying to Duxford with me? Are you getting ready for a World War Two movie?"

"Didn't they tell you? I'm helping you open a new wing of the aviation museum. It'll be fun. Lots of hot British men and cold French Champagne." She winked at the major. "You look sexy in that flight suit, Major."

He smiled and stood a little straighter—if that were possible. "Ready to depart, ladies?"

"Sure, what could possibly go wrong?" I grinned at them.

He handed Carlene a helmet. "Miss Jensen, we have this special helmet for you with a small video camera mounted on top. It's connected to the airplane's intercom. It'll record what you see and everything you and Sam say during the flight. Later, the video will be used to promote the museum."

"We'll have a bird's-eye view of castles and manor houses along the way," I said. "Should be fun. Just remember to be respectful of the airplane so it doesn't buck off us girly girls. It's normally flown by manly men."

"What's the big deal?" She cocked her head. "It's just an airplane."

"Oh no, *that's* just an airplane." I pointed at a C-130 cargo plane parked on the ramp. "*This* is a testosterone-filled, fire-breathing, mighty warrior of the sky."

"*Really?*" She giggled.

"Hey, it may be hard for a non-aviation person like you to understand, but this airplane has a soul. The Bearcat comes alive whenever its engine is started." I patted the side of the tall, single-engine

American fighter preserved from WWII. "You'll see."

I climbed onto the wing and into the front tandem seat while the major fussed over Carlene, strapping her in behind me.

When she was settled, I spoke into the voice-activated helmet mike, "Testing," to ensure Carlene could hear me on her helmet's intercom.

"Gotcha loud and clear," she said.

As soon as the Lancaster's engines were running, I lit the fire in the Bearcat. Its radial engine roared to life, and I slid the glass canopy forward to the closed and locked position. The airplane vibrated like an eager racehorse ready to burst from the starting gate, and its life force surged through me when I released the brakes.

"This'll be a nice, relaxing flight over the English countryside," I said as we taxied behind the perfectly restored old bomber. "Let me know if you want a closer look at anything along the way."

The major had just become airborne, and I was about to taxi onto the runway, when Carlene screamed.

"Arggh! There's a spider as big as an armadillo back here!"

"Bearcat, cleared for takeoff," the tower controller said.

"Standby, Tower, we have a problem," I said as my passenger shrieked.

"Bearcat, this is Lancaster. Is there a mechanical issue?" the major asked.

"Uh, no, the passenger has a spider issue. I'll deal with this and meet you at Duxford. I know the way. Bearcat out."

After I set the brake and opened the canopy, it took a moment to unbuckle my harness and turn around. A spider the size of a fifty-cent coin was crawling across the top of her instrument panel. Before I could do anything, she pulled a small can of hairspray out of her handbag and drowned the spider, gluing it to the panel.

I hate spiders, but my flight gloves gave me the confidence to grab the now gooey arachnid and fling it out of the cockpit.

Problem solved, or, as the Brits would say, "Done and dusted."

"You okay, Carlene?" I strapped in again.

"I was freakin' out until I remembered my secret weapon and killed the big bastard." She zipped up her bag. "Let's roll."

"Alrighty, crisis averted, although the Brits aren't going to like that hairspray on the instrument panel."

"Don't worry, it's jasmine-scented. This ol' cockpit smells better already."

"*Great.*" I closed the canopy and keyed the radio. "Bearcat ready for takeoff."

In seconds, we were airborne and headed for the Imperial War Museum Duxford. Britain's famous aviation museum was situated on its own airport where many of its vintage airplanes were flown in daily flight demonstrations for the public.

I throttled back so we could enjoy the sights below. "Check out that big castle on the right," I said, banking so Carlene could see it better.

A minute later, she said, "Ooh, look at that huge mansion on the left surrounded by all the green hills."

Not concerned about catching up to the major, I dipped the left wing for a closer look.

A loud roar rattled our canopy and shook our aircraft.

"Sonofabitch!" she screamed. "That plane almost hit us!"

"A Focke-Wulf FW190! What a beauty!" I said as it streaked over us in the clear blue sky. "Its low wings probably blocked his view."

"How can you be so calm?" Her voice had shot up two octaves. "I about had a heart attack."

"He missed us. I'm sure it was an honest mistake."

"Oh yeah? Then why the hell is he coming back?"

The Focke-Wulf had turned around and was diving straight for us. When he was too close to react, I banked sharply to the right. As he blew by, I turned on course and hoped that was the last of him.

"Do you think he's gone?" she asked.

As if on cue, he passed over us much too close and rattled our canopy again. The Bearcat snapped over in the Focke-Wulf's wake, and I righted it.

"Sam, that guy's gonna kill us! Call for help!"

My mind raced as I struggled to understand what the other pilot was trying to accomplish. Then it came to me.

"Oh geez, I get it. He's in a German World War Two fighter, and we're in an American one. He's trying to goad us into a dogfight."

"Why the hell would he do that?"

"Because that's what men do for fun. Believe me, they love playing fighter pilots."

"*Fun?*" Carlene screeched. "Our airplane don't even have guns, does it?"

"Not anymore, but I don't think he'll stop dive-bombing us until we engage with him in mock aerial combat. If we don't, the fool might accidentally kill us."

"Do you know how to dogfight?"

"Not really, but neither does he, judging by the way he flies. I can take him. The Bearcat can out-climb any piston-engine warbird." I rocked my wings as he came at us.

When we were abeam the FW190, I pulled straight up, and so did he. We easily outpaced him in the climb. I kept climbing after he lost momentum and pivoted to a nose-down attitude. Then I pivoted and zeroed in on his tail.

Caught up in the moment, I yelled, "Eat lead, *kraut heimer*!" and made machine-gun sounds. Then I dove past him, pulled up, and executed a victory roll.

Problem solved…or so I thought.

Apparently, he wanted a rematch. He charged us again and banked hard, trying to get behind us. Visions of *Top Gun* danced in my head as I turned and scanned the sky.

"Talk to me, Goose. Where is he?" I said, channeling my inner fighter pilot.

"Who you calling a goose?" she snapped.

"Oh my God, Carlene, haven't you ever seen the movie *Top Gun*?" I searched the sky, looking for the Focke-Wulf and thinking that Maverick didn't have to deal with a shrieking radar intercept officer.

"I don't like war movies unless I'm in 'em," she snapped. "When are you gonna stop this insanity and land?"

"I've got him at two o'clock. Keep him on camera in case we need evidence later." I banked toward him.

"Who the hell cares what time it is when a maniac is trying to kill us?"

"I meant his location as it relates to the positions on a clock." Good thing she was behind me and couldn't see my eye-roll. I pointed. "Twelve o'clock is directly ahead of us, six o'clock is directly behind us, and so on. Ten o'clock high would be in our front left quadrant above us. Get it?"

"In that case, he's at twelve o'clock and fixing to hit us head-on. Do something!"

Dammit, not again! I banked right and pulled up as he did the same. Like before, I got on his six and pretended to shoot him down. But this time, I dove on him and rattled his canopy before I pulled up—a taste of his own medicine.

He disappeared low over a forest.

"That should convince him to back off." I turned back on course.

"Just in case, I sent an emergency text to the major," Carlene said, her voice shaky.

"You did *what*? He might scramble fighter jets or send an SAS team in a Super Lynx. I have to call them off!" I pulled out my cell and texted him: *Disregard Mayday. Stand down. ETA 5 mins. Need alcoholic beverage for Carlene.*

"Don't tell him what happened. Let me handle it, okay?" I spotted Duxford up ahead.

"Fine, just get me the hell outta here!" she yelled. "My nerves are shot."

"I asked him to have a stiff drink ready for you when we land."

"That and a stiff man and I'll be good to go."

"I'm sure there'll be plenty of men waiting for you on the tarmac."

We landed a few minutes later.

"See? Loads of men." I pointed at a large group

of guys wearing military uniforms as we taxied to the ramp. "Remember, I'll do the talking."

I scanned the men. "Oh no, there's a Special Air Service team waiting for us. I hope their leader isn't a hard ass. I'm counting on you to charm the hell out of them."

"How're you so sure they're Special Forces?"

"Have you forgotten my boyfriend Ross is an SAS captain? Believe me, I can spot them a mile away." I sighed. "Geez, I hope they don't tell him about your emergency text."

"Relax, we didn't do nothin' wrong."

"Hold that thought." I shut down the engine. "When you take off your helmet, leave it on the seat. Maybe Major Ferguson will forget about the video recorder. I don't want to be embarrassed in front of all those fighter pilots."

Earlier at Duxford

The major stood on the ramp and scanned the sky. "Where are they?" he said to no one in particular.

His cell chimed. He pulled it out of a zippered pocket in his flight suit and read Carlene's text: *Emergency! Enemy aircraft attacking! Send help!*

"Bugger!" He glanced around, spotted the Special Air Service team, and waved them over.

The team leader, a broad-shouldered lieutenant with short brown hair and a square jaw, trotted up. "What can I do for you, Major?"

"I'm glad your team happened to be here, Lieutenant. We may have a situation."

"We're here on orders to guard Sir Lady Samantha when she arrives. Trouble seems to follow that woman wherever she goes."

"Apparently, that hasn't changed. This just came in from her passenger." The major showed him the text.

The lieutenant keyed his radio mike and called the helicopter pilot assigned to his team. "Fire up the Lynx. Are the cannons loaded?"

"Always. Wheels up in five. What's the mission?" the pilot asked.

"Intercept and rescue. An aircraft is attacking Sir Lady Samantha in the Bearcat."

"How far away is she?"

"Uh, standby." The lieutenant turned to Major Ferguson. "Where is she?"

"Probably somewhere between here and the RAF base at Oxfordshire. She was supposed to follow me, but her takeoff was delayed a few minutes."

"Think they'll have her on radar, Major?"

"Maybe not. She planned to fly low and admire the castles and whatnot. I'll go with you and point out her planned flight path to your pilot."

Just as the Lynx taxied up to them, the major felt his cell vibrate. He read the text from Sam and made a slashing motion across his neck, giving the cut-engines signal to the Lynx pilot.

The lieutenant turned to him. "What happened?"

He showed him the text.

"How do you know which one to believe?"

"The emergency text came from an excitable actress, and the stand-down message came from an airline pilot. Who would you believe?"

"Right." The lieutenant stuck his head in the Lynx and gave his men the stand-down order. "But be ready when she lands, just in case."

The SAS team stood beside a group of fighter pilots waiting to greet Sam and Carlene. It wasn't long before the major spotted the Bearcat on final approach.

"Anybody have a flask?" he asked. "The lady passenger had a bit of a fright and could use a strong drink."

Two men in civilian clothes reached into their jackets and pulled out silver flasks.

One said, "Scotch," and the other said, "Rum."

"Perfect, I'll mix the rum with a large cola from the concession stand." The major sent a soldier to buy the soft drink.

When the man returned, Ferguson poured out half the cola and replaced it with rum from the flask. "This should calm her down."

He held the drink as he watched the Bearcat taxi to the ramp.

I opened the canopy and climbed out so I could help Carlene. She dropped the video helmet on the rear seat and stepped onto the wing.

Major Ferguson stood beside the airplane with the drink in his hand. "One strong drink, as requested." He handed it up to her.

"Thanks! Good thing there's a straw. My hands are still shaking like crazy." Carlene took a big gulp. "Ooh, rum and Coke, yummy!"

He looked up at me. "Well, Sam, what happened?"

"Uh, no big deal. A guy in a Focke-Wulf buzzed us a few times." I glanced at the row of fighter pilots standing ramrod straight.

She took another big gulp and turned to me. "Whaddaya mean, *buzzed* us? He almost killed us."

The major crossed his arms. *"Really?"*

Carlene hiccupped and took a long drink. "Yeah—lucky for me, Sam's a real good fighter pilot. She shot him down twice."

"Shot him down?" he asked.

"Yeah, he forced us into one of them doggie fights," Carlene said.

He looked up at me. "You don't know how to dogfight."

"True, but my opponent knew even less, and we had the better airplane." I poked Carlene. "I am *not* a fighter pilot." I glanced sideways at the real fighter pilots.

She cocked her head. "But you told me this here's a World War Two fighter plane."

"It is."

"Well, you piloted this fighter, so that makes you a fighter pilot. Right?"

"Wrong!" I pointed at the row of men. "Those men are fighter pilots, not me. I wouldn't last five seconds in aerial combat with one of them."

"Why not?" She looked confused. "You shot down that Fuck-Wolf pilot."

"These pilots are professional predators of the sky. I'm just an airline pilot with a little aerobatic training."

Carlene stood on the wing, looking down at them. "Well, how do ya even know these guys are fighter pilots?"

"Gentlemen." I waved them forward and said to her, "Look at their eyes. Don't you see it?"

She crouched on the wing and squinted. "See what?"

"The ultra-high intensity. You'll see it in the eyes of every fighter pilot who's ever lived, and it's still there long after they retire." I elbowed her. "You must've seen it in Lance's eyes. God knows you spent plenty of time close to *his* face."

Her eyes widened. "Oh, *that!*"

"Right, see it now?"

She looked down into the nearest man's intense eyes. "Ooh, yeah, that's real sexy."

The major cleared his throat. "Best hand over the video helmet so I can see what happened."

I grabbed her drink and took a long pull. The alcohol burned my throat, and I gasped, not accustomed to hard liquor. Wine was my drink of choice —especially red.

"Uh, you don't need to see the video." I smiled. "Everything turned out okay."

"It's no trouble. I have a laptop right here. We'll plug in the camera's memory drive and watch it together." He opened the laptop on the wing.

I helped myself to another gulp.

The SAS lieutenant stepped forward. "I'll need to see that for my report."

Just then, Carlene squealed and pointed up. "He's gonna attack us again! Quick, we have to hide!"

The Focke-Wulf flew over us.

I grabbed her arm. "Calm down. He'll never recognize us."

"Why the hell not?"

"We were wearing helmets. And if he comes over here looking for the Bearcat's pilots, I guarantee you he won't be looking for two blond bimbos." I pointed at the fighter pilots. "He'll assume it was two of them."

"Good." She grabbed the drink and took another swig.

I glanced down at the major. "Please tell me that FW190 doesn't belong to the museum."

He glanced in its direction as it wobbled around the landing pattern. "Nope, not an authentic paint scheme. Must be privately owned."

"Thank God for small favors." I wondered if the Focke-Wulf would survive the unstable-looking approach.

The major's voice hardened. "Hand over the video, Sam."

I sighed and handed him the helmet cam. "Would one of you handsome gents please help me down?" Anything to distract them from the embarrassing video.

Several men reached for me, but the SAS officer elbowed them aside. "You're the pilot. Can't you get down without help?"

"I could, but what would be the fun in that?" I grinned, trying to soften his stiff attitude.

I failed.

A total hard ass, he looked peeved when he lifted me down from the wing.

The major helped Carlene down, and then he plugged the memory drive into the laptop. The video began playing, and I wished I could disappear as the fighter pilots crowded around us.

There were collective gasps the first time the Focke-Wulf buzzed us. But as the dogfight progressed, the snickers grew louder. Soon, raucous laughter drowned out the Focke-Wulf's engine as it taxied closer to us.

The major leaned in to me and said, "Eat lead, *kraut heimer?*"

"I got caught up in the moment," I said, blushing.

By then, the men were laughing so hard I was almost worried they might hurt themselves. They barely noticed when the FW190 parked beside the Bearcat.

Carlene elbowed me. "What do ya think he'll look like?"

I shrugged. "He's probably a typical civilian warbird pilot with way more money than flying skills. He'll be short, bald, and wearing a fancy flight suit with lots of important-looking patches. He'll have it unzipped halfway down his chest, revealing a heavy gold chain or two around his neck, and he'll have a big gold watch and a diamond pinky ring."

A few minutes later, a man matching my description stomped over to our group and scanned the men. "I demand to know who was flying that Bearcat!"

Carlene's jaw dropped. "Whoa, Sam, you nailed it right down to the pinky ring! How'd you know?"

I glanced at the major and Lt. Hard Ass. "She's new to aviation." I turned to her. "If you spend enough time at aviation events, you'll see that some things are quite predictable."

The slightly paunchy little bald guy glared at me, annoyed I'd interrupted him. "Well, who flew this airplane?" He thrust his hands onto his broad hips.

The fighter pilots grinned and pointed at Carlene and me.

One of them said, "The blondes flew it in. What's your problem?"

The major put Carlene behind him, and the lieutenant did the same with me. He gave me a stern look and said, "I'll handle this."

I knew better than to argue with an alpha male. I said, "Okay," and peeked out from behind him.

The Focke-Wulf pilot said, "I want those women arrested. They're a danger to the public."

The major crossed his arms. "Really? What did they do?"

"They tried to kill me with that airplane." He jutted out his chin. "And they made me late for this event. They should be locked up."

"Are you sure about that? We have the entire encounter on video." He smirked and hit the PLAY button.

Oh God, not a replay!

When the video finished amidst more loud snickers, the bald guy said, "Those bitches must've turned off the camera during the part when they forced me into a dogfight."

Carlene and I shoved our protectors aside and dived at the nasty little jerk, our claws extended. Strong hands grabbed my waist and yanked me back, my long legs kicking at air.

Carlene managed to get in one good slash before the major pulled her off.

Just then, a stretch Rolls-Royce limousine pulled up, and a man in a tuxedo stepped out and grinned. "Ladies and gents, the Bollinger is chilled. Everyone ready for the opening ceremony?"

The lieutenant released me. I gasped when another man exited the limo. Short and balding, my nemesis, Lord Edgar Sweetwater, looked enough like the Focke-Wulf pilot to be a relative.

His cold, dark eyes were riveted on me. "Lovely to see you again, Sir Lady Samantha." He cocked his head. "Interesting contacts—makes your eyes look mysterious."

I didn't correct him; I was pretty sure he didn't know I'd been in the enclave.

Sweetwater glanced from me to Carlene. "Please introduce me to your beautiful friend."

Carlene had heard about Sweetwater's evil exploits, but she'd never met him.

When I made the introduction, she said, "Wait a minute!" and yanked her hand away as he was about to kiss it. "Aren't you the guy who kidnapped Sam—twice?"

"Allegedly." Sweetwater smirked at me. "That has never been proven."

I nudged the hard ass. "Now would be a good time to shoot him."

Major Ferguson stepped forward. "That would

be ill advised. Lord Sweetwater is the primary donor for the new wing of the museum."

Sweetwater and I locked eyes.

Oh God, what fresh hell does he have planned for me this time?

TWO

The chauffeur held the limo door open. "Ladies, may we give you a lift to the festivities?"

The distance across the broad concrete ramp to the new hangar was about the length of a football field.

I glared at Sweetwater. "No, thank you, we'll walk with the Special Forces team."

Sweetwater disappeared inside the gleaming silver Rolls-Royce.

Carlene latched onto a tall sergeant with a body like an Australian *Thunder from Down Under* dancer. (Not that I've seen them dance in Vegas more than a few dozen times.)

"You'll escort me, won't you darlin'?" she said.

He smiled and flexed his biceps. "Of course, Miss Jensen."

"I'll meet you in the new hangar," the major said as he slipped inside the limo.

The Focke-Wulf pilot followed him and slammed the door.

I grabbed Lt. Hard Ass's arm. "Hang back until they leave. We need to call Captain Sinclair."

He raised a brow. "What for? I'm in charge here. Don't you think my team can protect you?"

"Maybe, if you understood the situation." I watched Sweetwater's fancy limo glide away.

"You're afraid of a chubby little bald guy?" He crossed his arms. "*Seriously*?"

I pulled out my cell and called my boyfriend. When he answered, I hit SPEAKER.

"Sam? Is everything all right?" His deep voice had an edge.

"Ross, I have you on speaker. Sorry to bother you in the middle of maneuvers, but this is an emergency. Sweetwater is here. He's the primary donor for the new wing of the aviation museum at Duxford." I tried to sound calm.

"Has he seen you?"

"He took great pleasure in taunting me. By the way, Carlene Jensen is with me."

"I hope to hell you're with the London team."

"Yep, the team leader is standing next to me, but he doesn't seem to grasp the gravity of the situation."

"What's his name?"

I held my phone in front of the lieutenant, who'd never told me his name.

"This is Lieutenant Bryce Manning, Captain Sinclair. Your girlfriend is upset that Sweetwater is here, but I assured her…"

"Call for reinforcements now," Ross interrupted. "There's a high probability the event you're attending will be attacked by mercenaries. Their primary objective will be to capture or kill Sam, and they won't care how many people die in the process."

"You're sure of this?" Bryce asked.

"Aye, Lord Sweetwater is a billionaire arms dealer who considers Sam his number-one enemy. He employs a small army, and his attendance there is no coincidence. Watch him closely. If he leaves, that means an attack is imminent," Ross said.

"Captain, how will I explain calling for reinforcements without any hard intel?"

"Just keep your team tight around Sam and Carlene. I'll call our DSF in Credenhill and ask him to send more teams. Sam, stick close to him and be ready for the assault."

"But Ross, I don't have a weapon."

"Manning, give her a pistol. I'm vouching for her. I'll call General Barnes now." Ross ended the call.

Bryce's eyes bored into me. "What aren't you telling me?"

"Plenty, but we don't have time for a full recap. Suffice it to say Sweetwater doesn't like to lose, and I've cost him millions. I also foiled a plot that had taken him years to set up. Revenge is his favorite activity." I touched his arm. "This could get deadly real fast."

He sighed and pulled a Glock 26 out of his boot and handed it to me. "It has ten in the magazine and one in the chamber." He handed me an extra magazine. "Ever killed anyone?"

"More than I care to admit, but most of them weren't killed with bullets." I ejected the magazine, checked that it was full, reinserted it, and eased the slide back far enough to verify there was a round in the chamber.

His eyes widened. "Really? How many?"

"Too many to count, but all were in self-defense and the defense of others. I'm sure you understand."

He looked at me like I'd suddenly transformed into a stranger. "All right then, stick close to me."

I called to Carlene, "Stay close to the soldiers. We might be in for a rough time."

She nodded at my Glock. "I assume you don't mean the fun kind?"

"Nope. Sorry."

She held out her hand. "I want one too."

I nudged Bryce. "Carlene was the East Texas Pistol Champion. You can trust her with a weapon."

She grinned. "Don't worry, sugar, I can shoot flies off a watermelon at twenty paces."

He crossed his arms. "Not after all the rum you drank. Besides, shooting people is quite different from shooting flies or paper targets."

She thrust out her chin. "I'll have you know I've shot plenty of people."

"*Really*? Who'd you shoot?"

"Last fall, I shot a bunch of bad guys who attacked us during our round-the-world charter flight with Sam—and my ex-husband still has a bullet scar on his ass from when I caught him humpin' Becky Sue Harper." She glanced at me. "Right, Sam?"

"Carlene's not that drunk, and I'd trust her to have my back in a shootout." I nodded at her. "I've seen her in action, and she never misses."

Bryce sucked in his breath. "Don't make me regret this." He motioned to the soldier with Carlene. "Sergeant, loan this woman your spare pistol."

The soldier handed Carlene the weapon, and she checked the magazine and racked the slide.

"Let's roll." She stuck the Glock 26 in her jacket pocket and resumed strolling toward the new hangar with her hot escort.

"Eh, Bryce, shouldn't we come up with a defensive plan? There's only four of you, plus Carlene and me. If the mercs show up before reinforcements arrive…"

"My men know what to do. Just follow my orders and you'll be fine."

I sighed and followed Lt. Hard Ass into the new hangar.

The spotless painted concrete floor sparkled in the bright overhead lights. Sweetwater was holding court in the center, where a buffet table was adorned with aircraft ice sculptures and sterling platters piled high with delicious looking gourmet meats and vegetables. Several linen-covered tables and padded chairs bordered the buffet. Waiters with silver trays of Bollinger Champagne in crystal flutes circulated through the crowd of dignitaries. Captains of industry mingled with members of the nobility, fashion models, and movie stars.

Newly restored airplanes representing military aircraft from early designs up to WWII airplanes in use at the end of the war stood proudly throughout the giant hangar. A German Me-262 twin-engine jet fighter with a swastika on the tail looked ready to takeoff. If the war had lasted longer, that jet might've turned the tide in Germany's favor. A Russian Yak-9 sported blue and gray camouflage paint with the distinctive red stars on the tail and sides of the aft fuselage. A satin ribbon stretched between the two venerable WWII fighters, ready for us to cut it, and an oak pedestal table under the ribbon held two pairs of gold-plated scissors.

I worried that a gun battle would ruin all these rare and beautiful airplanes, not to mention what could happen to all the VIPs. I longed for a return to normalcy in the left seat of a Boeing 767. Flying for Luxury International Airlines was far less stressful than what I'd been through the past several months. I'd be back in the cockpit soon if I managed to survive this day.

I glanced at the podium. Sweetwater made a brief speech about preserving military aircraft and their role in world history.

"And now, Sir Lady Samantha Starr and Actress Carlene Jensen will cut the ribbon," the MC said.

We faced each other with our scissors poised and simultaneously cut the red satin ribbon. As everyone cheered, I glanced around and couldn't see Sweetwater anywhere.

I turned and looked through the open hangar door just as his Rolls pulled away.

Uh oh.

I glanced around at all the people and airplanes, searching for a plan that would avoid bloodshed and destruction if Sweetwater's mercenaries burst in. *Dammit! No one would be in danger if I weren't here.* I focused on the smallest member of the four-man SAS team. He was my height—five-nine—and lean but broad-shouldered.

I grabbed Carlene and faced the soldier. "We can avoid an attack here, but I'll need your help."

Bryce was right behind me. "And just what did you have in mind, Sam?"

"I'm about the same size as this guy." I smiled at the soldier. "What's your name?"

"Kyle."

"Kyle, I'll wear your uniform and sneak out before the mercs arrive, which might be any minute. You and Carlene will be undressed in the back office, pretending to fool around. The soldiers will waste time searching for us, allowing me time to get away."

"I can't do that," Kyle said. "I'm on duty."

Bryce frowned. "What is Kyle supposed to wear?"

"He can put on my flight suit after the soldiers find him. It might be a little tight in the shoulders, but it'll fit. When they discover I'm gone, there'll be no reason for them to hurt anyone."

Carlene slid her hands up Kyle's muscular chest. "Fine with me, but we don't need to *pretend* anything." She nibbled his ear and grinned.

Kyle stiffened and took a step back.

"Forget it, Miss Jensen," Bryce said. "This is a potential combat situation."

"When the mercs ask about my whereabouts, tell them I was last seen in the ladies' room." I glanced from Kyle to Bryce. "This way, there won't be any shooting."

Bryce's eyes skewered me. After a brief pause, he said, "Fine, but I'm going with you." He waved the hot sergeant over and said, "We have a plan for Kyle to switch clothes with Sam and pretend to bed Carlene in the back office so Sam and I can sneak out. We're trying to avoid a shootout with Sweetwater's soldiers, so tell Chris not to fire unless fired upon. If they ask about Sam, say she went to the restroom. Got it?"

The sergeant frowned, clearly disappointed he wasn't the one chosen to get undressed with Carlene. "Aye, sir, understood."

"Sorry, sugar, but you're too tall and muscular to fit in Sam's flight suit." Carlene gave him a soft kiss.

"The office is near the restrooms." I grabbed Kyle's arm. "Let's hurry."

Carlene grabbed his other arm like we were headed off for a threesome. Bryce hung back and watched the hallway, and the sergeant and other soldier remained vigilant in the hangar.

I shrugged out of my flight suit and stood in lacy red undies—my attempt to stay connected to my femininity, and Carlene stripped down to her sheer pink bra and panties.

Kyle stood frozen in visual overload. It was obvious he wasn't comfortable with my unorthodox plan.

"Hey, Kyle! Hurry up and strip. We may not have much time." I handed him my flight suit.

I hung onto my leather bomber jacket with the call sign "Bombshell" emblazoned on the left breast. My brother Matt's Navy fighter squadron had given it to me after I landed a Boeing 727 on their aircraft carrier, and that jacket meant a lot to me.

Carlene helped Kyle get undressed while I put on his uniform. She was quite adept at peeling off a man's clothes.

Usually, SAS soldiers wore all-black uniforms and black helmets with tinted visors to look extra intimidating. But this was supposed to be a fun event with lots of dignitaries, so the team wore camouflage fatigues and matching berets. I stuffed my hair into the beret and buttoned the shirt.

By the time I was fully dressed, Kyle was dancing around in his boxers, struggling to fend off Carlene. An aggressive maneater, she was accustomed to getting her way.

I pulled a tapestry off the wall. "Get under this and wait for the assault."

Bryce met me in the hall. He followed me inside the ladies' room and guarded the door, while I opened the window and shoved an upturned trash bin under it.

"One more thing." I stepped into a toilet stall, locked the door, and slid out under it. "Maybe the locked stall and window ploy will slow them down. Let's go."

Bryce led me to a door in the back of the hangar. We slipped out and sprinted to an employee lot where we found a Triumph 800XC dirt bike with a helmet on the dual seat.

"I'll look for a key in the saddlebags." I unbuckled the left bag.

He raised a brow. "You're wasting time." He pulled out his combat knife to work on hotwiring the ignition.

I found a key in a zippered side compartment. "Try this." I handed him the key.

He stuck it in the ignition, turned it, and hit the start button. The engine purred.

"I'll drive so you can shoot at bad guys." I pulled the big helmet on over my beret and straddled the bike.

He stood with his hands on his hips. "Are you sure you can handle one of these?"

"I rode one exactly like this in Scotland last summer, and I have a Ducati Diavel back home." I revved the engine. "Let's go."

We zoomed out of the lot and raced south on the two-lane highway. After a few minutes, I glanced back toward the airfield and spotted four unmarked black helicopters converging on Duxford.

Damn!

I turned off onto a dirt path and sped deep into a forest to give us cover from the helicopters. We parked under a huge oak tree surrounded by mature trees and bushes.

"We can shove the bike inside these bushes and hide up in that tree until your buddies from Credenhill arrive." I pointed up at the old, well-formed boughs in the oak.

"No one will know we're here until I call them." Bryce sat sideways on the Triumph's seat. "We can relax."

"If only that were true." I shook my head. "When the mercenaries discover I'm not at Duxford, they'll come looking for me in their well-armed helicopters. Their infrared sensors will paint us and the warm motorcycle engine, and then they'll send men to investigate."

He studied the tree. "The density of surrounding trees and bushes will prevent the enemy shooting from a distance at an angle. We'll wait from above and take them out when they enter the kill zone."

"My thoughts exactly, and your SAS mates will know our position thanks to my new watch with a GPS locator." I tapped the DOXA dive watch DARPA had sent me last week. It replaced the one Sweetwater had thrown in the ocean a few months ago.

I pulled back some branches so he could shove our stolen bike into the bushes. Then we arranged the branches to cover it. Afterward, I unbuckled my helmet strap.

He glanced at me. "May as well keep the helmet on in case you fall out of the tree."

"Seriously? I admit I tend to be a danger magnet, but I'm *not* a klutz. And I'll aim better without this oversized helmet obstructing my view." I pulled it off, shoved it into the bush, and rearranged my hair inside the beret.

The helmet maneuver earned me an angry glare. He stood next to the oak tree. "Ready? I'll give you a boost up."

I climbed up and found a thick branch protruding from the west side of the trunk. It had lots of side branches and would protect me from bullets fired upward. Bryce settled opposite me on the east side of the trunk so we could cover both sides of the tree. It wasn't long before we heard the thumping blades of an approaching helicopter.

We rechecked our weapons and waited in silence.

Fifteen minutes passed before the helicopter flew over us. It hovered above us and then flew a short distance away, probably to land in the open field bordering the forest.

"They're coming," he whispered. "Wait until I fire."

"Understood." I peered down from the wide bough, my heart hammering my chest.

It wasn't long before men seemed to materialize out of nowhere. They crept closer, slowly moving from tree to tree as they focused their green laser sights on the bush with the motorcycle. Their leader held up a fist, signaling stop. Looking out from behind a nearby tree, he swung his MP7 with an infrared scope upward and paused with it pointed at our hiding place.

"We have you surrounded. No use being a hero. Send the woman down and we'll let you live. Nobody needs to die today." Speaking with a Russian accent, he had his face covered with a balaclava like the other men who briefly peeked out from behind trees.

There were six of them.

I knew my boyfriend and his team well enough to know that SAS soldiers *never* back down or give up. Bryce would be the same. This had to be a one-shot-one-kill mission for us if we had any chance of surviving.

"You've got five seconds to send her down or we start shooting. One...two...three...four..."

When the leader peeked out, Bryce took him out with a head shot.

Another guy leaned out for a shot, and Bryce put a bullet in his head too.

I ducked as they sprayed our tree with bullets. When they paused to reload, I shot a guy under me and a man to his right. They must've thought they were safe on my side of the tree, having assumed I wasn't armed.

Now it was two against two, but not for long.

They blasted out another barrage of bullets our way and then ducked behind trees.

When the guy on my side peeked out, I shot him. Bryce hit the other guy. I still had eight rounds in my Glock and another full magazine.

"What now?" I whispered.

"Stay here. I'll climb down and hand the weapons up to you. They're sure to send more men when this team fails to report." He dropped down and gathered the weapons.

In a few minutes, we had six MP7 submachine guns with extra magazines and six Sig Sauer pistols. I piled the pistols on my lap. The MP7s had straps, so they were easier to manage.

Bryce slung the nearest dead guy over his shoulder and carried him up into a nearby tree. He did the same with all the bodies, distributing them in several trees on our perimeter.

He climbed back up to me. "Let's hope they get here while the bodies are still warm. They won't know where to shoot."

I handed him three MP7s and waited for him to sling them over his broad shoulders. Then I gave him extra magazines. I still had all the pistols on my lap. "Do you want any of these?"

"Give me four. It's times like this when all my zippered pockets come in handy. Use the thigh pockets for the pistols and the extra mags." He pointed as he began shoving weapons in pockets. Then he pulled out his cell and sent a text to Ross, even though he'd already know our location from my GPS watch.

A reply came back almost instantly. "They know we're here. Ross said to hold out a few more minutes. Uh, Sam, have you ever fired an MP7?"

"Yeah, I've had a lot of experience with MP5s and MP7s."

"Were you in the military?"

"No, but I have twin brothers in the U.S. Navy. One's a SEAL and the other is a fighter pilot. They taught me a lot. So did Ross." No need to tell him they had nothing to do with my automatic weapons expertise. Too long a story.

Our quiet conversation was interrupted by the thundering blades of several helicopters. I prayed they were from the SAS headquarters in Credenhill.

Trees shook, and their leaves fluttered like crazy as deafening rotor blades filled the forest with artificial thunder. The sun sank low on the horizon, darkening the kill zone.

"Oh God, it sounds like the other three helicopters are overhead. If each one has the same number of men as the first team, we'll be up against eighteen bad guys," I said.

"Relax, we have the high ground and automatic weapons with plenty of ammo. Just sit tight and wait." He sounded calm and confident. "The warm bodies will confuse them. Be ready to open fire when I do."

I'd had plenty of experience with SAS soldiers. One thing they had in common was fearlessness in combat. Me...not so much.

"Okay, I'll fire the submachine guns first and hope we don't run out of ammo before the good guys arrive." I arranged the shoulder straps so I could easily switch weapons.

"About that," he said. "When you hear more helicopters arrive, hunker down behind these thick limbs and stay out of the line of fire while our guys destroy the enemy."

"Uh, they know not to shoot up in this tree, right?"

"Yes, but we don't want to confuse anyone by firing while they engage the enemy."

"Understood." I held an MP7 and tried not to tremble.

Enemy combatants moved silently through the bushes and trees, their green laser sights searching for us. They pointed their weapons at the bodies arranged in the trees. It seemed like the ruse was working.

Then blood dripped onto a nearby soldier, and he focused on the body in the tree above him. He must've recognized the face. He said, "Our missing team is in the trees. I think they're all dead. Victor's up there, dripping blood."

Another soldier said, "There are eight targets.

Figure out which two aren't dead. Try to take the woman alive."

It wasn't long before all the lasers were pointed in our direction. They couldn't aim without peeking out from behind the trees.

Bryce opened fire, taking out two men in seconds and wounding some of the others. I sprayed the men on my side with bullets. Two went down. The others ducked back behind trees.

They fanned out slowly and flanked us, firing from all directions while we took cover behind the thick boughs. I didn't dare peek out with bullets splintering the wood near me. They seemed to be focusing all their fire in one place on the underside of my tree limb. Could their bullets cut down the branch?

The sound of fast-approaching helicopters was nearly lost in the fusillade of automatic weapons firing. We waited until some of them had to reload. When there was a pause, we peeked out and took aim.

I managed to nail two more bad guys when they poked their heads out, and Bryce took out four in rapid fire. Then the barrage started again. My branch made a cracking sound and dropped two inches.

I barely heard Bryce say, "Stay down."

The forest lit up with gunfire like strobe lights flashing on the trees. SAS teams surrounded the enemy and a fierce battle ensued. The deafening gunfire didn't last long. After a brief silence, I heard several men shout, "Clear!"

The forest was silent again. Then my boyfriend yelled, "Manning, report!"

"We're in the big oak. The other bodies up in the trees are dead."

I leaned my head around the trunk and looked at Bryce. His shoulder was soaked with blood.

"You're bleeding!" Shaking, I lurched up, heard a loud crack, and fell out of the tree as my branch split in half.

Luckily, Ross was standing below us and caught me.

"Sweetheart, are you all right?"

Bryce dropped down and looked at me. "You should've worn the helmet."

"Ross, call an air ambulance. Bryce has been shot!"

They replied simultaneously, "It's just a graze."

My eyes filled with water and my lips quivered. "B-but he's bleeding."

Ross set me down and said to Bryce, "She gets really upset if one of us is injured. Best let her make a fuss or she'll never stop blubbering." He kissed my forehead and handed me a handkerchief.

I unbuttoned Bryce's shirt and pulled it down. A bullet had grazed his left shoulder, leaving a bloody groove. I blotted the wound gently with the folded handkerchief and looked up at him. "Does it hurt a lot?"

"I didn't even notice it until you pointed it out." He stroked my cheek. "Relax, Sam, it's nothing."

I sighed and hugged him. "I'm really sorry you got shot. Thanks for saving me."

He smiled. "I couldn't have done it without you." He nodded at Ross. "Your girlfriend is one hell of a warrior. I'd go into battle with her at my side any day."

Ross pulled me into his arms. "Lately, she's had more combat experience than most soldiers. We need to figure out a way to put a stop to that." He hugged me and kissed the nape of my neck, sending shivers down my spine. The good kind.

I looked up at Ross. "Do you know if Carlene and the rest of Bryce's team are all right?"

"They're fine. When Sweetwater's men realized you weren't there, they left without firing a shot." He nodded at Bryce. "That was a good plan."

"Actually, the whole thing was Sam's idea. I was worried about taking her away from my team, but it all turned out okay, thanks to you chaps." He shook hands with some of the men.

Ross glanced around at all the dead mercenaries. "Sam, the body count around you keeps getting higher. We need to stop Sweetwater, permanently."

"I wish I could've shot the bastard at Duxford. I'm sick and tired of him targeting me, and I hate having to kill people. I want this to end." My hands were shaking.

"The DSF told me MI5 has been trying to find a legal way to stop him," Ross said.

Bryce had been listening. "There's another option. If you need volunteers for a black ops mission to make him disappear, I'm up for it."

"Thanks. I'll look into it, but first we have to deal with this mess." Ross waved at the twenty-four bodies. He pulled out his cell and called General Barnes.

After a mostly one-sided conversation with the Director of Special Forces, Ross pocketed his cell. "The other teams will head back to base. My team will escort you and Bryce back to his team and Carlene. Then we'll all go to Credenhill for the debrief."

A Super Lynx took us back to Duxford, and Bryce's team met us on the ramp.

I glanced from Carlene to Kyle. The poor guy looked like Carlene had put him through the ringer. His hair was tussled and he had on my flight suit but was unable to zip it up over his broad chest. "Looks like those two were in a different kind of combat."

Kyle said to Bryce, "Next time, send me into battle and you stay with the hellcat."

Carlene shrugged innocently and grinned.

Bryce and I took a few minutes to wash up in

the restrooms, and then Kyle and I swapped clothes. His uniform was dirty with a smidgen of blood, and my flight suit smelled like Carlene's perfume.

We boarded two Super Lynx helicopters with the teams and flew to the SAS headquarters in Credenhill.

After a tedious debriefing, I said my goodbyes to Carlene, Bryce, and his team. Then Ross and I flew back to Scotland where he lived in a castle built by his ancestors.

We snuggled up in front of a roaring fire in his study, and he lit a fire inside me that slowly built into a blazing inferno. Afterward, we sipped merlot, and I nibbled on chocolate truffles. My man knew everything I needed to calm my jangled nerves.

"Has anyone called my mom or Duncan? I don't want them to hear about us on TV and worry." I pulled out my cell.

"I thought it best to wait until I had you back in Scotland. Call her now." Ross kissed the top of my head.

My mother was staying with her boyfriend, Laird Duncan MacLeod, at his huge castle near Craigervie. Wedding bells were definitely in their future. Mom had been a widow for five years when she met Duncan, the spitting image of a Highland chieftain on the cover of one of her steamy medieval romance novels. He was perfect for her, and Ross was perfect for me.

Ross's castle was smaller than Duncan's, but it had a moat and drawbridge. He was laird of the Sinclair clan, although he rarely used his title. He took pride in his rank as a captain in the UK's elite Special Forces.

I called Mom's cell and hit the SPEAKER button. "Hi, Mom, I'm with Ross at his place, safe and sound, so disregard anything you might see on the nightly news or read in tomorrow's paper."

"What happened?" Her voice cracked.

"I was in a little dustup with Sweetwater's mercenaries, but the SAS ruined their day."

"Tell Ross thank you for saving my only daughter, yet again."

"No worries, Loren. We're working on a plan to end Sweetwater's attacks," Ross said.

"Good. The sooner the better. That man is pure evil. And Ross, we want you both here for dinner before Sam flies back to the States."

"Count on it. We'll see you soon." Ross clicked END and pulled me close.

Whenever I was in his arms, everything felt safe and good. If only that feeling could last when I returned home to Florida in two days and resumed my airline career.

THREE

Palm Beach, Florida

After having been away from the cockpit for the past six months, I completed mandatory re-qualification training in the B767 flight simulator. I just needed one sequence of passenger flights with a check captain before I could resume my regular flight schedule.

My boss, Chief Pilot Jeff Rowlin, who was tall, blond, and Nordic-looking, was in the copilot's seat. He'd observe my return to flying and sign me off after this multi-day trip.

I eased the 767's throttles forward and taxied to the active runway at Palm Beach International Airport.

"Luxury 422, cleared for takeoff, runway 10 left," the tower controller said.

"Luxury 422 is cleared for takeoff, runway 10 left," Jeff replied with a deep Texas twang as I pulled onto the runway and slid the throttles up to takeoff power.

Jeff liked to maintain the hands-on proficiency of his pilots, so we started every flight sequence using manual controls up to cruise altitude and again during approach and landing. I eased back on the yoke, and we climbed into the sunny Florida sky, our charter flight destined for Hong Kong with an overnight stop first in San Francisco.

My employer, Luxury International Airlines, was unique in the airline world. Our 767 jumbo jets were configured with one hundred fully-reclining seats, each covered in butter-soft leather and ensconced in large private cubicles with comprehensive individual entertainment centers and free in-flight phones.

Gourmet food, premium alcoholic beverages, entertainment options, and posh bathrooms with showers were included in the ticket price. The intent was to be even more appealing than a typical private jet by offering an ultra-luxurious experience with one flight attendant for every ten passengers in the roomy atmosphere of a jumbo jet.

After we leveled off at cruise altitude, Jeff said, "What's the deal with your eyes?" He stared a moment. "Are those colored contacts?"

"I'm not wearing contacts." I sighed. "My eyes

were affected by what happened to me in the Himalayas."

He raised a brow. "But how could your eyes change color?"

"Impossible to explain." *And I don't want anyone to know the truth.*

He chuckled. "I should know by now that abnormal is *your* norm. That reminds me, Max isn't happy you returned to flying. He wants you on *Leviathan*, helping him deal with all the weird stuff underwater in Atlantis."

"Sorry, but your son and the Navy will have to wait. They have no right to screw with my airline career." I glanced down as we passed over portions of the southern states west of Florida. "Damn, I really missed flying."

"I'm happy to have you back, Sam. I hate breaking in new hires. We have a nice mix of seasoned pilots who all get along great." He grinned. "Why mess with perfection?"

I smiled, nodding. "I owe you and Lance free drinks for life after your stealth mission in that floatplane over Atlantis. Not many people could've pulled that off. You really saved my butt." I reached over and patted his shoulder. "Thanks, Boss."

"We did what we could, but most of the credit should go to Ross. Now I understand why you chose a badass warrior for your boyfriend." He chuckled. "Seems like he spends most of his time rescuing you."

"Yeah, well, I intend to avoid all that nonsense from now on. Usually the bad stuff happens when I'm *not* in an airliner." I took a sip of bottled water and checked our course.

"By the way, Lance will be our relief pilot for the long flight to Hong Kong," Jeff said. "He's meeting us in San Francisco."

"Great—I haven't seen him since we landed that top-secret 727 you-know-where."

He nodded. "Um, I guess you know he has a thing for you."

"Nah, Lance just loves women, especially blondes." I twirled my long ponytail. "And he's a chick magnet, so women fawn over him everywhere he goes."

"Yeah, but *you* don't, so keep it that way, and respect his feelings. Don't give him false hope."

I raised a hand. "Hey, no problem here. I really like Lance, but he knows I'm in love with Ross. And you guys won't have to worry about me stumbling into danger again. From now on, I'll be extra careful everywhere I go."

"And stay out of curio shops in Hong Kong." He chuckled.

"You don't have to tell me twice. In fact, I'm seriously considering staying in my hotel room in Hong Kong so I don't risk running into Dragon Master again."

"Oh, right, I forgot about him. Wasn't he there

when our military bombed the shit out of the en-clave?" Jeff asked.

"Nope, but he's the one who pulled me into that mess." I shook my head. "I definitely don't want to see him again."

He blew out a sigh. "I sure am glad that crisis is over."

"You and me both." I held up my water bottle like a toast. "Here's to boring flights and dull overnights."

Jeff laughed. "I'll second that."

San Francisco, California

Jeff and I walked into the restaurant in our layover hotel, and I breathed in aromas of fresh-baked bread and sizzling steaks. Lance waved at us from across the dining room. We weaved our way through the linen-covered tables and joined him. He stood and pulled back my chair, always a gentleman.

Lance Bowie was the epitome of tall, dark, and handsome with liquid-green eyes and a sexy Texas accent.

I had to admit there was something special about Texas men—at least all the ones I'd met. They seemed to have a deep sense of honor and an easygoing atti-tude with tons of swagger. And Texas men had more than their share of tall genes. Jeff was at least six-four,

51

and with his blond hair and blue eyes, he looked like a Viking. So did his son, Max. Fun guys, including Lance, but also the kind who would always have your back. I was fortunate to have friends like them.

"Sam, it's good to see you." Lance's face reddened. "Okay if I give you a hug?"

"Of course." I reached for him, wondering why he looked embarrassed. "Something wrong?"

"Um, well, no, it's just that a lot has happened since the last time I saw you." Lance shot a glance at Jeff, then he gave me a quick hug and froze. "What the hell happened to your eyes?"

I blew out a sigh. "Hard to explain, but I'm okay. Thanks for helping save my butt again." I kissed his cheek and sat beside him. *What was he hiding?*

"Anything for you, darlin'." He glanced at Jeff again and mouthed, "WTF?"

I wanted to take the attention off me. "Did you guys meet the triplets?"

Lance blushed again, and his eyes filled with panic.

Jeff said, "I never met them, but they spent some time on my son's ship, and Lance met them in Key West when they were there with your brothers."

"My brothers were totally smitten with the redhead and the brunette for a while. They fooled me too." I looked into Lance's eyes. "What did you think when you met them?"

He swallowed hard. "I couldn't get used to how much they looked like you. It was bizarre. And they kept talking telepathically about us to each other. Then they'd giggle, and Mike would scold them about using telepathy."

"But did you like them?" I asked.

Lance hesitated. "They seemed okay at first, and like you said, Mike and Matt were hot for Blaze and Luna."

"Everyone said Solraya looked exactly like me and was pretending to be me. I never saw her in person. Did you think she was me?"

Lance turned crimson. "Yeah, at first, but so did your brothers. My first clue should've been when she didn't ask to fly my newly acquired L-39 jet."

"Ooh, you bought an L-39?" I couldn't hide my excitement.

"She's a real beauty and flies like a dream." He grinned. "You're welcome to fly her when we get back to Florida."

"Thanks, Lance, I'd love to." I couldn't help wondering what he wasn't telling me about Solraya.

A waiter appeared, handed us menus, and took drink orders.

"So, what are you ordering for dinner, Lance?" I asked.

"The porterhouse with sweet potatoes and green beans. The steaks here are always super tender." He grinned.

"I think I'll go for the ribeye with the Caesar

salad. What about you, Jeff?"

"The New York strip, nice and lean. Better get your red meat before Hong Kong. Steak prices there are insane." Jeff shook his head.

"Yeah, especially since I'll probably just order room service so I can avoid trouble on our layover." I nodded at Jeff.

"That's ridiculous! You don't have to stay in the hotel. You can hang out with us. We'll keep you out of trouble." Lance glanced at Jeff. "Right?"

"That didn't work out so well last time you two were in Hong Kong." Jeff arched his brow. "Weren't you with her when she met Dragon Master? Remember he gave her that artifact? Then the shootout? Months of chaos?"

"Yeah, but the bad guys are dead now, so no worries." Lance patted my hand. "Sam will be fine."

I shrugged. "Dragon Master might still be in Hong Kong."

"The old guy with the Fu Manchu mustache? His masters are all dead, and he closed his curio shop right after he gave you the artifact. He's probably long gone and happy to be free of the Atlanteans." Lance took a swig of his beer. "Seriously, you should be safe now."

"I hope you're right. I'm looking forward to a calm, normal life for a change."

Jeff laughed. "There's never been anything normal about *your* life."

"Yeah, there's a good reason your brothers nicknamed you Danger Magnet." Lance chuckled. "But seriously, you should be okay in Hong Kong, unless…" He let his last word hang in the air.

"Unless what?" I didn't like the worried look in his eyes.

Almost in a whisper, Lance asked, "Uh, the Chinese don't know about that Himalayan enclave, right?"

"How would they know that?"

He leaned closer. "A couple of weeks ago, you told me on the phone that the Chinese army came after you on the Nepal border where the rescue team landed their paragliders. Could they have recognized you?"

I thought for a second. "I was wearing a long golden robe, which probably attracted their attention, and my face and hair were uncovered. But even if their soldiers got a good look at me, they didn't survive the flood."

Jeff leaned forward and asked in a low voice, "Any chance they might've taken your picture and sent it to their leaders before they got swept away?"

I looked up, remembering. "I suppose it's possible, but they were rushing to climb up to us right before all that water came roaring in."

Jeff said after a moment, "Maybe you flying to Hong Kong is a bad idea. China might have your name on a watch list."

"Why would they even care if I'd been in the

enclave?"

He looked around and whispered, "They're suspicious about the bombing near their border. Our government doesn't want China to know the truth because of the connection to the underwater city. They might think you have the answers, so keep a low profile."

"Like I said, I'll hunker down in my hotel room." I sat back. "I brought my Kindle loaded with novels by my favorite authors: Nancy Cohen, Dallas Gorham, Don Stratton, Fred Lichtenberg, Ray Flynt, and George A. Bernstein."

Jeff pulled out his cell. "I'll ask Max to have the DIA verify you're not on China's radar before we launch for Hong Kong. Better safe than sorry." He hit speed dial for Max's cell and selected SPEAKER.

Judging by the many pictures Jeff had shown me, Max looked so much like him that he could've been his clone. But instead of following his father's path on Navy fighter jets and airliners, Max had focused his energy on covert missions and commanding a five-hundred-foot Navy ship. The USS *Leviathan* was an espionage/research vessel equipped with missiles, deck cannons, mini attack submarines, a research sub, a diving bell, a SEAL team, Hardsuits, and a long list of unusual equipment.

"Hey, Dad, what's up?" Max said.

"I'm in San Francisco with Sam and Lance, and I have you on speaker. Sorry we didn't think of this sooner. We're fixin' to take a charter flight to Hong Kong tomorrow night, and I'd like you to have DIA check if it's safe for Sam to go to China. You know, in case those soldiers in the Himalayas identified her to their superiors."

"I have a better idea: Replace her now and send her to my ship. I'll keep her safe, and she can help me deal with this Atlantis nightmare. I'll have a Seahawk waiting for her in Key West." Max paused. "Scratch that, I'll arrange for a military jet to fly her straight from SFO to the Key West Naval Air Station."

"Nice try, son, but this is her first airline flight back in the saddle. She's not ready to jump ship on day one. You'll have to make do without her for a few months, but you can always consult her via satellite phone. Right, Sam?" Jeff slid the phone closer to me.

"Sorry, Max, but I really need some stick time. I've been gone six months. I'll help you via SAT phone, email, or whatever works. Of course, I won't be able to do that if I'm locked up in a Chinese prison."

"*Funny*. I'll try to have an answer for you later tonight. And if you could spend a long weekend on *Leviathan* sometime in the next month or two, I'd be eternally grateful. As far as we know, you're the only person left who knows anything about Atlantean technology."

"As long as you promise me, in writing," I joked,

"that you'll let me leave after three days, I'll visit you in May. I'd like to help you wrap up down there before hurricane season starts. See you then." I slid the phone back to Jeff.

After a leisurely dinner and plenty of conversation catching up with what had been happening with all my friends at LIA, Jeff got a call back from Max.

Jeff hit SPEAKER. "Hello, son, that was fast. What's the verdict?"

"No guarantees, but DIA couldn't find any intel on China targeting Sam. She should be okay in Hong Kong. Just tell her not to do anything that might draw their attention."

"Thanks for checking, son."

"Happy to help, and I'm looking forward to Sam's visit next month." Max ended the call.

Jeff smiled at me. "Looks like you're good to go."

"Great!" I grinned. "I'd better run, guys. I have to make some calls and check my email."

"So early? There's a good band playing in the lounge," Lance said.

"Thanks, but I want to hit the exercise room before I call Ross." I stood. "It's been great catching up. See you guys tomorrow." I strolled out to the elevators, still wondering what Lance was hiding. His behavior toward me had changed. Instead of flirting like before, he seemed more interested in protecting me. *Hmmn.*

FOUR

USS LEVIATHAN, Thirty Miles NE of Cuba

Commander Max Rowlin, Captain of the *Leviathan*, read the intel report and swore under his breath. He glanced at his executive officer, Lt. Commander Vance Lowes. "This is insane. We've got *Texas* cruising around the underwater city, dodging ancient structures and our research sub, while playing chicken with fast-attack nuclear-powered subs from the UK, China, and Russia, and diesel-electric subs from Iran and North Korea."

"At least the Brits are on our side, and the diesel-electric subs can't go as deep as the nukes," Lowes said. "One screw up and we could start World War Three on our country's doorstep. Does the structural engineer know yet if we can raise Atlantis's Hall of Records?"

"She's taking a final pass around the building in *Vanguard*. I ordered her not to report anything until she returns. We don't want to risk our foreign *friends* intercepting our communications." Rowlin stared out at the calm blue water.

"If they find out what we're after, we may have to fight them for it." The XO shook his head. "No way that would end well."

"Thousands of years of advanced scientific knowledge is stored in those vaults. The country that recovers it will have a huge technological advantage." Rowlin reached for his coffee.

"I guess the appropriate quote for this situation is: 'Failure is not an option.'" Lowes patted Rowlin's back. "We're all counting on you, Captain Kidd."

The XO's comment wasn't meant as an insult. Only thirty-five, Rowlin was the youngest officer in command of a U.S. Navy ship, but he'd earned the respect and loyalty of his crew.

"Hey, at least our missions are never boring." Rowlin glanced at his watch. "XO, you have the conn. *Vanguard* should be back by now."

Rowlin worked his way through lower passages and down deck ladders to the moon pool located in the belly of the ship. Two top-secret thirty-foot Scorpion attack submarines with clear canopies were poised in their lifts, ready to launch at a moment's notice. They looked like nautical fighter jets with mini torpedoes mounted under their wing stubs.

Fresh from a tour of Atlantis, *Vanguard,* the forty-two-foot research submarine with a viewing port in the nose, dripped sea water as the lift operator placed it in its berth. Rowlin waited as the crew emerged from the top hatch and climbed down the ladder.

First out was *Leviathan's* marine biologist, Dr. Kip Peterson, the image of a Norwegian sea captain with white hair, a neatly trimmed white beard, and ocean-blue eyes. His face lit up when he spotted Rowlin. "Captain, thank you for sending me down in *Vanguard.* I've been dying to see the entire city. What a fantastic view!"

"Glad you enjoyed it, Kip." Rowlin patted his back. "God knows you earned it after rescuing Banger from that megalodon last month."

Chief Marine Engineer Victoria Edwards, a long-haired strawberry blonde with high cheekbones and dancing blue eyes, beamed with excitement. Lean but curvy, she approached Rowlin and spoke in rapid-fire. "Spectacular view—white marble buildings, beautiful statues, pyramids, and sphinxes, especially the huge black obsidian pyramid." Out of breath, she grinned, then lit a cigarette.

Rowlin shook his head. "That cancer stick will kill you, Vicky."

She shrugged. "Hey, we all have to die of something."

"What's the verdict on raising the Hall of

Records?" Rowlin tried not to sound as impatient as he felt.

"Sorry, can't be done," she said in a matter-of-fact tone.

"It sank intact." Rowlin crossed his arms. "Why can't it be raised intact?"

"Captain, the last small chunk of the continent sank as one land mass, buildings and all. Those buildings have foundations which are rooted into the seabed. We can't detach a marble building from its foundation without causing it to crumble to pieces."

Rowlin sucked in his breath. "So, you're saying there's no way to recover the treasure trove of scientific data in those vaults? Come on, Vicky, you're supposed to be the best."

She smiled. "I said we can't raise the *building*. Your ship has everything we'll need to raise the sealed vaults. Of course, I'm assuming they're self-contained and able to be separated from the interior walls. I'll need to go down in a Hardsuit and study how they're attached before I can make a final recommendation."

"Great. Give me a list of the equipment you'll need on the dive and I'll have my SEAL commander make the arrangements," Rowlin said. "And Vicky, the sooner the better. That underwater city is crawling with foreign submarines."

"The Hardsuits are well-equipped. I'm good to go whenever the SEALs are ready." She grinned.

"Don't worry, Captain. The Atlanteans went to a lot of trouble to preserve those records. We'll find a way to raise the vaults."

Hong Kong

After ten hours of sack time in my king-size hotel bed, I met Jeff and Lance in the lobby. Our ten flight attendants had already left the hotel for an extensive shopping mission. I intended to stay away from the shops after what had happened last time, so the guys suggested we have a late lunch at a floating restaurant in Kowloon. The spring air felt balmy as we crossed the street to the bustling harbor and searched for a water taxi.

In China, a five-nine blonde standing between two tall guys in jeans was like having a neon tourist sign flashing above us. Eager men in little boats yelled and waved. We chose the sturdiest-looking vessel and climbed aboard.

"Kowloon," Jeff said. "Take us to the best floating restaurant."

"No worries," the boat captain said. "I know good place. You like."

We sat back as he negotiated through the nautical obstacle course. Small boats cut in front of larger, slower ships, triggering loud horns and angry shouts.

"It's a miracle they don't have hundreds of collisions in this chaos," I said, my head on a swivel.

"I'm glad they don't let their aircraft operate like this."

"There's probably a method to their madness that's not obvious to us foreigners," Jeff said. "I bet most of the small-boat operators know each other and their routes."

"Hey, so long as we don't end up swimming in this filthy water, let them have at it." Lance grinned and pointed at an ornate Chinese junk. "Look at that beautiful sailboat."

Our kamikaze water-taxi ride ended a few minutes later when we docked near a one-hundred-foot, multi-colored floating restaurant. Aromas of sizzling beef, chicken, and fish swirled around us as we walked up the boarding plank. A young woman in a red silk dress greeted us and led us to a water-view table.

"Front-row seats to the nautical demolition derby," Lance said.

"I hope we can get the same guy for the trip back rather than roll the dice." I watched our water taxi take on new passengers. "He did a good job getting us here in one piece."

A waiter appeared and handed out menus printed in both Chinese and English. Thank God for the British. They had controlled Hong Kong for centuries, so English was prevalent throughout their former colony.

"Peking duck our special today," the waiter said

as he set a large teapot and three cups on the table. "I come back soon."

I waited until he was out of earshot. "I heard the Peking duck in Hong Kong is actually from New York."

"Don't they have ducks in Peking?" Jeff asked.

I laughed. "Not anymore, but they might have ducks in Beijing."

"Sneaky—new name, same city." Lance shrugged. "I'd rather have seafood."

The waiter returned and took our lunch orders. We sipped Oolong tea and enjoyed watching the constant bustle of the busy harbor as we waited for our meals.

I glanced around at the tourists on board. "I guess you were right, Lance. No reason for me to hide in my room. Thanks for inviting me to lunch."

"Happy to oblige." He scanned the boat. "Not a bad guy in sight. Things are looking up."

"Yep, just keep sending out positive vibes and the universe will reward us," I said.

"Sam, I didn't know you believed in that New Age bull crap," Jeff said.

"I don't, but I'm trying to adopt a positive attitude and change my karma. It's better than expecting bad things to happen all the time, don't you think?"

"True, but don't let your guard down. In the current political environment, all Americans are targets—especially in foreign countries," Jeff said.

I stood. "Fear not. I'll now make a cautious trip to the ladies' room."

Lance stood. "I'll walk with you, just in case."

We headed for the restrooms on the lower deck. I entered the tiny ladies' room, and Lance was waiting for me when I came out. Things happened pretty fast after that.

USS LEVIATHAN

Captain Rowlin stood beside the lean and steely eyed SEAL Commander, George Bern, who said, "Cleared to lower divers."

Two divers encased in Navy Hardsuit 2000s were winched over the side via heavy cables with integrated power, data, and communication lines. The Hardsuits remained at one atmosphere of air pressure to a maximum depth of two thousand feet, eliminating a need for decompression on the ascent.

"Comm check," a mocha-skinned African-American SEAL nicknamed Banger said into the voice-activated mike in his helmet.

"We have you five-by-five," Bern said.

"Loud and clear," Vicky said. "I feel like an astronaut in this suit. I can't wait to use the thrusters. It'll feel like flying."

"Dial your enthusiasm down a few clicks," Banger said. "The warning on ancient nautical charts is true in Atlantis."

"What warning?"

"Here there be monsters," he said. "I'm not joking. Stay sharp, Vicky."

"But Navy Intelligence assured me your people killed the megalodons," she said, peering through her viewing port.

"There's no guarantee we won't encounter another one. And there's no telling what other deadly creatures might be lurking down there. *Leviathan* is using passive sonar because of all the submarines sneaking around the city. They might not detect a threat until the creature is right on top of us."

"Stupid me," she said, her tone a pitch higher. "I thought this dive would be fun."

"Maybe it'll be different this time," he said. "Just watch out for booby traps and be extra careful."

The tension in Banger's voice sent goose bumps over Vicky's skin as their floodlights illuminated a giant black pyramid standing sentinel at the edge of the ancient city.

As they descended deeper, magnificent white marble buildings in circular and octagonal shapes were illuminated by their spotlights in the crystal-clear water. Huge sphinxes guarded the inner city, and beautiful pyramids of varied sizes adorned the metropolis, some covered in gold, others embedded with gems.

Marble statues of sea life and various deities decorated what appeared to be public parks throughout the city. The statues and structures were smooth and free of growth because the deep water was too cold, and life-giving sunlight couldn't reach down two thousand feet to the city.

"There's our objective: the octagonal marble building with the white columns around it. Follow me and be very careful what you touch. A British marine archaeologist was killed inside the giant pyramid when he activated a defense mechanism. I saw it happen," Banger said, his voice tense.

"What killed him?" she asked.

"Long spears pierced his suit, and the immense water pressure compressed him into Jell-O." He sighed. "It wasn't pretty."

"That's awful!" She hesitated. Her voice quivered when she said, "Banger, please don't let that happen to us." She looked around and then pointed at a large opening in the ancient Hall of Records. "There's the entry." It looked to be about a ten-foot square.

"Don't zoom around inside with your thrusters. Could be booby traps." Banger eased into the gleaming golden interior.

Vicky followed close behind. "Wow, the Atlanteans had tons of gold!" She pointed at massive gold vaults lining the walls. "I need to check if these are freestanding or bolted in place."

Banger pointed at a nearby section. "Check this one first."

She shined a spotlight on the front. "Looks like

it could be freestanding, but I'll need to see the top to be sure."

According to Vicky's digital laser measuring device, each vault was six feet high, nine feet wide, and three feet deep. The ceiling measured fifteen feet high, leaving nine feet of vertical wall space for ceramic pictures and marble wall sculptures. Seven vaults lined the outer walls, and four stood in the room's center around the base of a huge gold statue of Poseidon.

"Give me a minute to check for traps." Banger used his thrusters to ascend above the rectangular gold storage unit. He scanned the top side and the ceiling nine feet above it. "It looks safe. Come on up."

Vicky mimicked Banger's movements as she ascended. She found eyelets embedded in the vault's top near each end with heavy chains that fastened to the eyelets in the wall.

"These chains kept them secure. All we have to do is disconnect them and connect tow lines to the eyelets and drag the vaults out of here. Then we'll—"

Banger cut her off. "Not here! We'll discuss this when we're topside."

"Sorry, I got excited."

They eased around the perimeter, checking each vault and unhooking the chains. After finishing, they examined the ones around the base of the statue.

"The eyelets are on the back sides with chains attached to the statue's base. Once we unhook them, we're good to go," Vicky said.

Just as they disconnected the final chain, a call came in on their comm lines.

"Divers, cut your cables and move to the back of the building, now!" Bern said.

Banger activated his cutting tool and severed his cable. He was about to do the same for Vicky's when something yanked it, pulling her toward the open doorway.

"Help!" she screamed.

"Hold on!" He snagged her cable with his suit's claspers and thrusted upward, pulling her above the open door.

Vicky wrapped her arms around an Atlantean king's bust protruding from the wall over the entrance, while Banger rushed to cut her cable. Once the line was severed, he clipped a tether to her suit and zoomed deep into the interior with her in tow. He pulled her atop a vault on the back wall.

"Quick, grasp the left chain with your claspers." He did the same on the right end.

"What's happening?" She asked, her voice rising to a panicked pitch.

"I don't know." He shined a spotlight at the entrance. "Watch the door."

"Oh my God!" Vicky screamed. "It can't be real!"

FIVE

Kowloon

I walked ahead of Lance down the narrow passage leading from the restrooms to the stairwell. An elderly man with a Fu Manchu mustache stepped out from a side door.

I was face-to-face with Dragon Master. He held a long, black wig in his hand.

"Golden Twin," he said, his face grim. "I serve you now. Ministry of State Security come for you." He pulled the wig over my head, covering my blond ponytail. "Hurry!"

Thudding footsteps pounding down the stairs verified his warning.

He nudged Lance. "Quick, pin her against wall and kiss her so they can't see her face." He acted like he was hobbling to the restrooms at the other end of the passage.

I'd barely straightened the wig before Lance pinned me against the wall and kissed me like he hadn't had a woman in ten years. I guess he saw this as his chance to kiss me with impunity.

I peeked, my eyes slits, during his hot kiss. Four fit looking Chinese men in civilian clothes rushed past us.

Although the kiss *was* necessary, and Lance was insanely handsome with his Adonis face, broad shoulders, and rock-hard abs, the imminent danger made my heart race more than his skillful kiss.

Moments later, Dragon Master returned and shoved us through a side door. He was surprisingly strong for an old guy. The tiny cabin had an open porthole. Despite his age, he shimmied through the window and dropped into an idling boat tied alongside.

"Help her through porthole," Dragon Master commanded as he reached up for me.

I wobbled, not quite recovered from the triple shock of the mesmerizing kiss, the imminent danger, and meeting Dragon Master again. Lance lifted me and fed my legs through the opening, and I dropped into the boat.

Dragon Master said, "You go to hotel now. I bring her to airplane tonight."

Before Lance could reply, the old man released the line and accelerated away.

Lance rushed up the stairs, taking them two at a time. He shoved money into the waiter's hand. "Sorry, we're late for our trip." He waved at Jeff, who rushed to join him.

They ran down the gangway and leaped into the nearest water taxi.

"Lotus Blossom Hotel. There's an extra twenty if you get us there in ten minutes," Lance said. "Family emergency."

The boat captain untied the dock line and accelerated away.

Lance glanced at Jeff. "My sister was in an auto accident."

Jeff nodded. He knew Lance didn't have a sister, and Sam's absence meant something major had just happened.

In moments, their water taxi had blended into a maze of boat traffic. Lance glanced at his watch.

Ten minutes later, their boat docked across the street from their hotel. Lance paid the fare plus twenty dollars and thanked the captain.

Lance raced into the lobby elevator with Jeff close behind. A family stood inside.

When the two men stepped out onto their floor, Jeff said, "What happened?"

"We need to put on our uniforms and head for the airport. I'll grab my stuff and change in your room so I can explain." Lance opened his door and rushed inside.

Moments later, he knocked on Jeff's door. He held his uniform on a hanger in one hand and his suitcase in the other.

"Get in here and tell me what the hell happened," Jeff said as he pulled his shirt off.

Lance told him the sequence of events as he rushed to change into his uniform. "The old guy said he'd bring her to the plane tonight."

As Jeff knotted his tie, he said, "We can leave a message for the flight attendants that we went early to check maintenance items."

"Those Chinese spooks will look for us here. If we leave now, we'll have time to come up with a plan." Lance shoved his civilian clothes into his suitcase.

"How do you know we can trust Dragon Master?" Jeff asked. "I mean, those men might be on *his* team."

"Shit! It all happened so fast, but they wouldn't have rushed past us if they were working with him. If he's on our side, how's he going to sneak her onto our airplane tonight?"

Jeff closed his suitcase and grabbed his captain's hat. "The spooks are looking for a blonde. The black wig will help, but Sam's a lot taller than most Chinese women, and her unusual eyes and big breasts will be hard to conceal."

"Maybe she'll get a message to us through a mechanic or a baggage handler." Lance pulled on his uniform jacket. "Let's go."

They grabbed their bags and headed down in the elevator. After leaving their keys at the front desk with a message for their flight attendants, they caught a cab for the airport.

They breezed through Customs and boarded the jet. After powering up the electrical and air-conditioning systems, they ran through their cockpit checks and discussed a plausible reason for Sam's absence. Every scenario sounded lame.

Jeff got out of his seat. "I'm going to the galley to brew some coffee. When you do the walkaround, look for a hidden message from Sam or Dragon Master."

Lance pulled on his jacket and grabbed his hat. "I'm on it." He headed down the jetway steps and started his inspection at the nose gear.

A Chinese man in a reflective vest and orange hardhat tapped his shoulder. Lance turned. The man held out his right arm and showed him a tattoo on his forearm. It was a dragon clutching a trident.

Lance recognized the tattoo. Dragon Master had one just like it.

The man ducked inside the wheel well. Lance joined him. He opened his hand and slipped a folded note to Lance, then nodded and left.

Lance casually slid the note into his pocket and continued his outside check of the aircraft.

His heart raced as he tried to focus on the walkaround. Were Chinese secret agents watching? He finished the inspection and hurried up the jetway steps.

USS LEVIATHAN

"How big is it?" Captain Rowlin asked the sonar operator over the intercom.

"About a hundred and sixty feet when it was swimming toward the Hall of Records. Then it seemed to become part of the building, so it's hard to tell."

"What the hell is it?" Rowlin asked.

"I don't know, sir. Never seen anything like it. All I can say is it's not manmade. Definitely a biologic."

Rowlin called Dive Ops. "Bern, did the divers sever their cables?"

"Affirmative, Captain, cables are severed, but their backup radios can't get reception inside that stone building. They still have forty-four hours of air."

"Good." Rowlin hit the PA button. "Dr. Kip Peterson, report to the bridge." He turned to his XO. "I hope our marine biologist can tell us what we're up against."

A few minutes later, Peterson entered the bridge.

"Ah, Kip, looks like we may have another sea

monster. This one's too big to be a megalodon, and it can change its shape."

Peterson nodded to Rowlin and then stared down at the placid sea. "How big and where is it?"

"Sonar said it was a hundred and sixty feet long when it swam to the Hall of Records, but then it appeared to become part of the building. What the hell?"

His eyes widened. "Oh shit, this time it really is a kraken—better known as a giant squid. He probably perched on the roof with his tentacles draped over the building. That would make him hard to see on sonar."

"Seriously?" the XO said. "Is that even possible?"

"After our encounter with the megalodons, I believe almost anything is possible down in Atlantis," Peterson said.

"So how do we kill it before it gets our divers?" Rowlin asked.

Peterson thought a moment. "Well, if it's on the building the divers are in, we can't torpedo it. And if it's in open water, torpedoes won't explode on its soft flesh. They'll go right through it and maybe hit one of the subs."

"So how do we turn it into shark food?" This from XO Lowes.

"Don't send in the Scorpion subs," Peterson said. "Too dangerous. They're only thirty feet. The squid could crush them in its tentacles or pierce their hulls with its beak."

Rowlin shook his head. "A breach at that depth would implode a Scorpion."

"Can it reach inside the building with a tentacle and grab a diver?" Lowes asked.

"What are the building's dimensions?" Peterson pulled out his cell and tapped the calculator function.

Rowlin looked upward. "As I recall, it has an eighty-foot perimeter, the roof is eighteen feet high with a fifteen-foot interior ceiling, and the open doorway is ten feet square."

"Assuming the beast is perched on the roof and allowing for the body section, or mantle, as it's called, that leaves about a hundred and twenty feet for the long feeding tentacles." Peterson tapped numbers on the keypad. "The longest distance inside the building is twenty-six feet diagonally. Add the eighteen-foot roof and half the diagonal width for draping over it before entering, and that's only fifty-seven feet total. The giant squid won't be able to fit more than one tentacle inside, but it's plenty long enough to reach anywhere in there." He pocketed his cell. "Our divers won't stand a chance."

Rowlin raked his buzz cut. "Maybe *Texas* can draw it away. She's almost four hundred feet of double-hulled steel—should be safe, right?"

"How good is their navigation officer?" Peterson

asked. "Could they do a low pass and still miss everything down there?"

"I'll send an emergency message to *Texas's* captain, but even if they can draw it away, they can't fire one of their torpedoes. Their weapons aren't designed for biologics, and we can't risk hitting those other subs." Rowlin dictated the message to his comm officer.

Minutes later, Rowlin received a reply from the USS *Texas*. "He said they'll dive at it, hit it with an active ping, and then blow their ballast and lead it to the surface so we can smoke it with our deck cannons."

Lowes grinned. "Sweet."

Peterson nodded. "That could work."

"It could, but Atlantis is full of surprises. No way it'll be that easy." Rowlin called the moon pool operator. "Get both Scorpion crews ready to launch with full armament and have them standby. I'll brief them in person if the mission is a go. Tell them we're trying something else first."

A comm operator sprinted up to Rowlin and thrust a satellite phone at him. "Emergency call for you from Samantha Starr."

A giant tentacle snaked inside the Hall of Records, probing around like a blind man feeling his way.

Paralyzed with fear, Vicky's heavy breathing was

broadcast to Banger through the voice-activated intercom system that allowed the divers to talk to each other.

Banger tapped her suit. "Stay calm and keep your floodlight on the tentacle. It probably won't find us up here on top of the innermost vault, and I have the cutting tool ready. But keep still in case it can track vibrations."

"You warned me there were monsters down here, but I thought you were just hazing the new girl." She paused. "Oh God, it's checking the top of that vault!"

"It's still a long way from us. It probably can't reach this far," he said for her sake. He held the rotary cutter in front of him and hoped he had enough battery power to fight the inevitable battle.

An enormous tentacle with huge, pulsating cups crept closer.

SIX

Hong Kong International Airport

Lance entered the cockpit and closed the door. "I met a guy outside with a tattoo like the one on Dragon Master's forearm. He gave me a note."

Jeff glanced back over his shoulder. "What's it say?"

Lance pulled out the note and read aloud. "Golden Twin will come during loading dressed as mechanic. She will hide in electronics bay. This note written on rice paper. Eat now."

"Could be poison. You'd better flush it." Jeff checked his watch.

A loud knock on the cockpit door jarred them. "Ministry of State Security, open door!"

Lance shoved the paper into his mouth, chewed

it, and swallowed it. He grabbed a bottle of water and took a swig before he opened the door.

"Pilots, come out now!" A Chinese man in civilian clothes waved an MSS ID at them.

Three men waited with him in the passenger cabin. Lance recognized them as the ones who'd come for Sam on the floating restaurant. They flashed their MSS credentials.

After the leader searched the cockpit, he said, "Where is Captain Samantha Starr?"

Before they could answer, the cabin crew boarded. Cindy, the curvaceous blonde lead flight attendant, shoved a suitcase through the cockpit door and hung a coat bag in the cockpit closet. She then strolled up to Jeff. "I put Sam's stuff in the cockpit."

Jeff and the lead MSS agent said simultaneously, "Where is she?"

"She left me a note at the hotel asking me to bring her stuff and said she'd meet us on the airplane." Cindy glanced at her watch. "She should be here any minute."

"Okay, good." Jeff towered over the short MSS agents. "Gentlemen, how can we help you?"

"We want to talk to Captain Starr. I will wait in cockpit, and they will wait in boarding area. You may go about your duties." The lead secret service agent nodded to his comrades.

Jeff and Lance entered the cockpit and ran all their checklists again for the agent's benefit. They kept everything professional and refrained from chitchat.

Thirty minutes passed, and no Sam.

The passengers began boarding. Fifty high-tech industry executives and their spouses were returning from a four-day business conference. They were scheduled for a two-day stop in Hawaii before continuing to San Jose International Airport and their jobs in Silicon Valley. The passengers Luxury International Airlines had brought in the previous day had left on a thirty-day VIP tour of China, so the timing had worked out perfectly for the two charter flights.

As Lance stood in the cockpit door and greeted passengers, the lead MSS agent slid past him, checked his watch, and strode out to the jetway. He called another MSS agent, who hurried down the jetway and took the stairway door to the ramp.

Lance stuck his head in the cockpit and whispered, "The spook that was in our cockpit is on the jetway, and another one just went down to the ramp."

"Be cool. He's probably checking the cargo bays. Sam will be in disguise if she's out there." Jeff glanced out the side window.

Lance turned back to the cabin and smiled at the weary-looking passengers. A vibration under his feet indicated the cargo doors had closed. Not long after that, an MSS agent came up from the ramp and reported to the lead man. It was obvious from their facial expressions that he hadn't found Sam.

A LIA passenger service representative handed the passenger manifest to Cindy and smiled at Lance. "All passengers are on board, and you're cleared to depart." She noticed the MSS agents. "Gentlemen, it's departure time. Please step off so we can close out the flight."

"One of your pilots is missing," the lead MSS agent said. "Aren't you going to wait for her?"

"That's up to Captain Rowlin, but we have strict rules about departing on time," the airline's representative said.

After Lance settled in the copilot seat, the LIA rep entered the cockpit. "Captain Rowlin, the MSS agents want to know whether you intend to wait for Captain Starr or depart on time?"

"We have a schedule to keep, and we don't need a relief pilot for the flight to Hawaii. She'll have to catch a commercial flight home. Button us up." Jeff waved her out.

After the boarding door and galley doors were closed, Lance called Cindy on the interphone. "Did the MSS agents get off?"

"Yep, we're good to go, except I haven't seen Sam."

"Hang on a sec." Lance looked over at Jeff. "The spooks are off, but Cindy hasn't seen Sam. What do you want her to do?"

"I'll talk to her." Jeff selected the interphone

button. "Cindy, carry on as normal and we'll discuss Sam on the way back to the States." He released the parking brake and began the start procedure for the right engine as the ground crew pushed them back.

"Jeff?" Lance asked, his voice cracking.

"Wait 'til we're airborne." He held his right thumb up and grinned. "We're good."

Lance nodded and continued his normal duties, his jaw clenched and his body rigid.

After takeoff, they were given a turn on course and cleared to their cruise altitude. Jeff switched on the autopilot and released his shoulder harness. "You've got the airplane. I'm going to let Sam out of the electronics bay. She's probably waiting for us to tell her the coast is clear."

"How'd you know she was in there?"

As Jeff stood, he said, "I saw the door light for the electronics bay blink on right after that MSS agent left the ramp. The door closed a few seconds later. Has to mean she's on board."

"Dang it, Jeff, I about had a heart attack thinkin' we'd left her stranded." Lance blew out a sigh. "Get her. I won't relax until I see she's here."

Jeff lifted the floor panel that accessed the electronics bay beneath the aft end of their oversized, specially designed cockpit.

An elderly man with a Fu Manchu mustache looked up at him.

USS LEVIATHAN

The USS *Texas,* a huge nuclear-powered submarine, shot out of the water and made an enormous splash when it landed on the sea.

Rowlin focused his binoculars on the area behind the submarine. "Where's the friggin' kraken?"

The words had no sooner left his mouth when his comm officer burst onto the bridge.

"Captain, the Iranian submarine, *Ghadir* 962, is sending out a Mayday. They were cruising near the path *Texas* took on its way up, and the giant squid attacked them. It's wrapped around their hull, and one of its tentacles must've fouled their propeller. They're dead in the water."

"That's a ninety-five-foot diesel-electric sub, right?" Rowlin asked.

"Yes, sir."

Lowes shook his head. "That Iranian sub is sixty-five feet shorter than the squid, and it's only rated for a maximum depth of one thousand feet. If the kraken pulls it to the bottom, it'll implode."

"Why the hell don't they blow their ballast?" Rowlin asked, frustrated.

"Maybe they did, and the immense weight of that squid is holding them down," Peterson said.

Rowlin turned to his comm officer. "Ask *Texas* if they can maneuver beneath the Iranian sub and lift it to the surface."

"Aye, Captain." He rushed out.

"Even if they push them up to the surface, we still can't fire at the giant squid while it's wrapped around that sub," Kip said.

"I have an idea." Rowlin keyed the PA system. "Commander Bern, report to the bridge."

The comm officer's voice filled the bridge speakers. "Captain, *Texas* will try and lift the Iranian sub."

"Good," Rowlin said, keying the mike. "Keep me informed."

Tall and toned, SEAL Commander George Bern entered the bridge. "Yes, Captain?"

Rowlin explained the situation. "Gather your SEALs on the port rail armed with flare guns and as many flares as you can find. When the sub breaks the surface, fire flares into the kraken so it'll release them." Rowlin glanced at the sea. "Hurry!"

George raced from the bridge.

"Brilliant!" Lowes said. "As soon as the giant squid is clear of the sub, we'll blast it with our deck cannons."

Rowlin, Lowes, and Peterson scanned the placid sea from the bridge.

Nothing.

Ten minutes later, a comm officer entered the bridge and handed Rowlin a message.

"Sonofabitch!" Rowlin said after he read it. "*Texas* hit the kraken with an active ping to verify its exact location, and the squid dove to two thousand feet clutching the Iranian sub. *Texas's* sonar operator recorded sounds of *Ghadir* 962 imploding."

It wasn't long before flotsam from the destroyed Iranian sub littered the surface.

"XO, you have the conn," Rowlin said. "I'm going down to meet with the Scorpion crews." He waved at Kip. "With me."

LIA Flight En Route to HNL

"Who the hell are you?" Jeff asked.

"I am Dragon Master." He glanced behind him. "Tell him, Golden Twin."

Sam nudged the old man aside. "It's okay, Jeff. He's with me. Is the coast clear?" She wore a baggy mechanic's uniform, a short black wig, and an orange hardhat.

"The spooks are gone, and we're over the Pacific. Come on up." Jeff moved back.

Sam started up the ladder and grasped Jeff's hand when her head emerged above the cockpit floor.

"Welcome back, Sam," Lance said over his shoulder. "I'm glad you're okay."

"I hope you have a plan that doesn't involve smuggling this guy into our country," Jeff said to Sam as he reached down and helped the elderly Chinese man up.

"Don't worry, Boss. I called Max, and he said the

State Department would have the political asylum paperwork ready by the time we land in Hawaii. His plan is to have Dragon Master help him with Atlantis." She hugged Jeff. "Thanks for getting me out of China."

Jeff's frown turned to a smile. "Good plan, but will your tattooed buddy go along with it?"

"I serve Golden Twin now." Dragon Master bowed. "I will obey her."

Jeff raised a brow and faced Sam. "Is he referring to you?"

"Yep. I look identical to the Atlantean sun goddess, Solraya—hence the name Golden Twin. It was part of an ancient prophecy from Atlantis." I shrugged. "Lucky me."

"Sam! Get your ass over here and give me a hug," Lance said, half-turned in his seat.

From where he stood, Jeff was blocking Sam's view of the copilot. She side-stepped around his tall frame and leaned in for a hug.

Lance pulled her close. "I was worried sick." He planted a kiss on the nape of her neck.

She kissed his cheek. "Thanks for saving my butt *again*. From now on, anytime you're drinking, I'm buying."

He grinned. "I can live with that."

"You can sit here." Jeff directed the old man to a seat behind Lance and helped him secure his seatbelt.

The huge modified cockpit had a big closet, a

lavatory with a shower, and a sleeping chamber with two bunk beds.

"Did Cindy bring my uniform and bag aboard?" Sam asked. "I can't wait to get out of this dirty uniform and itchy wig."

Jeff slid into the left seat. "Your things are stowed in the closet. Go ahead and change in the head. When you come out, we'll order food and drinks."

"Great, I'm starved. I missed lunch and dinner." Sam grabbed her suit bag and slipped into the cockpit lavatory.

Lance glanced back at Dragon Master. "Welcome aboard and thanks for saving Sam, uh, I mean, Golden Twin."

The Chinese man bowed his head. "It is my honor to serve her."

SEVEN

USS LEVIATHAN

Two Scorpion submarines were poised over the moon pool, ready for launch. *Scorpion One* was piloted by Lieutenant Jane Hoebich, a curvaceous five-foot-three blonde expert at mixed martial arts and the only female submarine pilot in Special Operations. Sitting behind her in the tandem seat was her weapons officer, Ensign Scooter McCoy—pale, skinny, and sandy-haired with a slight case of acne.

Lieutenant Fred Lichten, tall and movie-star handsome with dark-brown eyes and hair, piloted *Scorpion Two*. His brash weapons officer, Ensign Bull Simmons, was of medium height and had bold hazel eyes, dark hair, broad shoulders, and a barrel chest.

Both crews were strapped in with their canopies open, awaiting launch orders when Rowlin strode onto the catwalk separating them. "Climb out and join me." He motioned to where Kip was standing at the edge of the moon pool.

Rowlin waited until the sub crews were gathered around them. "Our divers are trapped inside the Hall of Records by another sea monster." He paused. "It's a hundred-and-sixty-foot giant squid."

Jane shook her head. "And we thought the biggest biologic we'd ever see was that eighty-foot megalodon we killed."

"Damn, Atlantis has to be the most bizarre place on Earth," Fred said. "Captain, I don't think we can use our torpedoes on the squid."

"You're right, torpedoes only work on hard targets, not biologics," Rowlin said. "We need a plan to save our divers without putting the Scorpions at risk. That beast just destroyed a ninety-five-foot Iranian submarine. Your little boats wouldn't stand a chance. Any ideas?"

"How long are the tentacles?" Scooter asked.

"The two longest ones are the feeder tentacles," Kip said. "I'd estimate about a hundred and twenty feet. The rest are maybe ninety to one hundred feet long."

"That rules out harpoons," Scooter said. "We'd have to get within fifty feet for an accurate harpoon shot."

"Yeah, a longer distance underwater would slow the harpoon too much," Bull said. "Too bad we can't get it to move away from the building and then sit still while we drop a depth charge on the bugger."

"We don't have depth charges," Rowlin said.

"No, but that gave me an idea," Kip said. "We can rig an autonomous underwater vehicle with explosives and a remote detonator. If the kraken moves away from the building, we'll send down the AUV and blast it to bits."

"Sounds like a good plan as long as a foreign submarine doesn't get in the way when it goes boom," Fred said.

"The UK won't be a problem, but China, Russia, and North Korea don't trust us and probably won't believe an enormous squid destroyed the Iranian sub," Rowlin said. "They'll think we're trying to trick them into leaving."

"I can see how this could easily start a war if we're not careful," Jane said. "Why don't we use the ROVs to verify nobody is near when we detonate the AUV?"

"Alright, Jane and Scooter will help Kip and his techs operate the remote vehicles, while SEALs rig the autonomous vehicle with explosives and a remote detonator," Rowlin said. "Fred, you and Bull standby in *Scorpion Two* to bring up our divers when the coast is clear."

"Uh, Captain," Bull said, "what if there's more than one giant squid down there? We all remember what happened with the megalodons." He turned to Jane and Scooter, and they nodded.

Rowlin said, "Well, Kip, you're the expert. What are the chances there's more than one?"

"The odds for one squid that size are almost zero. But it's there. And don't forget there were three megalodons, even though *one* should've been impossible." Peterson shrugged. "There's no way to predict whether more krakens are down there."

"Well…shit!" Bull said.

"I have an idea," Jane said. "Kip, does a giant squid have any natural enemies? Another sea creature it's afraid of?"

"Sure, sperm whales feed on normal-sized giant squids, but there aren't any nearby."

"What if we rig our Scorpions with loudspeakers that can broadcast sounds made by sperm whales?" Jane asked. "Could that work?"

"Maybe, as long as the squid doesn't see how small your subs are," Kip said. "I have recordings of sperm whales stored on my computer."

"Good idea, Jane," Rowlin said. "Kip, get someone to copy the sperm whale sounds onto two flash drives while you get busy finding that kraken. Killing it is priority one. You all have your orders. Get going and keep me informed."

Two divers in foreign-made atmospheric dive suits eased through the entrance door and shined their bright lights around the Hall of Records. Large flags consisting of three equal horizontal fields of white, blue, and red were emblazoned on their front torsos.

"Russian divers," Banger said, recognizing the flags. "The kraken must be dead."

Vicky waved at the divers. "Thank God! They must be here to save us."

The Russians pointed high-powered spear guns at the American divers.

Vicky froze. "Why are they aiming at us?"

Just as the Russians fired, a huge tentacle yanked them out of the building.

"Holy shit!" Banger yelled as ballistic spears impacted the wall, barely missing them.

An inky substance filled the building.

"Our lights can't penetrate that black water," Vicky said, her voice shaky. "No way to see if it's coming."

"Keep still and hang onto the chain," he said. "The water will clear eventually."

"That monster squirted its ink in here because it doesn't want us to see its tentacle when it reaches in and grabs us!" Her voice had risen to a panicked pitch.

"Squids release ink to hide from enemies," he said. "Our shipmates must be attacking it. Relax. They'll have us out of here soon."

Not believing his own words, Banger held the rotary cutter and prayed it would be powerful enough to save them—assuming his internal battery wasn't too depleted.

As he struggled to see through the inky water, he thought, *I hate this friggin' city!*

Kip controlled the first remote-operated vehicle sent into the depths, SEAL Commander George Bern operated the second one, and Jane and Scooter operated the last two.

"Besides worrying about the kraken, we have to safeguard our tethers from being ensnared by submarines cruising around us," Kip said. "*Texas* and the British sub *Audacious* are steering clear as requested, but we can't count on the Russian, Chinese, and North Korean subs to do the same."

"Commander Bern, you have a call on the interphone," the PA system announced.

George picked up the handset.

"Bern here." He listened a few moments.

"Understood." He scanned the small group. "That was the captain. He said Russia and Cuba just sent in spy ships disguised as fishing trawlers. They're not buying our story about the sea monster, which means all the commie subs are still cruising around down there."

Kip shrugged. "Let's hope they don't learn the truth the hard way. The sooner we find the kraken, the better." He focused on his video screen as his ROV neared the ancient city. "I'm directing mine to the Hall of Records since that's the squid's most likely location."

As his little robotic vehicle neared the building, the video feed became clouded by an inky substance in the water.

"Uh oh!" Kip said. "The big guy released an ink cloud. Visibility just went to zero."

Seconds later, something yanked the line so hard the tether was severed.

"Shit!" Kip said. "The kraken just destroyed my remote vessel."

"We can't detonate the autonomous vehicle until we lure the squid away from the building our divers are in," George said. "Any suggestions?"

"Do we have something noisy we could drop in the water to lure it to the surface?" Jane asked.

Scooter glanced at the marine biologist. "Would a sonic buoy work, Kip?"

"That would get its attention. Let's see if it'll draw it away from our divers. Use your ROV to observe from a distance." He nodded to George. "Advise the captain to ready the deck cannons in case we get a clean shot."

Ten minutes later, Rowlin watched from the bridge as the crew deployed a high-pitched sonic buoy. Scooter's remote vessel tracked it from twenty yards aft as the current pushed the buoy away from *Leviathan*. A screen in the bridge displayed the video feed. Rowlin ordered the ship's cannons trained on the buoy.

Jane called the bridge. Her tense voice filled the overhead speakers. "Captain, the Russians must've deployed divers from their submarine. I'm sending an image to your video screen."

The bridge video monitor displayed a split-screen view of two crumpled dive suits with Russian flags on the fronts. Cables were still attached, and a dark liquid trailed from cracks in the metal.

"Jane, follow the crushed divers with your remote vehicle and see if the Russian sub reels them in," Rowlin said.

Scooter's voice boomed over the bridge speakers. "Captain, the kraken's coming!"

Rowlin trained his binoculars on the buoy. "Looks like we'll get a chance to smoke its ass after all."

"Maybe not." Lowes put his hand on Rowlin's shoulder and pointed at a Russian spy trawler racing toward them.

"Dammit! XO, tell our radio operator to get them the hell out of here," Rowlin said as he picked up the interphone and called the weapons control officer. "Hold fire until that trawler clears the area."

As the spy boat neared the buoy, huge tentacles thrashed the water, sending spray in every direction. They snaked around the trawler and pulled it under, fracturing its fiberglass hull and shattering it into pieces. Crewmen screamed as the beast plucked them off the surface and fed them into its huge beak, chomping them to bits. Blood and guts oiled the roiling surface. Another tentacle crushed the sonic buoy, and it sank.

The carnage took less than a minute, leaving a scattering of severed limbs, sections of ragged fiberglass, and debris bobbing on the gently rolling waves.

Scooter had recorded the kraken's rapid attack and followed it downward as Rowlin and Lowes watched from the bridge.

Rowlin scanned the area with his binoculars and spotted two survivors struggling to grab hold of floating debris.

George hurried onto the bridge. "Captain, my SEALs have a boat with a deck-mounted .50-cal ready to launch. Should I order them to pick up the survivors?"

"Hell no! I won't risk our people for those friggin' Russians. Fire ballistic rescue buoys at them and pull them in."

"Aye, Captain." He rushed from the bridge.

Rowlin called Kip on the interphone. "As soon

as the survivors are rescued and we ensure the Cuban trawler stays clear, we'll launch another sonic buoy."

"Understood, Captain. Scooter is following the kraken on video. We'll call if it takes the bait again."

Rowlin watched his crew reel in the survivors from the Russian trawler. "XO, arrange for those men to be transferred to the Cuban trawler, and make sure they warn their commie buddies to stay the hell away from here so we can shoot the kraken."

"Aye, Captain." The XO called the radio operator and gave the orders.

Thirty minutes later, the Cuban trawler pulled alongside *Leviathan* and picked up the Russian sailors.

Rowlin watched them pull away. He waited until they were a mile out on a course away from his ship. "Good riddance." He picked up the interphone. "Launch another sonic buoy."

Rowlin and Lowes scanned the sea. Gentle rollers belied what lurked beneath.

Scooter's voice boomed on the bridge speakers. "It's on the move, heading for the surface."

Rowlin grabbed the interphone. "Fire the cannons as soon as it comes into view." His eyes riveted on the sea, he watched and waited.

Nothing.

Scooter's voice filled the bridge speakers. "Captain, big problem! Check the video screen."

The North Korean sub had wandered into the path of the ascending squid. It wrapped itself around the Sang-O Class Shark submarine, which was about sixty feet shorter than the sea monster.

Its massive body and tentacles obscured most of the submarine on the video. After churning the water and tumbling around with the stricken boat, the giant squid succeeded in pulling the North Korean sub to the bottom, well beyond the boat's crush depth.

When the submarine imploded, the bone-crushing pressure at depth compressed the crew into a gelatinous mush. Small bits of buoyant, interior materials were the only things that reached the surface, forming a spotty debris field.

Rowlin swore under his breath. "Launch another sonic buoy. This time, make sure there aren't any small boats nearby."

Jane's voice filled the bridge speakers. "Captain, I have video of the Russian nuclear sub, *Kazan*, reeling in their divers. That sub is huge—almost as big as *Leviathan*."

"I guess they'll start believing us now that the giant squid has killed their divers and destroyed their spy trawler," Rowlin said. "Good work, Jane. Save that video."

"Aye, Captain. I also saved some closeup views

of the crushed Russian divers in inky water near the Hall of Records."

"I'll review the footage later." Rowlin looked up at the live video screen. It was blank. He called Scooter on the interphone. "Where's the kraken?"

"It vanished into the depths, sir. My ROV wasn't able to match its speed."

EIGHT

LIA Flight to HNL

After changing into my airline uniform, I flew the rest of the flight to Hawaii from the left seat, and Jeff observed from a seat behind me. He kept one eye on Dragon Master, seated behind Lance, who'd stayed in the copilot seat and answered all the radio calls.

I didn't say anything to Jeff about Lance's steamy kiss on the floating restaurant, which had been necessary to hide me. Better to forget the whole thing now that we were out of China. Besides, it was obvious Lance had been worried about me. He really was protecting me. But what had happened that made him stop trying to seduce me? It was like he was a different person now. Better, actually.

As we sped along at cruise altitude, I glanced back at the little Chinese guy. "Have you ever spent any time on a boat, Dragon Master?"

"Yes, Golden Twin, I served as captain on sailing junk that fished you out of Weddell Sea. I prefer sailing ships, but I also have expertise on power boats."

"Wait a minute, the Weddell Sea? Are you saying you were the captain on the boat that kidnapped me?" My voice shot up an octave.

He nodded. "So sorry."

"Why should she trust you?" Jeff asked, his voice tight.

"Atlanteans all dead. I serve Golden Twin now. She last heir to throne." He bowed his head.

"What throne?" I arched my brows and half turned.

"Throne for ruler of Atlantis," Dragon Master said.

"You're kidding. Rule an abandoned underwater city?" I asked. "I'm not a mermaid."

"Weapon is already activated in black pyramid. Fire it and raise city." He said it like it was no big deal to drown millions of people in the giant tidal waves that would be created by raising Atlantis.

"Forget it. My loyalty is to America. I won't drown my fellow countrymen so I can rule a dead city," I said. "If you really do serve me now, you'd better make damn sure Atlantis stays at the bottom of the sea."

He nodded. "As you wish, Golden Twin."

Lance glanced at me with wide eyes and mouthed, "WTF?"

"Sam, are you sure we can trust this guy to help my son?" Jeff asked.

"Dragon Master is an expert on dragon currents, or ley lines, as the Brits call them, and all things Atlantean, but he doesn't have super powers. I'm sure Max and his SEALs can handle him." I reached up and switched on the seatbelt sign, then made a brief arrival announcement before beginning our descent for Honolulu.

I flew a hands-on approach and made a smooth landing. After I taxied to the gate, we finished our checklists and waited for someone from the State Department to bring the necessary paperwork for Dragon Master to enter the USA.

Jeff opened the cockpit door and said goodbye to our passengers as they disembarked for a two-day stop on Oahu.

After the last person deplaned, an admiral decked out in a white uniform with full regalia boarded with a man in a dark suit.

"Captain Rowlin, I'm Admiral Ruth Jacobs, and this is Richard Leach from the State Department. Please allow Captain Starr and her friend to step out."

I exited onto the jetway with my Asian charge. "This is the man known as Dragon Master," I said. "He has sworn to serve me."

Mr. Leach pulled out a camera and took a few pictures. "This will do for now." He handed Dragon Master a State Department ID.

Our head flight attendant, Cindy, stood nearby, taking it all in.

"All right, Captain Starr, grab your bag," Admiral Jacobs said. "It's a matter of national security. We have two fast movers waiting on the tarmac to fly you two to Key West and get you to the USS *Leviathan* as soon as possible."

A man in a G-suit appeared with two G-suits in hand. "Put these on."

"What this for?" Dragon Master asked.

"The suit helps you tolerate G-forces in a fighter jet." He thrust one at me and one at the old guy.

I looked out the jetway window and spotted two F/A-18F fighter jets parked nearby. They were the two-seat trainer version of the single-seat Super Hornet my brother Matt flew in his Navy squadron.

I nudged the guy who'd given me the flight suit. "Are you one of the Hornet pilots?"

He nodded. "Lieutenant Don Dixon at your service, Captain Starr. Callsign Jackpot."

I crossed my arms. "I'm not going unless you let me do the takeoff, some fun stuff on the climb, and the landing in Key West."

Stunned, he glanced at the admiral, clearly not wanting to fail in front of the woman in command of the Pacific fleet. "Uh, we're not allowed—"

Admiral Jacobs interrupted him, "Let her fly the

damn plane." She turned to me. "Hurry, Captain Starr. Every minute counts."

I grinned as I stripped off my uniform jacket, shoved it and my hat into my bag, and pulled on the G-suit.

"Wait!" Cindy handed me a tiny velvet pouch. "My sister is a marine engineer on that ship. Her name is Vicky Edwards. Please give her this necklace I bought in Hong Kong for her birthday."

I shoved it in a zippered pocket. "Alrighty, I'll find her after I deal with the big emergency." I grabbed my bag and paused. "I'll be back ASAP, Boss." I waved goodbye to Jeff and Lance and trotted down the jetway stairs to the ramp.

It's rare for a non-military pilot to get a chance to fly a fighter jet that's still in active service. If the Navy was going to mess up my flight check on the 767, the least they could do was let me have some fun in the Super Hornet.

Jackpot tapped my shoulder. "Uh, this is considered an emergency, so we're waiving the usual ejection-seat training and pre-flight lecture, but I can explain everything on the way to Key West."

"No need," I said. "My brother checked me out in an F/A-18F last fall. I'm good to go, but I'm pretty sure the old guy has never flown in a fighter."

As Jackpot led Dragon Master to the other Navy pilot, I texted Ross my new route so he'd know why my watch's GPS signal was making a supersonic track to Key West.

It wasn't long before we were on the takeoff roll. The Super Hornet pinned me in my seat as we rocketed down the runway. We continued to accelerate as I pulled back on the stick and executed a rolling vertical climb. Woo hoo!

The overwater portion of our flight was way faster than Mach 1. We slowed for in-flight refueling and the overland portion. Then it was back to supersonic speed over the Gulf of Mexico to Key West Naval Air Station.

Fun stuff.

As we rocketed across the Gulf of Mexico, Jackpot asked, "How did your brother get permission to give you a check out in an F/A-18F?"

"This isn't for public knowledge, but it was a reward I earned for landing a Boeing 727 on the deck of an aircraft carrier last fall."

"That was you? There must be more to the story if they let you fly a fighter."

"Oh yeah, that airliner held key enemy combatants and a treasure trove of intel. The *Lawrence Lee's* captain will probably make admiral soon thanks to me, which is why he let me fly one of the carrier's Super Hornets."

"Wow, that airliner landing must've been tight. I'd love to see the video," Jackpot said.

"It's in the Navy archives. It was the scariest landing I've ever made," I said.

He laughed. "I guess I don't have to sweat your landing in Key West." He paused. "On another subject, are you dating anyone?"

Sitting in front of him, I nodded. "My boyfriend is a captain in the UK's Special Air Service."

"Good to know. I'm not about to piss off an SAS badass. Be sure and tell him I was real nice to you. Oh, and slow the hell down. We're only eighty miles from Key West."

"Roger that—slowing the hell down now." I pulled back the throttles. Before long, we were cleared to land.

I landed the Super Hornet as though my twin brothers in the Navy were watching. They were two years older, and we'd always been competitive. I knew news of my fighter flight would get back to them. Matt, the fighter pilot, would hear about it first. Then he'd tell Mike, a tier-one SEAL. I made a smooth landing to keep up my good reputation with Matt's carrier squadron.

As I climbed down from the cockpit, I couldn't stop smiling. Controlling the massive power and speed of a modern jet fighter had been an exhilarating adrenaline rush.

And Jackpot had been "real nice to me." When we stepped onto the tarmac, I hugged him.

"Thanks for the fun flight. I'll tell Admiral Jacobs you were a total pro."

He grinned. "Looks like the Seahawk is waiting for you. Keep the G-suit. You never know when you might get another flight in a fast mover." He handed me my bag and saluted.

I saluted Jackpot and trotted to the waiting helicopter. Dragon Master looked a little wobbly as his pilot escorted him to me. A crewman handed us helmets and life vests. We pulled them on and climbed aboard. The instant our seatbelts were fastened the Seahawk took off and zoomed low over the sea.

We landed on *Leviathan's* helipad about twenty minutes later. The crewman who'd given us the life vests and helmets took them back and ushered us off the helipad.

I'd never met Max, but Jeff had shown me plenty of pictures. When I spotted a tall blond guy, I recognized him right away. He was almost an exact copy of his father.

As he approached, his jaw dropped. "Sorry, Sam, it's just that you really do look exactly like Solraya, the blond triplet," he paused, "except your eye color is a little different." He offered his hand. "Thanks for coming. I wouldn't have whisked you away like that if it wasn't a life or death crisis, and frankly, I'm out of options."

I squeezed his hand. "Good to finally meet you,

Max, and this is Dragon Master." I thumbed at the small man beside me.

Dragon Master bowed. "An honor to meet you, Captain."

Max glanced at his watch. "I hate to cut this short, but my divers only have about twenty minutes of air left. They're trapped inside a building that's two thousand feet down, and there's a giant squid down there that'll kill them if they try to leave."

Stunned, I asked, "How big is it?"

"About a hundred and sixty feet long," Max said. "It's already destroyed two foreign submarines and a Russian spy trawler, and it killed two Russian divers."

I glanced at Dragon Master. "Any suggestions?"

"All sea creatures are yours to command, Golden Twin." He bowed his head.

"I remember the times the triplets telepathically commanded orcas to do their bidding, but what makes you think I can do that—especially with a sea monster that's way bigger and a lot dumber than an orca?" I asked, my mind racing.

"Golden Twin now Atlantean queen." He bowed. "Sea monster guards your city. It will obey you."

"How could you possibly know that?"

"Atlantean masters told me years ago."

I turned to Max. "Take me to Dive Ops."

We rushed through the ship to the area where

they launched divers in Hardsuits. A suit was attached to the winch.

I nudged Max. "What was the objective in that building?"

"We've been ordered to retrieve all the vaults. The divers had already unhooked the chains securing them to the walls. Then we spotted the giant squid on sonar and ordered them to sever their cables and move to the rear of the building."

I bit my lip. "I'm going to test something. If it works, I'll have your divers up here before their air runs out. Is there an open spot on the deck?"

Max pointed. "The forward deck is clear."

"I need quiet with no interruptions, and don't shoot the squid. We need it." I closed my eyes and concentrated on contacting the monster telepathically.

Forget there's a ticking clock. Relax. Visualize the kraken and call out to it.

God, am I really doing this?

Focus!

Max grabbed an interphone and gave the hold-fire order.

Five minutes later, I heard yelling.

Oh God, did it work?

I opened my eyes. The water beside the ship churned, throwing up a fountain of spray as a huge tentacle burst through the surface, clutching a rectangular gold vault. The massive appendage gently deposited it on the deck and then slithered beneath the waves.

"If I send the kraken to retrieve your divers, they'll think it's coming to kill them and fight it," I said. "Can you contact them and explain it's there to rescue them?"

"We lost comms when they cut their cables." Max frowned. "Their radios can't receive our signal inside the stone building."

I sucked in my breath. *I have to find a way to save the divers without anyone knowing the triplets transferred all their knowledge to me before they died.*

"Put me in a Hardsuit so I can go down there and tell them myself." I unzipped my G-suit. "And give me two cables to tether the divers to me."

Can't believe I'm doing this.

"There's no time to winch you down two thousand feet," Max said.

"Then disconnect the winch cable, and my new pet will take me down. How much time do we have left?" I shrugged off my G-suit and kicked off my shoes.

Max glanced at his watch. "Eight minutes." He motioned to his SEAL commander. "George, put her in the Hardsuit and disconnect the cable. Hurry!"

"If that squid makes a mistake and squeezes you

a little too hard at depth, you'll end up a blob of Jell-O," George said.

My gut twisted into a knot.

"Hey, if this was easy, anybody could do it." I grinned, trying to hide my terror.

"When you're in the suit, you'll have hand controls for the graspers, foot controls for the thrusters, and a voice-activated mike to talk to the divers via radio interphone once you're inside the building. Questions?"

I glanced at my watch. Six minutes. "Just get me out of this metal coffin as soon as I get back." I turned to Max. "Uh, Max, promise me that if I pull this off, you won't tell your superiors what I did. I'd like to have a life after this. They probably wouldn't believe you anyway." I stepped into the suit.

"I'll promise to keep your secret if you promise to come back alive," Max said. "My dad would never forgive me if I got you killed."

"It's a deal," I said right before they locked the suit shut. I looked at them through my much-too-small viewing port and forced a smile.

Five minutes left on the dive clock.

Now I have to somehow forget about being claustrophobic and concentrate on communicating telepathically with a terrifying sea monster. Holy crap!

I took another deep breath and tried to ignore a wave of fear-induced nausea as a giant tentacle snaked toward me and gently wrapped around my Hardsuit. Once it had me in its grasp, it raced downward to the ancient city. It moved so fast I saw nothing but giant suction cups and a blur of rushing water as my heart jackhammered my chest.

My tentacle ride stopped in front of a white marble building shaped like an octagon. The small viewing port in my suit wasn't big enough for me to see the rest of the monster somewhere behind or above me. Just as well—I'd probably have a heart attack. I gasped as the tentacle holding me cleared the door and snaked inside the building.

The divers were on top of the rearmost vault. They had maybe four minutes of air.

"Attention, *Leviathan* divers! I'm here to rescue you," I said over my radio intercom. "This is not a hallucination—the kraken is helping me."

A man replied weakly, "Who are you and who sent you?"

"I'm Samantha Starr. Captain Max Rowlin sent me. You're almost out of air. The kraken will take us up to the ship really fast, so I'm going to attach these tethers to keep us together." I clipped the cables to their suits. "Hold still while the tentacle gathers us."

The woman screamed, "Don't let it get me!"

I heard the man say, "Vicky, let go of that chain!" He tapped her. "Now!"

Her grasper released the chain. "This is too scary," she said, almost out of breath.

"Hang in there. We'll be topside soon," I said as the tentacle withdrew us from the building.

Two minutes before they'd run out of air.

The trip up was as blurry as the trip down had been. We burst above the surface, and the tentacle curved over the rail, lowered us onto the deck, and paused.

I unhooked the tether cables with my graspers, leaving the divers on the deck. Then I took another nauseating trip down to the Hall of Records.

Might as well seize the opportunity and recover the vaults for Max. Then maybe I won't have to get in this torture chamber again next month. A few more minutes of terror and I'll be done. The worst is probably over—I hope.

Once I was back inside the building, the kraken's tentacle released me and began gathering vaults according to my commands. It pulled one through the door and handed it to another tentacle, then returned for another one. I sent the kraken to the surface with six gold vaults.

That left four more and me. One last trip to the ship and we'd be done.

I glanced at the entrance and saw two divers enter wearing odd-looking dive suits with Russian flags on their chests. Their suits had cables attached. I hadn't seen any other surface ships, so I assumed they'd come from a submarine. One big enough to survive a kraken attack.

Just in case they weren't friendly, I hit my thrusters and zoomed behind a big statue of Poseidon in the center of the dark room. My suit had a closed oxygen system that wouldn't expel air bubbles, but I didn't know how to switch off my external light. Could be they wanted those gold vaults for Mother Russia and wouldn't want me telling anyone they'd been here. That damn light on my suit was like a beacon for them to find me.

A ballistic spear zipped past the statue, barely missing my right shoulder.

Oh God, they're coming for me! And my only weapon is topside making a delivery.

The two divers could easily flank me. One spear into my Hardsuit and I'd be reduced to a gory soup.

NINE

Honolulu, Hawaii

"She not here. Never checked into hotel," the Chinese agent said into an encrypted satellite phone. "And no record of her going through U.S. Customs."

"She might still be in Hong Kong. We will widen search," the agent in Hong Kong said. "Go to her airline's headquarters in Palm Beach and find out where she is."

"I have a flight booked to Los Angeles connecting to Fort Lauderdale. I will call when I get to my hotel in Palm Beach."

"Good. We must find Samantha Starr and learn her government's secrets."

USS LEVIATHAN

"Where the hell is she?" Rowlin stood beside Bern as they watched the kraken deposit huge rectangular storage containers made of gold onto the deck nearby.

"She must be down there, directing the beast to bring up all the vaults."

Rowlin yelled to the deck crew, "As soon as the squid dives underwater, cover that cargo with tarps."

Bern's SEALs had pulled the divers out of the Hardsuits with seconds to spare. Banger and Vicky sat on deck chairs with blankets wrapped around them, trembling but not wanting to miss the kraken spectacle. Wide-eyed, they sipped orange juice from a safe distance and watched the deck activity as Rowlin stood nearby.

"She'd better come up with the last four." Rowlin ran his hand over his blond buzz cut, pacing. "Man, if she doesn't come back, I don't know what we'll do."

A crewmember rushed up and handed Rowlin a printed message.

He swore under his breath. "Sonar's got *Kazan* sitting on the bottom near the Hall of Records, and they heard a hatch open. Could be they sent in divers."

Rowlin snatched up the interphone and called CIC. "Send a message to *Texas*. Tell them to intimidate that Russian sub any way short of starting a war. We need a little help to get our diver away from there."

Rowlin watched the kraken slip beneath the surface. "It'd better get her out of there fast."

The Russian divers flanked me and aimed their weapons. I hit my thrusters and shot straight up. Their ballistic spears brushed my inner thighs. Their next shots wouldn't miss. To buy time, I circled around the far side of Poseidon's huge statue.

I looked down as the Russians took positions on my right and left front. Where the hell was my kraken buddy? I knew I shouldn't have been gulping air, but I couldn't help it.

The divers looked up at me and aimed their spears at my torso.

At that moment, a huge tentacle snaked into the room and snared their cables. It yanked hard just as they fired. Both spears flashed by, barely missing me. My protector pulled them into its grasp as they desperately stabbed and kicked at its tentacle. In one quick movement, it crushed their suits and dragged them out of the building, leaving behind a dark cloud of blood and guts.

It was a horrifying display of gore—but better them than me. I struggled to get my panicked breathing under control. I felt sick but managed to stop myself from puking inside the suit.

The kraken gathered the four remaining vaults. I was terrified to have it grab me again after witnessing what it had done to the Russians, so I wrapped my arms and legs around Poseidon's upper torso and commanded the beast to yank the statue off its five-foot base and carry it and me to the ship.

Bad idea. When it jerked the statue off the base, it severed Poseidon's ankles, leaving the statue's feet secured to the base and sending me tumbling backwards. I recovered and thrusted back to the statue just as the tentacle pulled it through the door. I grabbed the mythical god's head and then hooked my arms under his arms. My feet scraped the doorjamb on the way out.

Outside the building, I spotted two huge submarines facing off in what looked like a game of chicken.

This was a good time to say goodbye to Atlantis.

I watched the city recede in a blur of rushing water as we sped to the surface. My heart raced as the monster plunked the statue onto the deck, pinning me beneath Poseidon's head and upper torso. My squid buddy vanished into the depths before I could think of what to do, and I didn't want to risk calling it back.

Crewmen swarmed the statue and rolled it off me. It was a relief to feel strong hands pulling me out of that claustrophobia-inducing metal prison.

I stood on wobbly legs and wrapped my arms around Commander Bern. Shivering like a victim of extreme cold, I was actually soaked in sweat. "Don't let go," I said.

George held me close. "You're okay now. The kraken's gone."

"I'm alive, but I'm definitely not okay. I feel like I'll never stop shaking."

"Relax and take some slow, deep breaths." He rubbed my back.

"I don't suppose you have any red wine on this tub? I could use a drink to calm my nerves."

"No wine, but the captain has some incredibly smooth forty-year-old Scotch the Brits gave him. Will that do?"

"Uh, no hard liquor. My stomach is already queasy." I loosened my grip and looked up at him. "Do you have a fitness center on board? Maybe a hard workout will burn off the adrenaline."

"We do—a good one. Our captain likes his crew to keep fit." George accepted a towel from a crewman and wrapped it around me.

Max put his hand on my shoulder. "You okay, Sam?"

"She wants to use our gym. Take the edge off."

"Sam, first I need to ask, did you see any Russian divers when you were down there?"

"Yeah, and the bastards tried to kill me." I sucked in my breath, trying to erase the carnage from my memory. "The monster saved me from them. It wasn't pretty."

"It crushed them?" Max asked.

"Well, the water pressure crushed them after the beast cracked open their suits. Nothing left but a gory gelatinous mush and crumpled metal still attached to cables. I assumed they came from the Russian sub that was playing chicken with ours."

"When the crew reels them in, maybe they'll finally believe us about the giant squid," Max said.

"Maybe not," I said. "There's nothing left there that would prove the squid did it."

"They might assume their guys lost the battle with our divers," George said.

"The survivors from that Russian spy ship saw the kraken sink it," Max said. "They must've reported it."

"In any case, I suggest you make it your number one priority to get those vaults onto U.S. soil before our enemies realize what you have on deck," I said to Max.

"The gold alone would pay down a sizeable portion of our national debt," George said.

"The crew covered them with tarps as soon as they hit the deck," Max said. "I have one major task remaining. Do a quick workout and meet me in the conference room in thirty minutes. An ensign will show you the way."

I glanced at my DOXA dive watch. "See you in thirty."

After a brief, hard work-out and a hot shower, I put on jeans and a T-shirt. I had just texted Ross that I was alive and well when an ensign arrived to escort me to a conference room.

I still felt shaky. Massive amounts of adrenaline will do that. It had all happened so fast I hadn't had time to really think about what I was doing. If I had, I probably would've talked myself out of it—but then *Leviathan's* divers would be dead.

Dragon Master, Max, and George sat at a long, rectangular table with a white-haired guy who looked like a Viking, an African-American man built like a chiseled block of granite, and a lovely woman in her late-twenties who looked a bit shell-shocked.

Kind of like how I felt.

"Sam, I'd like you to meet the divers you saved." Max nodded at the woman. "Marine Engineer Vicky Edwards and her dive partner, Banger, one of our SEALs."

My jaw dropped. "Oh my God, you're Cindy's sister! She's on the crew I left to come here."

"Yep, I'm her sister, but please don't tell her about what happened." Vicky stood and hugged me. "Thank you for saving us and for getting the vaults. You made a hard job easy, but I have to admit it scared the crap out of me."

"Yeah, well, seems like everything has a down side." I smiled. "I'm just glad we made it back."

Max turned to the Norseman. "And this is our marine biologist, Dr. Kip Peterson."

I nodded at Kip. "It's a pleasure to meet everyone, especially now that our underwater nightmare is over." I smiled and settled in across from Max.

"Lucky for us, that kraken killed the Russian divers. Bastards tried to shoot us," Banger said.

"The Russians sent divers to kill me too, but the monster crushed them into mush."

"We thought it was coming to kill us when we saw you riding the tentacle," Vicky said. "Even though you explained why it was there, I still thought we were going to die."

"How did you manage that rescue?" Banger asked.

I glanced at Max. "Uh, I'd rather not get into that. In fact, I'd like you to forget the whole thing and pretend you were rescued by other means. That goes for the vault retrieval too."

Max jumped in. "Sam did us a huge favor at great personal risk. It would be better for her if no one finds out what she did. No one would believe it, anyway."

"We're going to have to admit the giant squid is real since we already told several foreign countries about it," Kip said. "No other way to explain the loss of their ships without bringing the blame on us."

"Which is why we can't tell anyone Sam can control it," Max said. "Those countries would think we sank their subs and spy ship on purpose."

I added, "It rescued the divers and retrieved the vaults in less than ten minutes. Only your crew saw what it did, so make sure they keep their mouths shut. You need to come up with an alternate explanation for the Navy."

Max nodded. "Alright, how about this? We tried our best to kill the kraken and have no idea why it destroyed those vessels and killed the Russian divers. We lured it away with an AUV and rescued our divers with the research sub. And we won't mention the vaults."

"Perfect," I said. "And the dead Russian divers can't refute your account."

"I have one more major task to complete in Atlantis." Max glanced at me. "I've been ordered to deactivate and then disable the weapon housed inside the black pyramid."

"Can our pet squid reach it with one of its tentacles?" I asked.

"The weapon is in a circular chamber well over three hundred feet from the entrance. The giant squid is much too big to fit inside, and its tentacles aren't long enough," Kip said.

"Too bad. I know from past experience the pyramid's defense mechanisms aren't programmed to attack sea life," Banger said.

"Defense system will not attack Golden Twin.

She now ruler of Atlantis," Dragon Master said as he nodded in my direction.

Great. He had to open his big mouth and tell them I can enter safely. There has to be another way.

Vicky glanced from me to Max. "Captain, why can't you just destroy the pyramid with torpedoes and crush the weapon?"

Max shook his head. "Too dangerous. The weapon is already powered up and ready to fire. There might be a failsafe that would trigger it if we attack the pyramid. It would only need a second or two to fire enough energy into the ley lines beneath it to set off a major earthquake that would compress the tectonic plates and raise Atlantis."

"Massive amounts of water would be displaced, which would create enormous tsunamis that would kill millions of people on both sides of the Atlantic," Kip added.

"That's why we need to disarm the weapon before we destroy it." Max nodded at Vicky.

I tried to change their focus. "I think delivering those vaults to U.S. soil should be the top priority. In the meantime, our nuclear sub can guard the pyramid, and you can send me back to Hawaii on another fast mover so I can finish my flight check." I glanced at my watch. "If I go today, I'll get there in time to rest and resume my trip on schedule. Dragon Master can stay here and assist you." I raised a brow. "You owe me, Max."

"All right, but promise you'll return and help me deal with that weapon."

"Agreed." I stood. "I'll go put on my G-suit."

"Thanks. I'll arrange to have an F/A-18F waiting for you in Key West and order a Seahawk to fly you there." He glanced at his watch. "Be ready in fifteen minutes."

"Thank you, Max." I hesitated. "Uh, any chance you can get me some chocolate?"

The men looked bewildered, confusion clouding their faces.

Vicky laughed. "I've got plenty. The phenyl-alanine in it helps take the edge off all the stress," she explained, glancing at the men.

"Lucky for me there's a woman on this ship." I grinned at her.

I rushed out, pulled on the G-suit, texted Ross about my supersonic flight back to HNL, and met Vicky and Max on the helipad.

She handed over two bars of Godiva dark chocolate and hugged me. "Thanks for saving me, Sam. I'll see you back here soon."

"Wait, I have a birthday gift for you from Cindy." I unzipped a thigh pocket, pulled out the velvet pouch, and zipped the candy bars into the pocket.

She opened the pouch and pulled out a silver-chain necklace with a silver kraken pendant dangling on it. "Holy crap! How did she know?"

"Sister's intuition?" I laughed. "Now you'll never forget that giant squid."

"As if I ever would!" She grinned and hugged me.

I hugged a bewildered-looking Max and waved goodbye.

TEN

My ride back to HNL was in another F/A-18F, piloted by a guy with the call sign Gunslinger. En route at supersonic speed over the Gulf of Mexico, I asked, "How'd you get that call sign?"

"Ever hear of a shooting organization called SASS?" he said.

"The Single-Action Shooting Society? My brother, Matt, used to compete in it doing Cowboy Action Shooting before he joined the Navy. He won a bunch of trophies."

"Then you know all the shooters had competition names. Mine was Gunslinger, and I won National Champion three years in a row before I joined the Navy. My squadron found out about it, and the name stuck."

"Then you must be Paul Dupree, the guy who kept beating out my brother. Matt won National

Champion the year you joined the Navy. He joined the year after."

"Matt Starr is your brother? What's he doing now?"

"He flies Super Hornets based on the carrier *Lawrence Lee*. His call sign is Rodeo. I think they're still in the Mediterranean Sea."

"No kidding? What are the odds?"

"I guess you guys have a lot in common. I'm surprised your paths haven't crossed in the Navy."

"You're an airline pilot, right? That's what they told me in Key West."

"I fly Boeing 767s for Luxury International Airlines based in Palm Beach."

"Would you like some stick time in the Hornet?"

"Another pilot—Jackpot—let me fly one from Hawaii to Key West earlier today. I'd love to do it again, but I'm afraid my nerves are shot. My hands are still shaking from a terrifying experience that happened a little over an hour ago. If I take the stick, we'll be all over the sky."

"No kidding? What happened?" he asked.

"It's top secret, and you wouldn't believe me anyway, but I really appreciate the offer. Maybe next time—if there ever is a next time."

"I understand. I figured you must be somebody important. The Navy doesn't order fast-mover transport for just anybody. You relax, and I'll get us there ASAP."

And he did.

I fell asleep and dreamed of sea monsters. When I awoke, we had just touched down in HNL.

"Thanks for the ride, Gunslinger. Give my best to Jackpot if you see him." I handed him my helmet.

I took a cab to the layover hotel on Waikiki Beach and checked in. Then I grabbed the phone in my room and called Jeff. He answered on the second ring.

"Hey, Jeff, I'm back in Hawaii, and I'll be ready to finish our flight sequence tomorrow."

"Great! Everything turn out okay?"

"Yep, the divers are safe, and your son's mission is now way ahead of schedule, so he sent me back here on another Super Hornet."

"Want to join the crew for dinner? We're going to a luau."

"I'm pretty beat. I think I'll just get room service and crash, but I'll see you for breakfast."

"Okay, I'll call you in the morning. Glad to have you back, Sam."

I opened a split of red wine from the mini bar and called Ross. Hearing his Scottish baritone always made my heart race.

The next morning, I strolled into the restaurant and found Jeff and Lance seated with three of our flight attendants at a table for six. Lance had kept the seat next to him empty.

I had to admit I might have responded a bit too favorably to his hot kiss in Hong Kong, but hey, I was only human. I was pretty sure the majority of women would've ripped his shirt off in the first five seconds. I'd handled it better than most. All clothing had remained on. And we'd had a good reason for the kiss anyway.

On the other hand, my actress friend, Carlene Jensen, would've had Lance right there in the hallway of the floating restaurant. (It wasn't like she hadn't had him plenty of times in the past.) The man never had to do without. There was no reason for me to ever feel guilty about turning him down. He knew I loved Ross.

"Welcome back, Sam. How was your trip?" Lance said as he stood and pulled back my chair, always a gentleman.

I settled in and greeted everyone. "The flight to Key West was a thrill. I got to do the takeoff, some of the flying, and the landing. It was also the first time I've gone supersonic. I loved it!"

"What did you think of Max?" Jeff asked.

"I recognized him the moment I saw him. He looks like your clone—and he's an amazing captain. It's obvious he has the respect and trust of his crew."

"What was the big emergency?" Cindy, the head flight attendant, asked.

"Two Hardsuit divers were trapped inside a building that was two thousand feet beneath the surface, and they'd run out of options." I honored Vicky's request and didn't mention she'd been one of the divers.

"But why did they need you?" Sonia, a blonde flight attendant in her mid-twenties from Spain, asked.

"Because it happened in the underwater city of Atlantis." I paused. "I might be the only person left alive who knows a lot about the Atlanteans, and that little Chinese guy who came with me is an expert on their energy systems."

"Did you figure out how to save them?" Cindy asked.

I nodded. "I tried something Dragon Master suggested, and it worked." I glanced at Jeff. "It's considered top secret, so I can't share the details, but the main thing is the divers made it back safe and sound. Oh, and Vicky loved the necklace you gave her."

Lance put his arm on the back of my chair. "Did you at least enjoy the experience?"

"God no, it was terrifying—not to mention I felt claustrophobic in that damn Hardsuit." I bit my lower lip. "I'm not looking forward to going back there, but I promised Max I'd return for a few days in May after I'm back on regular flight duty."

"Did you at least get a good view of Atlantis? That must've been awesome," Sonia said.

"My trip down and back up was so fast, all I got was a quick glimpse—and don't ask any more questions. Sorry." I grabbed my plate. "I'm going to the buffet. Anybody need anything?"

"I'll go with you," Lance said. "I haven't eaten yet."

As we worked our way down the buffet table, Lance asked, "Any injuries?"

"No, mostly just terrified." I looked around. We were alone at the buffet. "Deadly situations are playing out in Atlantis. Russian divers tried to kill our divers, and they tried to kill me, but we can't disclose that without opening a dangerous can of worms. World War Three could be at stake. There are nuclear-powered subs cruising around down there, along with some other scary stuff."

"Dang, woman, you're lucky you survived. No wonder you're so glad to be back." He hesitated. "Do the Chinese have a sub down there?"

"Yeah, I think so. Why?"

"All the more reason for you to stay the hell away. They won't give up just because they missed taking you in Hong Kong." He squeezed my shoulder. "You need to keep a low profile for a while."

I nodded, staring absently at the buffet. "That's my plan."

Later that day, we flew to California and spent the night in San Jose. The next day, we flew home to Palm Beach where we were greeted by the usual blue skies and bright sunshine.

USS LEVIATHAN

Rowlin ripped open the sealed orders from SEC-NAV. "I can't believe we've been delayed almost two days waiting for the brass in D.C. to make a decision about the vaults."

Executive Officer Vance Lowes settled across from Max in his stateroom. "Maybe they've decided we deserve a posting in Stockholm or Naples. I'd settle for anywhere with hot chicks and no sea monsters." Lowes grinned, trying to ease the tension.

"Fat chance." Rowlin read the orders. "The delay was to allow time for two destroyers to join us early tomorrow morning. One will escort us to Mayport where we can unload the vaults away from public view, and the other destroyer will remain on station until we return."

"I thought SECNAV didn't want to draw attention to our cargo," Lowes said. "Sailing all the way up to Jacksonville instead of Key West will most certainly make all our commie friends suspicious."

"They're also sending *Texas* to guard us from enemy subs. Apparently, North Korea thinks we sank their sub. They're making the usual nuclear threats, but they may also be planning an attack on our ship."

Lowes leaned forward. "If *Texas* shadows us, who'll guard the weapon in the black pyramid?"

"That was another reason for the delay. Washington negotiated a deal with the Brits. Their nuclear-powered sub, *Audacious*, will handle it."

"Can they launch Hardsuit divers from that sub?" Lowes sipped his coffee.

Rowlin nodded. "Banger met with their divers and warned them about the Russians. They'll be armed with ballistic spear guns."

"How do we know their divers won't mess with the Atlantean weapon and accidentally fire it?" Lowes shook his head.

Rowlin thought a moment. "That would annihilate Ireland and a big chunk of England, including London, so the Brits won't risk it. And they haven't forgotten their marine archaeologist got killed messing with that weapon."

"Let's not forget the giant squid. Aren't the Brits concerned for their crew's safety?"

"I'm sure they are, but they know the lives of their people back home depend on them." Rowlin hesitated. "They asked me to loan them Banger."

Lowes straightened. "And did you?"

"Not a chance in hell. I told Banger he's not going down again unless Sam is down there with him. Besides, he's a SEAL. We need him to defend our ship."

"One SEAL team isn't enough to defend a ship this big. Good thing you requested a full platoon." Lowes glanced at his watch. "They should be arriving in Seahawks any minute."

"My gut tells me the North Koreans will send in

an assault team tonight. Notify the officers to arm our crew and plan on going to general quarters at sunset."

Lowes stood. "Aye, Captain."

"And XO, you have the conn while I meet with the SEALs." Rowlin pulled on his captain's hat and strode down the corridor.

ELEVEN

Palm Beach, Florida

"Hi, Mom," I said into the phone. "I'm back home now and cleared to resume my flight schedule. How's everything with you and Duncan in Scotland?"

"We're good, but aren't you leaving out a few things? Like flying a fighter from Hawaii to Key West? What have you gotten yourself into this time?"

"How did you…oh, Matt must've told you."

"You know how quickly news travels in the military. Are you okay?"

"Yeah, and I'm working another flight as soon as I get my mandatory crew rest." I hesitated to tell her, but decided it was better if she knew. "The Chinese may be after me to find out why the US bombed the Himalayas near their border. I want to keep moving until they lose interest."

"Then for God sakes go to my house. The security system is far better, and Romeo can protect you. Besides, he really misses you."

"That's actually a good idea. They're bound to look for me at my condo, and I miss our big cuddle bear. It's a shame the UK has such strict rules about bringing in pets. Romeo would love Duncan's castle and grounds."

"Hurry and pack. Call me when you're settled at my place," Mom said and hung up.

Her "place" was a huge oceanfront mansion. The local police were known for keeping careful track of everyone entering Palm Beach who didn't live there. They'd know if Chinese agents were sneaking up on me.

I put several uniform items on hangers into my clothes bag and packed my luggage. Fifteen minutes later, I headed to my mother's manse.

A black SUV with darkly tinted windows pulled behind me seconds after I left my condo's parking garage. It followed me through town to A1A and stayed on my bumper all the way to Mom's oceanfront home about a half mile south of Trump's Mar-a-Lago.

Damn.

The SUV kept going down A1A when Mom's iron entrance gates closed behind me.

Rosa, my mother's longtime domestic helper, greeted me when I entered the house.

"Sam, *mi corazón, cómo estás?*"

She reverts to Spanish when she's excited.

"I'm fine, and you? I've missed you."

We hugged.

Before she could answer, Romeo galloped across the polished marble floor and skidded into me, yowling with glee.

He covered me with sloppy dog kisses as he stood on his hind legs. A honey-colored German shepherd, Romeo was almost my height standing with his front paws on my shoulders.

I kept petting him until he'd had time to calm down. Big dogs are the best—so warm and huggable.

"Your mother called and told me you were on your way. Where is your luggage?"

"In the car. I didn't want my hands full when Romeo greeted me." I turned and headed out the door.

Rosa helped me with my bags while Romeo supervised. We took the elevator to the third floor and deposited the luggage in my old bedroom.

"How long will you stay?"

"Just until my next flight in a day or two, but I'll come back again after that."

"Good. We've missed you," Rosa said as she patted Romeo's head.

I stepped out onto the balcony overlooking the

ocean. Below, I spotted a lone figure with binoculars looking up at me from the shadow of a palm tree.

How did he get past the security system?

I backed out of view, pulled out my cell, and called the cops.

My next call was to my brother, Mike. Luckily, he answered. "Hi, Mike, no time for chitchat. How can I contact your SEAL buddy Tim Goldy—the one who has the security company?"

"Sounds like another Danger Magnet mission," he said. "Who's after you this time?"

"The Chinese Secret Service."

USS LEVIATHAN

Rowlin stepped out onto the bridge's port wing and scanned the dark water with night-vision binoculars. Humid salt air shrouded him like a wet blanket in the still night.

"It's almost midnight, and they're out there somewhere, XO. I can feel it." He stepped inside and keyed his mike. "Commander Bern, report."

"The moon pool is locked down, and SEALs are stationed at potential boarding points throughout the ship," Bern said. "We're ready, Captain."

Rowlin turned to XO Lowes, who stood beside him. "Am I missing anything?"

"All battle stations are manned, and the crew is armed. I think we're good."

"Unless a skirmish here triggers World War Three." Rowlin clenched his fist.

"That nut in North Korea thinks we sank his submarine," Lowes said.

"He wants payback—tit for tat, with an attack on my ship."

"And Washington is okay with that as long as we win…so no pressure, Captain."

Rowlin pounded the console. "I wish we could use our Scorpions. Inflatable boats might sneak in under the radar, and *Texas* wouldn't be able to take them out."

"Can't risk our Scorpion crews with that giant squid out there, but maybe it'll do the job for us." Lowes grinned. "That'd be poetic justice."

"We should be so lucky. Too bad Sam isn't here to make it happen." Rowlin scanned the calm water. "This is the perfect night for an amphibious assault—heavy cloud cover and no moon. Kraken or no kraken, we're ready for the North Koreans."

"Unless they vaporize us with a nuke."

"Nice to know I can always count on you to be the optimist," Rowlin said.

Earlier in Palm Beach

I was relieved when Palm Beach cops arrested the Chinese intruder, but they couldn't hold him because he had diplomatic immunity. He claimed he didn't know he was on private property.

Yeah, right!

I stepped out on the third-floor balcony of my bedroom and scanned the back lawn, pool deck, and oceanfront. Nothing seemed to be there but palm trees swaying, sea gulls squawking, waves breaking on shore, and balmy breezes caressing me. When I returned to the air-conditioned room, my cell rang. The caller ID indicated Luxury International Airlines, my employer.

"Captain Samantha Starr, at your service," I answered.

"Hello, Captain Starr, we need you for a charter." It was crew scheduling. "Flight 515 departs at noon tomorrow for Rio de Janeiro. Your passengers will attend the two-day Rio Film Festival, and you'll fly them back the next morning."

"Great! I was hoping for a trip as soon as my crew rest was over. Thanks!"

I'd no sooner hung up when Tim Goldy from Trident Security returned my call.

"Hello, Tim. Thanks for getting back to me so fast."

"When my men heard you'd called, they were eager to join another Danger Magnet mission. Protecting you is like being back as an active-duty SEAL. That first time sure was exciting."

"Yeah, well, this one might be a lot worse. The Chinese Secret Service is after me."

"What? Here in the US?"

"Yep, the local cops caught one spying on my mom's house in Palm Beach."

"If he's in custody, why do you need us?"

"They had to let him go—diplomatic immunity. He's probably one of many. I need you guys to guard Mom's house just for tonight. I'm leaving the country tomorrow."

"Are you sure you need a full team? Wouldn't two men suffice?"

"It's a twenty-thousand-square-foot oceanfront mansion with three full floors and a circular glass-enclosed office on the roof deck. I'm guessing they'll approach from the ocean so they can escape in a fast boat."

"How many people will we be protecting?"

"Three—Rosa, Romeo, and me."

"Romeo?"

"He's a German shepherd—and a treasured member of my family," I said in a firm voice. "Make damn sure nobody shoots him."

"Understood," Tim said in a reassuring tone. "My security company has several service dogs. I can put a bullet-proof vest on Romeo if you like."

"That'd be great. How many men can you bring?"

He hesitated. "Look, this is really short notice. I can only spare five men, plus me, but we can bring two service dogs."

"Are the men former SEALs?"

"All the guys in my company are from the teams."

"Six SEALs can fight off a small army. I'm satisfied."

"Good. We'll be there at 4:00 p.m. to familiarize ourselves with the property before dark. Uh, is Romeo good with other dogs?"

"Romeo is good with any person or dog if I tell him to be, so no worries there. Thanks for doing this on short notice, Tim. I'll see you in a few hours."

My next call was to Ross. "Hey, handsome, how's it going in Scotland?"

"Better now that you're safe at home," he said in his deep, sexy voice.

"Um, about that…" I explained the situation and the precautions I'd taken.

"Bugger! I never thought China would go this far to find out why America bombed the Himalayas. I don't think they have assets in Brazil, but who knows? Best not to wander about in Rio."

"Okay." I sighed. "I miss you."

"I miss you too, lass. Be careful tonight and call me in the morning so I'll know you're safe. General Barnes told me MI6 is trying to sort out what China's up to. They're working with the CIA to find a way to end this."

"I hope it's over soon. Bye, love." I clicked off and scanned the placid sea.

They're coming. I can feel it.

TWELVE

USS LEVIATHAN

Rowlin strode into the Combat Information Center—the nerve center of the ship where all weapons were controlled. "Anything on radar or sonar?"

"Four nuclear-powered fast-attack subs cruising around—ours and the UK's, Russia's, and China's," the sonar operator said. "And one slow-moving barge about four miles to our east in a shipping lane. It makes the same run every week."

"Radar shows one high-altitude aircraft." The radar operator pointed to his screen as the aircraft blip continued north directly overhead. Then it suddenly reversed course toward South America. "Huh, that's odd."

"Put our defense missiles on high alert in case

that aircraft dropped bombs and move the ship five miles northeast. Now!" He watched as his crew sprang into action. "I'll be on the bridge. Keep a close watch on that plane."

He left CIC and rushed up to the bridge.

Rowlin stood beside his XO as the engines went to full stop. The ship slowly drifted five miles northeast of its previous position.

"It's too still out there." Rowlin scanned the water on the port side. "I'm going out on the wing. Maybe I'll hear something."

He stepped into the balmy night air and listened. At first, there was nothing but the gentle slap of waves against the hull.

A loud splash drew his attention.

"What the hell?" He scanned the water near the ship.

It was pure luck that he spotted the billowing black chute a second before it was pulled underwater.

Rowlin dived inside and grabbed a microphone as bullets peppered the front windows on the bridge, showering him with shattered glass. "HALO jumpers attacking!"

A bullet hammered XO Lowes in the left shoulder and spun him around. He ducked behind the control console beside Rowlin as a metal storm slammed into the electronics panels.

"Vance, you're hit!" Rowlin ripped off a sleeve and wrapped it around his upper arm.

"It's just a flesh wound. My trigger arm's still good."

The two officers fired M4 carbines at paratroopers dropping onto the bridge wings. Both men were bleeding from numerous small puncture wounds inflicted by flying glass shards.

Dozens of dark chutes fluttered onto *Leviathan* with black-clad commandos firing before they even touched down. A few of the high-altitude low-open jumpers missed their landing spots on the ship and hit the water.

SEALs and sailors stationed throughout the ship opened fire on the assailants. Screams and staccato blasts from automatic weapons echoed off the water.

"XO, how're you holding up?" Rowlin noted the makeshift bandage was soaked with blood.

Lowes slapped a full magazine into his weapon. "I'm good."

A paratrooper crashed through a broken glass panel and shot Rowlin square in the chest. The Kevlar vest stopped the bullet, but the force of it knocked him into the back wall.

Lowes took out the attacker with a head shot.

"You okay, Captain?"

"Just got the wind knocked out of me." He patted his vest. "Kevlar stops Atlantean spears *and* modern bullets."

Rowlin turned and tracked an attacker as he dropped down on the port side. After he drilled him with bullets, a round fired from somewhere below grazed his left shoulder.

He scanned the water. "RHIBs! Must've launched from that damn barge."

An armada of rigid-hull inflatable boats with silent electric motors closed in and opened fire with .50-caliber deck-mounted weapons.

Rowlin shot one of the last airborne commandos and then grabbed the mike in the bridge. "RHIBs attacking! Fire the deck cannons!"

Powerful cannons raked the water around the ship in an artificial thunderstorm of bright flashes and loud explosions, creating a strobe-light effect on the dark sea. The inflatable boats' attacks inflicted superficial damage, causing several casualties, but they were no match for *Leviathan's* powerful cannons.

Rowlin shouted, "XO, keep your head down. Those .50-cals are nasty."

"No shit! How's your shoulder?"

Blood ran down Rowlin's left arm. "Huh, didn't notice that one. Just a graze."

After a few minutes of booming weapons blasting into the enemy armada, Rowlin ordered a cease-fire while he assessed the battlefield.

"XO, check the starboard side." Rowlin scanned the sea on the port side.

Debris littered the water with destroyed attack boats. Smoke and the scent of gunpowder hung in the air.

"Looks like our deck cannons decimated the enemy," Lowes said.

Rowlin spotted four survivors clustered together, clinging to floating debris. Water foamed around them as their loud screams carried across the sea. An enormous tentacle rose up and crashed down on them. Then they were gone, debris and all.

"The kraken's feasting on leftovers." Rowlin scanned the water and pointed fifty yards south a second before more survivors were pulled under by the beast.

Lowes shook his head. "Why the hell didn't it attack them five minutes ago?"

"Maybe it didn't like the noise from the deck cannons."

Commander Bern called Rowlin on the radio. "Captain, the ship is secure. We have two RHIBs ready to pick up survivors."

"Negative! No RHIBs. The kraken is out there. Use ballistic floats. Acknowledge."

"Aye, Captain, we'll use floats."

Rowlin called CIC. "Give me a sitrep. Casualties? Damage?"

"No deaths on our side, Captain, but we have twenty wounded, some critical, and superficial damage to the ship. No aircraft on radar."

"Call Guantanamo and Key West for medevacs. Have them fly out everyone who needs surgery. And maintain readiness for a secondary attack."

"Aye, Captain."

Rowlin called Bern, "Order the SEALs to search the ship for enemy combatants."

He scanned the dark water and his ship with night-vision binoculars as blood soaked his left sleeve.

A few more screams carried across the water, followed by silence.

Palm Beach

Tim sequestered Rosa, Romeo, and me in my bedroom after fitting us with bullet-proof vests.

"Rosa, I know you're not good with guns, so if bad guys break in, get under my bed."

"*¡Dios mío!* You hide with me, *hija*." Rosa's widened eyes radiated terror.

"Romeo and I are trained for this. We'll protect you." I hugged her trembling body and felt guilty for putting her in harm's way.

Romeo had met Tim's team, including their security dogs. I was pretty sure he understood they were on our side, and his job was to protect the household, like always.

I racked the slide on Mom's Glock 19 and peeked out the window beside the balcony.

Rosa sat on my bed and wrung her hands. "Sam, are the bad men out there?"

"I can't see anyone. Too dark. Wish I had night-vision goggles like Tim's team. He probably doesn't want me to see the assault and maybe shoot at the wrong guys. SEALs don't trust civilians with stuff like that."

Rosa crossed herself and bit her lip.

"Don't worry, the security team will protect us. Try to relax, Rosa."

My DOXA dive watch gave off a faint glow in the darkness. We'd decided to keep the room lights off so our eyes would be adjusted to the night.

Tim had darkened the rest of the house so his team could use their NV goggles inside and out on the grounds.

I sat in a wingback chair near the French doors to my balcony and glanced at my watch. Romeo was beside me. I couldn't hear a sound, but it seemed he did. He nudged me with his nose and stared at the glass doors.

Uh oh.

It was after midnight, and Mom's silent mansion was suddenly alive with gunfire, loud thuds, and breaking glass.

"Rosa, get under the bed and keep quiet!"

She gasped and dived under my four-poster queen-size bed.

I peeked through the doors. Nothing. Too dark.

I grabbed Romeo's collar, and we hid behind the sofa that was along the wall near the balcony. Listening for intruders amongst the gunfire and explosions, I concentrated on slowing my breathing.

Please don't come in here.

Romeo crouched beside me, whined once, and stared at the glass French doors.

Not a good sign.

I released his collar, aimed my Glock, and waited. I knew Tim's men wouldn't enter through my third-floor balcony.

Seconds later, a man crashed through the glass doors and released his parachute. He aimed his green laser sight at my bed. He was only three feet from my hiding place. I jumped up and took him out with a red-lasered head shot as Romeo lunged at him. He sniffed the dead man and backed away.

Two more paratroopers crashed through the glass doors and landed on their comrade's body. They released their chutes and swept the room with their green laser sights. When one sighted on my fur missile, I jumped up, put my red laser sight on his forehead, and squeezed the trigger.

His buddy turned and aimed at me. Romeo launched himself at him and grabbed the guy's gun arm, making the shot go wide as the intruder fell backward. Fierce growling matched the high-pitched screams of my dog's wounded target.

My four-legged protector was moving back and forth too much for me to shoot the bad guy. When I saw the creep pull a knife, I pounced on him and clubbed his knife arm with my pistol.

Tim's men burst through the bedroom door in the middle of our battle on the floor. Romeo had bitten our attacker hard enough to make him drop his handgun, and I'd broken his other arm when I'd smashed my pistol butt into it.

Tim and another guy flanked us.

"Call your dog off," Tim said. "We'll take it from here."

"Romeo, stand down—good boy!" I grabbed his collar as he backed away, still snarling at the bleeding commando.

Tim had the guy in cuffs seconds later, despite the broken wrist. I didn't feel sorry for the intruder.

Sirens pierced the night. SWAT had been called. Good thing Tim's team had registered with the police and informed them of their security detail before they had begun their vigil. The SWAT commander would be aware of their presence.

"Rosa, you can come out now." I sat on the edge of the bed and held Romeo's collar.

Rosa crawled out from under the bed, and our beloved protector licked her face.

Tim flicked on the lights. I avoided looking at the dead guys. Didn't want those images in my head.

"Uh, Sam, you'd better put your Glock on the floor before SWAT gets here." Tim set his weapon on the floor in front of him and stood with his hands on his head and his foot on the back of his prisoner. His men did the same with their weapons and hands.

SWAT swept in with weapons pointed at us, yelled commands, and herded us into one corner.

Scary guys. I kept a tight grip on Romeo. No way in hell they'd shoot my fur buddy.

The Palm Beach police captain rushed in and separated the good guys and civilians from the live bad guy. Photos were taken of the crime scene, and soon the Medical Examiner would arrive and deal with the bodies on the grounds and in the house.

Tim put his hand on my shoulder. "You okay, Sam?"

"Yeah, but the night's not over. Think China will send more men?" I petted Romeo. "They were Chinese, right?"

"Definitely Chinese. The police will have to keep all the weapons that were fired during the assault, including your Glock, until they close this case."

"That's not good. What if another assault team attacks us after the cops leave?"

"We have extra weapons in lock boxes inside our SUVs. We'll stay and protect you until you leave for work in the morning, and the police will station a few officers around the house and grounds. Why don't you go to another bedroom and get some sleep? We've got you covered." Tim smiled and squeezed my shoulder.

"Sleep? Not tonight." I glanced at Rosa, who looked shell-shocked. The fact that I wasn't meant I'd been in this kind of situation way too many times.

"Try to relax. I saw a guest room on the

second floor with two beds. You'll be insulated from an aerial assault. Let's go." Tim took my arm.

"Not so fast," the police captain said. "We need her statement first." He handed me a clipboard and a pen.

I kept it short and simple. I wrote: *Armed bad guys broke in. I shot two, and my dog helped me disable a third one.* I handed back the clipboard.

"Thank you, Ms. Starr," the police captain said. "Some of my men will stick around and assist your security team."

"Thank you, Captain. We appreciate your help." I smiled, hooked arms with Rosa, and followed Tim to the stairway and down to another bedroom.

Rosa and I settled in our beds, wide awake, and Romeo sat on the floor between us. We were too tense to sleep, and I worried over every sound.

Romeo remained on guard duty.

Good doggie.

The remainder of the night passed without incident. In the morning, I donned my uniform and hugged everyone goodbye, including Tim and his intrepid team.

God bless Navy SEALs.

I pulled my cell out of my shoulder bag to call Ross, but it rang before I tapped his number. He was calling me.

"Good morning, lass. Any action last night?"

"Yes, but not the good kind." I filled him in. "I'm leaving now for the charter to Rio."

"Hard to believe China would risk an assault like that on U.S. soil. The heat they'll get from this should keep you safe for a while, but stay sharp."

"Alrighty. I love you, darling. Be careful out there," I said, sliding inside my car.

THIRTEEN

Earlier on USS LEVIATHAN

Rowlin had planned to interrogate survivors of the assault, but there weren't any. The SEALs and his crew had killed the commandos who'd landed on the ship, and the kraken had taken the ones in the water. He sent pictures of enemy casualties to the Defense Intelligence Agency and Navy Intelligence.

"Looked like North Koreans to me. What do you think?" The XO pulled a sliver of glass out of his forearm as the faint light of dawn filtered through the bridge's broken windows.

"They were using Chinese weapons, but that's not unusual. North Korea gets most of their goods from China." Rowlin adjusted the bandage on his left shoulder. "I just hope the assault on our ship doesn't start a war."

"I'm sure the Secretary of State and a bunch of diplomats are working overtime to prevent that. Good thing the news media doesn't know about this."

"Sooner or later, someone will ask questions about the wounded crewmembers sent to the mainland for emergency surgery," Rowlin said. "Then the media will circle like sharks smelling blood in the water."

"What do you think SECNAV will do?" the XO asked.

"The Secretary of the Navy is meeting with the President and Joint Chiefs." Rowlin moved aside while a crewman swept up the broken glass on the bridge floor. "As soon as they make a decision, he'll contact me about whether we sail to Jacksonville as planned or receive new orders."

"And what are we supposed to do with all the bodies?" Lowes glanced at a sailor washing blood off a console in the bridge.

"Seahawks are en route to load up the dead and take them to Key West." Rowlin took a cup of coffee from a tray held by a sailor. "Not sure what they'll do with them after that."

"Probably put them in cold storage because they're evidence North Korea attacked our ship."

An ensign entered the bridge and handed Rowlin a printout. "From SECNAV, sir."

Rowlin scanned it. "We're ordered to stop in Key West for provisions and temporary repairs. Then cruise to Jacksonville with air cover, a destroyer, and *Texas* guarding our six. I doubt the North Koreans will attack us on the way, but you never know with a crazy leader like theirs."

"Do the Brits know what happened last night?"

"I had CIC keep them informed. *Audacious* is guarding the black pyramid, and one of our inbound destroyers will guard them." Rowlin scanned the dawn horizon and pointed. "Looks like the ships are almost here."

"Can't say I'll be sorry to leave this place." Lowes drained his cup.

"Too bad we have to come back after we drop off the vaults." Rowlin looked down at the deceptively placid sea. "I'm keeping that platoon of SEALs."

"Good." Lowes nodded. "It's a long way to Jacksonville and back. A lot can happen."

"And with us, it usually does."

PBI Airport

I drove over the Southern Boulevard bridge to Palm Beach International Airport, walked into LIA Flight Operations in Terminal A, and found Lance waiting for me with the paperwork.

"Sam, you aren't going to believe who we're taking to Rio," he said. "Carlene Jensen and her new billionaire boyfriend. He's taking her to a big film festival there."

"No kidding? How many people are going with them?"

"Just a British singer-musician. Carlene's entourage went ahead on an American Airlines flight yesterday." Lance grinned. "I think he wants her all to himself."

"Well, that means you can breathe easy for a change." I laughed. "Or maybe not, since you're the only man on an all-female crew."

"Hey, as long as it's not Carlene. My back still has faint scars from that woman." He shook his head. "She's a real maneater."

"Oh, *please*." I raised a brow. "You make it sound like you were helpless."

"She doesn't respond well to rejection, and I remembered her saying she shot her ex-husband."

"In his butt!" I crossed my arms. "Geez, Lance, she wasn't even armed when she nailed you."

"Her fingernails should be registered as deadly weapons." He handed me the flight plan.

"I can't believe my big, strong copilot is afraid of a five-foot-nothing actress." I studied the flight plan and signed it. "Anyway, sounds like her new boyfriend plans to keep her busy. What's his name?"

"Renaldo Murciato, the Brazilian casino king. He has vast real estate holdings in South America—and maybe an illegal drug empire." Lance paused.

"He's quite the player—super yachts, exotic sports cars, private jets, the whole package."

"Then why didn't he take Carlene to Brazil in one of his own jets?"

"Carlene has flown in plenty of private jets. No big deal to her. But a huge 767 with professional flight attendants catering to them? Now that's impressive."

"She and I dedicated an aviation museum in England two weeks ago, and she never mentioned a Brazilian boyfriend. This relationship must be brand new."

"Well, you know Carlene." He grinned. "She moves fast."

I gathered up the paperwork. "Alrighty, let's go face the music."

We grabbed our bags and walked up the jetway to the airplane. I greeted the two flight attendants assigned to take care of our three passengers. Tiesha, a mocha-skinned Halle Berry lookalike, and Barbi, a statuesque blond from the Midwest, were both consummate professionals in their mid-twenties.

"Don't be surprised if our passengers decide to spend a lot of time alone together," I said. "I think the guy booked this flight with romance in mind, and Carlene's not shy about intimacy in unusual settings."

"It won't be anything we haven't seen before." Tiesha smirked.

"Don't be too sure about that," Lance said. "Carlene Jensen's a force of nature."

"You'd know that better than we would," Barbi said.

We snickered, enjoying teasing him.

"Yeah, well, good luck. I'm staying in the cockpit the whole flight." He turned and walked forward, and I followed.

We settled in our seats and ran through the checklists. We'd no sooner finished all our preflight duties when hurricane Carlene blew in with her Latin lover.

"Sam!" She breezed through the open door. "I was hopin' we'd get you." She glanced to her right and spotted Lance. "Ooh, we really hit the jackpot. This'll be a fun trip." She pulled her man forward. "I'd like you to meet my sugar pie, Renaldo Murciato. Isn't he a hottie?"

I grinned, stepped behind the seat to greet them, and offered my hand. "Pleased to meet you. I'm Captain Samantha Starr."

About five-ten, he bore a strong resemblance to actor Andy Garcia in his thirties. He kissed my hand with a flourish and gazed into my eyes like I was the only woman on Earth. "It is my honor to be flown to Brazil by such a beautiful lady."

Geez, what a player!

Lance shook Renaldo's hand and welcomed him aboard, then said, "Good to see you, Carlene."

"Have you met the British singer I booked to entertain us inflight?" Renaldo asked.

"Not yet. Is she on board?" I glanced behind him as a beautiful redhead peeked through the cockpit door.

Renaldo turned. "Ah, there she is. Lisa, come and meet our pilots."

A slender, green-eyed woman of medium height entered the cockpit. Dressed in a red satin formal, she appeared to be in her late twenties.

"Captain, allow me to introduce world-renowned musician Lisa Atwater." Renaldo bowed toward the singer.

"It's an honor to meet you, Miss Atwater. I hope I'll get a chance to enjoy a little of your music during our long flight."

"Thank you, Captain." She smoothed her gown. "As you can see, I'm dressed for my performance on board."

"Lovely dress." I moved aside. "This is my copilot, Lance Bowie."

Lance kissed her hand and turned on the Texas charm. "Pleased to meet you, Lisa."

She looked into his liquid-green eyes and then took in his hunky build. "The pleasure is mine, Lance."

I slid into my seat. "Alrighty, the flight attendants will show you to your seats, and we'll get this flight airborne. We expect good weather, except for the usual thunderstorms over the Amazon basin, and we'll circumvent those."

Barbi appeared and led the passengers out of the cockpit so we could get underway.

It wasn't long before we were headed south in blue skies.

Four hours into the flight, the sky ahead turned dark and stormy. Turbulence jolted the Boeing 767 jumbo jet like we were driving down a road covered with deep potholes.

I switched on the seatbelt sign and keyed the PA system. "This is your captain speaking. We've got a little bumpy air associated with thunderstorms along our route. Nothing to worry about. Just keep your seatbelts fastened while we navigate around the weather. Flight attendants, secure the cabin and take your seats."

A monster seventy-five-thousand-foot thunderstorm blocked our flightpath over South America near Brazil's northern border with Venezuela. The dark sky around it flashed with multiple lightning bolts.

I spotted an opening right of course. "Tell ATC we need to divert thirty degrees right to avoid that big boomer."

Lance made the call, and ATC responded,

"Luxury five-one-five, turn right to heading one-eight-zero for weather avoidance."

"Luxury five-one-five is turning right to one-eight-zero," Lance replied in his Texas twang.

As soon as we passed the storm, we got clearance to turn back on course and deviate as necessary to avoid storms along our route. It was a time of day with little air traffic on the airway.

"I'll go around this next one to the east." I banked left as Lance made the call to ATC.

Our jet rose and fell in the turbulent air like a boat going over waves in the ocean.

He finished the call and glanced at me. "All this deviating is cutting into our drinking time in Rio."

As I flew around the storm, I caught a whiff of something no pilot ever wants to smell on an airplane. "Is that smoke?"

"Smells like it might be electrical," Lance said. "Not sure where it's coming from."

I glanced behind him. "Multiple breakers are popped. Tell ATC we're investigating a possible in-flight fire and ask them to open a route to the nearest suitable airport. I'll check with the flight attendants."

I keyed the interphone to call the lead flight attendant.

Nothing. The interphone was dead.

My gut tightened as I hit the call bell three times in rapid succession.

"No radio response, not even on the standby radio," Lance said.

"Don't reset any breakers until you check the electronics bay. I hope we don't have a fire."

Barbi hurried into the cockpit. "What's wrong, Captain?"

"We're smelling a little smoke here in the cockpit. I need you and Tiesha to conduct a thorough cabin search to rule out a fire. Get back to me ASAP."

"I didn't smell any smoke in the cabin, but we'll check everything."

Right after Barbi left the cockpit, the autopilot disconnected.

"Autopilot failure. I'm taking over manually," I said, my hands gripping the yoke.

"We're not getting any warning lights, but the system could be compromised." Lance unbuckled his harness, moved to the back of the cockpit, donned a smoke/O2 unit, and grabbed a fire extinguisher.

"Be careful down there. I'll keep us away from storms."

He disappeared below while I waited several minutes in the silent cockpit.

No radios. No cell phone coverage. No autopilot. Plenty of lightning flashes, turbulence, and whiffs of that damn smoke.

Lance climbed up through the floor hatch and pulled off his oxygen mask. "We've been sabotaged."

My cheeks flushed with anger as I glanced back at him. "What did you find?"

"Someone must've entered the electronics bay after my preflight walkaround and rigged devices with timers. They fried our autopilot, all the comm and nav radios, the transponder, and our navigation computers."

"Is there a fire?"

"No fire, just some residual electrical smoke," he said, wiping black smudges off his hands with a napkin. "This was a professional job. We're in serious shit."

He clutched the side of the empty observer's seat as turbulence pitched us up and down.

"What about repairing at least one comm radio?"

Lance stowed the smoke/O2 unit as he said, "No way to fix it. All the circuits are melted."

"We're over the friggin' Amazon basin in the middle of nowhere." I held up my cell phone. "We can't even get a cell signal, which begs the question, why sabotage our avionics but not start a fire?"

"Or why didn't they destroy the airplane with a bomb?" He slid into his seat as another sharp jab of turbulence jolted the jet.

"Maybe we just haven't found the bomb yet." I bit my lip.

Barbi burst in, her eyes wide and her voice tinged with panic. "No fires in the cabin, Captain, but I think I found three bombs!"

FOURTEEN

USS LEVIATHAN

R owlin gazed out the newly replaced windows on the bridge as his ship cruised along the east coast of Florida en route to the Mayport Navy Base in Jacksonville. A destroyer, the USS *Wolverine*, flanked their starboard side, and *Texas* guarded them underwater, while U.S. fighters rode herd overhead.

"Good weather and plenty of firepower should make this a smooth journey." The XO scanned the turquoise sea on their port side, his high-powered binoculars briefly pausing on bikini-clad women sunning themselves on Fort Lauderdale's beaches.

"It should, so why do I have a knot in my gut?" Rowlin gripped his coffee mug.

"If you were anyone else, I'd guess too much

coffee or a greasy breakfast, but your gut's never wrong." Lowes turned and scanned dark-blue water feathered by white caps on their starboard. "Think the North Koreans will take another crack at us?"

The captain glanced at the destroyer surging through rollers on their starboard side. "If they come, my guess is they'll attack when we're about halfway to Mayport, probably assuming we'll be complacent that far from Atlantis."

Rowlin grabbed the interphone and called the moon pool operator. "Prepare the Scorpions for launch. Full armament."

"*Texas* or *Wolverine* can eliminate any enemy sub. What's your gut telling you?"

"Several subs might attack simultaneously. I don't know if *Texas* can handle multiple targets, and *Wolverine* has to be over the enemy to blast them with depth charges." Rowlin clenched his jaw.

"You could be right." Lowes focused his binoculars on the water closest to their port side.

"The Scorpions are our best defense underwater now that we're away from the kraken's territory." Rowlin keyed the PA mike. "All Scorpion crews report to the bridge."

Fred, Bull, Jane, and Scooter rushed up to the bridge and saluted.

"At ease," Rowlin said. "We may be approaching an underwater combat situation, only this time we won't be battling sea monsters. I'm guessing several North Korean Sang-O Class submarines will attack in unison."

"Their diesel-electric subs are about a hundred feet long," Fred said. "Our little Scorpions are much faster and more maneuverable."

Jane nodded. "Yeah, ours are silent and deadly."

"They won't even know we're there until they go boom." Scooter pulled his hands apart to simulate an explosion.

"The Scorpions were designed for multiple-target missions like this," Rowlin said. "There's a good chance the enemy will attack *Texas* and *Wolverine* first, then us."

"Why do you think that?" Fred asked, frowning.

"Because that's what I'd do," Rowlin said. "It's their only chance for a successful strike with a clean getaway."

"Captain, do the North Koreans know we're equipped with Scorpion attack subs?" Bull asked.

"No one knows, except the Brits after you saved their people from the megalodon," Rowlin said.

"Everyone else thinks our moon pool is just for launching the unarmed research sub," Lowes said.

An ensign from CIC rushed in and handed Rowlin a printout. "Emergency message."

Rowlin read it and clenched his fist. "A military contractor testing underwater sensors reported four unknown vessels, each approximately a hundred feet in length, fifteen miles east of the Palm Beach Inlet."

Lowes glanced at his watch. "We'll pass by there in twenty minutes. Too late to send a bird to drop a sonar buoy and verify the targets."

Eager for their first military combat mission, the Scorpion crews' eyes lit up as they did fist pumps.

"Prepare to deploy," Rowlin said. "I'll call with your launch confirmations."

LIA Flight 515

"Where are the bombs?" I asked, my heart pounding against my chest.

"In overhead compartments. One near the front, one about halfway back, and one near the aft end." Barbi bit her lip. "I'm not sure they're bombs, but they look scary. I've never seen anything like them on our airplanes."

"Lance, get back there and check them out. Take pictures with your cell phone." I looked into Barbi's frightened eyes. "We'll handle this. Prepare the cabin for an emergency landing. Secure everything and seat the passengers away from the bombs."

I focused on missing the storms while my mind raced, searching for solutions. Would we be blown apart in the next few minutes?

After a long twenty minutes, Lance returned with Lisa Atwater, the British musician. She had changed from her satin gown into jeans and a sweater.

His tone was grim. "Lisa says she's undercover with MI6. She checked the devices and confirmed they're bombs."

She gripped my seatback when turbulence jolted our jet.

"MI6? Do you know Hugh Owen?" I asked, testing her.

"You're smart to be careful." Lisa's lips were a tight slit. "Hugh was killed in Edinburgh Castle last summer, right in front of you."

"Right, so what can you tell me about the bombs? Any connection to your mission?"

"We had no concerns about this flight. I'm gathering evidence to prove Murciato has branched out from his drug cartel and is now selling illegal arms to African war lords."

"Carlene sure picked the wrong guy." I glanced back as our jet zoomed up and down like a roller-coaster. "How big are the bombs?"

A loud boom from a nearby lightning bolt made us duck involuntarily.

"There's enough C4 to destroy the aircraft. Lance told me about the sabotage. The bombs were activated with timers about the same time your radios were fried."

"So why didn't they explode?" I asked, hoping the bombs had malfunctioned in a good way.

"I've seen bombs like this before. The timers

were only meant to make them live. Each one has an altitude detonator, which means they won't explode until we descend to a preset altitude—2,000 feet above sea level." Lisa wiped her forehead with the back of her hand and glanced out the cockpit windows. "We need to find an airport above that altitude."

"Any chance you can defuse them?" I asked as I banked to avoid a storm.

"Afraid not." Lisa gripped my seatback as another patch of unstable air jarred us. "Once they've been activated, they're designed to explode if they're tampered with. Landing above 2,000 feet is our only option."

"Could these nasty air currents set them off?" I asked.

She hesitated. "The bombs are securely anchored inside the overheads, but...maybe."

"Then I'd better find a safe place to land before they get jarred into exploding."

"I'm on it." Lance slipped into his seat and scanned a flight chart. "The highest mountains are near the west coast. Where do you want to go?"

Before I had a moment to think, fate made the decision for me.

Both engines quit, and all the glass displays on the forward panel went blank.

The cockpit became deathly silent as lightning flashed outside and thunder boomed in the distance.

"Dual engine failures!" Lance shouted.

I glanced up at the overhead fuel gauges. "Shit! The tanks are empty."

"What the hell happened to all the fuel?" Lance asked. "We had plenty twenty minutes ago."

"I don't know." I eased the nose down and searched in vain for a safe place to land, my hands unconsciously tightening on the yoke.

"Whoever destroyed our radios must've sabotaged the fuel tanks too," Lance said, his eyes riveted on the fuel gauges.

"Doesn't matter now." I glanced at him. "Where's the nearest mountain?"

He sucked in his breath. "Way too far for an engines-out glide."

I glanced over my shoulder at Lisa. "Thanks for the help. You'd better return to the cabin now and strap in."

She bit her lip. "Sorry I couldn't disarm the bombs. I know you'll do your best."

I searched the ominous looking sky.

Thunderstorms everywhere, no mountains, and endless jungle below.

God help us.

USS LEVIATHAN

Rowlin grabbed the interphone and called CIC. "Send warning messages to *Texas* and *Wolverine* that there may be four North Korean subs lying in wait off the Palm Beach Inlet. Notify them I'm deploying the Scorpions."

Lowes tapped Rowlin's shoulder. "Captain, we're ten miles from the target area."

Rowlin keyed the radio and called Jane and Fred. "*Scorpion One* and *Scorpion Two* are cleared to launch. Locate the enemy subs and report back. If they attack, destroy them."

"Aye, Captain, *Scorpion One* is cleared to launch, locate the enemy, and destroy them if they attack," Lieutenant Jane Hoebich answered.

Lieutenant Fred Lichten gave the same reply for *Scorpion Two* and then asked, "Sir, any chance we can get permission for a preemptive strike?"

"I'll check with SECNAV and get back to you. Be careful down there."

Rowlin called CIC. "Sound the alarm for battle stations." He turned to Lowes. "XO, you have the bridge. I'll command from CIC." Rowlin rushed down to the Combat Information Center as the klaxon horn blared.

He entered the nerve center of the ship and strode up to the communications officer. "Ensign, get SECNAV on a secure line."

"Aye, Captain, I'm putting the call through now." The ensign snatched up a secure satellite phone. Moments later, he handed it to Rowlin.

"Admiral, this is Captain Rowlin on *Leviathan*. I believe we're about to be attacked by four North

Korean submarines. If that's the case, do I have permission to destroy them?"

"I was about to call you. I've already been notified about the possible enemy subs, Captain, and I just finished speaking with the President. We're on the brink of war with North Korea, and we're now at DEFCON 2. Do not engage the enemy unless they attack one of our ships. Understood?"

"Aye, Admiral, understood, but if we wait until after they fire torpedoes at *Texas*, we won't be able to save them." Rowlin crushed an empty paper coffee cup and tossed it.

"*Texas* can defend itself. Those commie bastards are accusing us of sinking their sub without provocation. Worse, they're denying responsibility for their attack on your ship. We're walking a fine line in the court of world opinion."

"Understood, sir," Rowlin said, clenching his jaw.

"One more thing: If you do get in a battle with enemy subs, destroy them all. No survivors."

"No survivors?" Rowlin's gut twisted. "Isn't that against the Geneva Conventions?"

"Screw that! We need deniability to prevent a war. The Navy will take care of any debris while you continue up to Mayport. If anyone from the press or public asks, we'll say we were testing weapons."

I hate doing that, but I understand why it's necessary.

Probably wouldn't be any survivors from a sunken sub anyway.

Rowlin bit his lip. "Aye, Admiral, total annihilation and no survivors."

"Good," the Secretary of the Navy said. "Keep me informed and Godspeed, Captain."

FIFTEEN

LIA Flight 515

We were descending through 26,000 feet when I turned to miss a huge thunderstorm and spotted a dark mesa poking up out of the middle of the jungle. Narrow and flat, it extended a few miles and looked like it might be higher than 2,000 feet.

"There's our runway." I pointed at it.

"It looks long enough. Maybe not as wide as I'd like, considering the steep cliffs, but way wider than real runways." Lance squinted. "Looks fairly flat, but if the elevation isn't high enough, nothing else will matter."

"With our rate of descent, the distance to the mesa should work out." I focused on the dark plateau. "I can always put the airplane in a sideslip maneuver if we're high."

The PA system still worked, and I used it to call the cabin crew into the cockpit.

"We only have a few minutes before we land there." I pointed at the mesa.

Tiesha gripped a cockpit seatback as turbulence buffeted the airliner, and a brief rain squall pummeled the windshield. She squinted. "It looks like the bow of a huge ship, except the sides have waterfalls shooting out near the top. Are you sure we can land there?"

"Positive. Now pack food and water in garbage bags and pillow cases. As soon as the airplane stops, open the doors on whichever side is farthest from the cliffs, evacuate the passengers, and toss out our luggage, the supplies you packed, and at least one life raft. The tanks are empty, so if the airplane is stable and not too damaged, gather blankets, pillows, and anything else to keep us warm and comfortable until help arrives. We're not staying on board with those bombs. Any questions?"

"Uh, Captain, you can land us safely with no engines, right?" Barbi asked, clutching my seatback in the bumpy air.

I scanned the standby instruments and struggled to hold my glide angle in the unstable air currents.

"Absolutely. Now prepare whatever you can in the next five minutes, do a final check, strap in, and brace for impact. With so many thunderstorms nearby, expect rough air all the way to touchdown. I'll see you on the ground."

After Tiesha and Barbi left, I turned to Lance. "Get the weapons duffel out of the secret locker and hand me a Glock with a thigh holster."

He unscrewed a floor panel and pulled out a canvas duffel bag. Seconds later, I strapped on a thigh holster and shoved a pistol into it.

Time was short. I barked orders in rapid fire.

"Grab our bags, strap in near the passengers, and secure the duffel in the seat next to you. I can't risk the passengers and cabin crew losing both of us."

"Dang it, Sam, I should be up here helping you."

"Pilots in the cockpit have the greatest odds of being injured in a crash. I need you back there with our people. Now go!" I turned my attention to the mesa looming ahead.

Another squall buffeted the airplane and hammered the windshield.

I heard the cockpit door close and glanced back. Lance had gone into the cabin.

Good. He'd try to keep everyone back there safe.

With no operating engines, I was saddled with what was known as a dead-stick landing. Energy management was key. If I put the jet in a steeper nose-down attitude, the airspeed would increase, but so would the rate of descent. I needed enough airspeed to control the airliner in the bad weather and enough altitude to reach the mesa.

Wind shear was treacherous during my landing approach. I gripped the yoke, making constant corrections in the updrafts and downdrafts, struggling to maintain a constant airspeed and rate of descent. I didn't want to fly too fast, but I needed a little extra speed to compensate for the crazy winds.

I adjusted my flightpath to keep the touchdown zone in the center of my windshield. Any other sight picture would mean I was too high or too low. I had to land on the centerline of the mesa and keep the rollout straight. If we slid off the side, we'd be toast.

I wiped my sweaty hands on my uniform slacks and gripped the control yoke.

Fear was an emotion I wouldn't allow myself during an emergency. Long ago, I'd trained myself to ignore fear and bury it somewhere deep in my subconscious. I'd let myself feel something after the danger had been dealt with and everyone was safe.

As I neared the granite runway, the turbulence intensified. Would all the violent jostling set off the bombs?

I bit my lip and dropped the flaps into the landing configuration but kept the landing gear up. I didn't want to risk catching a wheel on a big rock and flipping the airplane or spinning it off the cliff.

Dear God, please make that hunk of rock higher than 2,000 feet.

We passed through 2,500 feet. The landing elevation was going to be damn close to the detonation point.

Nothing I could do if it was lower.

I was out of options.

My heart raced as the big jet bobbed up and down passing through 2,400 feet. I made continual adjustments to the flightpath to keep us centered on the landing zone. The plateau was long enough that I planned a touchdown about a thousand feet past the approach end.

I glanced left and spotted another wall of rain approaching. Nasty wind gusts slammed into the jet as I scanned the standby instruments. The 767 was descending through 2,300 feet, and my rock-hewn airport was dead ahead.

Lightning flashed so close it temporarily distorted my vision. A loud thunder clap jolted me into thinking a bomb had exploded.

Nope, the airplane feels normal. No explosion. Not yet anyway.

I dried my sweaty hands on my pants again and gripped the control yoke.

Would the landing site be high enough to avoid detonation?

I grabbed the PA mike and announced, "Brace for impact!"

We cleared the approach edge of the cliff, but just as I flared for landing, a strong gust from the left blew us sideways and lifted the left wing. I instantly corrected with the ailerons and rudder, leveling the wings.

A quick glance at the standby altimeter told me the elevation was close to 2,000 feet.

The next moment, we were bounding along the uneven ground. It wasn't as flat as it had appeared from altitude. Lightning flashes, booming thunder, and screeching metal assaulted my senses. I wrestled with the controls as the five-point harness kept me firmly in my seat while the big jet bucked and swerved.

I fought to keep us in a straight path, but the thunderstorm had intensified the left crosswind. The rudder and ailerons were barely effective enough to counteract the powerful gusts as the right cliff threatened to pull us over the edge.

As we continued our shuddering deceleration, the rudder lost effectiveness, and I prayed full ailerons would keep the left wing down. Another massive gust pushed us even closer to the right edge.

The standby altimeter read a hair above 2,000 feet.

We were still bumping and sliding forward. If the ground slanted downward ever so slightly before we stopped...

USS LEVIATHAN

Rowlin handed the SATCOM to the ensign. "Contact the Scorpions."

The ensign made the call and handed Rowlin the microphone.

"*Scorpions One* and *Two*, SECNAV has ordered us *not* to fire unless they fire first. Acknowledge."

"Aye, Captain, no preemptive strikes," Fred said.

Jane gave the same response.

"And *Scorpions*, if you engage the enemy, SECNAV wants their total destruction with no survivors. Acknowledge," Rowlin said, his tone tense.

"Aye, Captain, total destruction, no survivors," the Scorpion pilots replied in unison.

"Good, now go radio silent and switch to digital messaging," Rowlin instructed.

Two minutes later, Jane's silent text message was received in CIC: 4 NK subs on bottom with torpedo doors open, tubes flooded, ready to fire.

Rowlin responded: Understood, Scorpion One. Send coordinates to Texas and Wolverine. Follow rules of engagement.

Rowlin prayed *Texas* would survive as he stood beside his communications officer.

He sucked in his breath. "Connect me with *Wolverine's* captain."

The ensign handed Rowlin a microphone. "Captain Benvenuto for you, sir."

"Captain, did you receive the enemy subs' coordinates from my Scorpions?"

"Affirmative, Captain Rowlin. I'd like to maneuver to your port side."

"Negative," Rowlin said. "I can't have you dropping depth charges over my Scorpions, but if an enemy sub makes it past my starboard side, blast them to hell."

"Understood. Increase to flank speed and we'll hang back with *Texas*."

LIA Flight 515

Just when I thought we were doomed, the nose slammed into a small rise, and we lurched to a stop. Our right wing hung over the side of the western cliff.

I grabbed the PA mike. "Evacuate on the left side only!"

I unbuckled my harness and rushed to the cockpit door. It was jammed shut. The frame had buckled—no way to open it.

The lower door panel was meant to be knocked out in an emergency. I tried kicking it hard. It wouldn't budge—no time to mess with it.

I pulled on my uniform jacket and slid open the left cockpit side window. It was a long way to the ground, even with the gear up. I stuck my head out and saw my crew unloading survival gear. I was amazed by how fast they'd accumulated a large pile of supplies. They'd even managed to drag out two ocean rafts.

Lance spotted me at the window. "Sam, get the hell out! Hurry!" He waved at a wall of rain roaring toward us.

The left wing suddenly surged up about thirty degrees. I popped open the panel holding my evacuation rope and climbed out the window. When I started down the escape rope, the airliner rolled right. A big gust had forced the left wing up to a vertical position. I stood outside the left side of the cockpit, which was now horizontal, so the ground wasn't any closer.

Wind whipped my hair as the big jet shuddered and the ground rumbled. Even with empty tanks and no cargo, the airplane's massive 200,000-pound weight crushed the cliff. The bombs were already almost level with the ground. Just a short fall would set them off.

With the ground about to fall away, there was no time to climb down a rope. I ran three steps across the cockpit's left side and jumped off a second before the big jet slid over the cliff. I hit the ground, rolled, leaped to my feet, and sprinted over tumbling rocks into the blinding rain.

I thought I'd covered enough distance, but the ground crumbled beneath me. Frantic, I clawed the earth above me, trying to stop my downward slide.

Three massive explosions within a nanosecond

produced a concussion wave that tossed me up into the raging thunderstorm.

I gulped air as I wondered how high I'd been thrown.

Would I land on the mesa?

Fear and anger surged through me.

I'd damn well better land safely after all I've been through!

SIXTEEN

The Scorpions

Jane maneuvered her two-man submarine between reefs as bright-colored fish scattered in all directions. The clear canopy allowed her a panoramic view of the underwater environment as a big sea turtle glided overhead. Four long, dark-grey submarines loomed ahead.

She checked her comm screen and read a text from Fred: How can we save Texas if we have to wait until a torpedo is fired? Not a lot of maneuvering room. Enemy subs are resting on reefs at 100 feet.

Jane responded: I have an idea, but timing must be perfect, and it won't work if they fire simultaneously.

Fred texted: What's your plan?

Jane replied: Get in position. When first torpedo is fired, start taking them out. We'll capture their torpedo in our ballistic netting and drag it away from Texas.

"Will that work?" Scooter, the weapons specialist seated behind her, had kept up with the messages to and from their wingman. "I'll have to snag it when it zooms by."

"The water's crystal-clear. The closer we are to where it's fired, the better our chances. The torpedo will take a second to accelerate," Jane said, thinking it through.

"That means we'll have to be in the center of the line of fire for all four submarines," Scooter said.

"I never said it'd be easy." Jane eased her little attack sub into a central position over the coral reef.

She texted: Ready, Scorpion Two?

Fred replied: Ready. Don't miss with that netting.

Jane replied: We'll save Texas.

"Shit! Torpedo away going high!" Scooter said. "Too late. It's headed for *Wolverine!*"

The torpedo had fired in a sharp upward angle from the northernmost sub.

"I thought for sure they'd fire at *Texas* first," Jane said as she glanced over her shoulder at Scooter. "It's the closest target they know about."

A powerful explosion near the surface rocked

their little Scorpion. Jane righted their sub after the shock wave passed.

"Incoming!" he said. "*Texas* just fired."

Jane banked left to dodge the friendly fire and stopped in front of the southernmost enemy submarine.

"Here comes one aimed at *Texas*!" Scooter said as he fired the ballistic netting.

The Mesa

I landed in a shallow pool of water and half-swam, half-crawled out. I collapsed on the ground face-down and waited for the storm to pass.

Heavy rain and fierce winds assaulted me as lightning struck so close it felt like a flash-bang grenade. My hearing had already been stunned by the explosions, and everything sounded far away.

At 2,000 feet above sea level, the downpour was much colder than it would've been in the jungle. I shivered as the chilly pellets stabbed me and soaked me to the skin. Then the shower ended as suddenly as it had begun.

I wiped water from my eyes and raised my head, searching for my crew and passengers as thunder boomed nearby.

Lance ran to me, yelling, "Sam! Are you all right?" He helped me up and wrapped me in a blanket he'd brought with him.

"How'd you get a dry blanket?" I asked as he hugged me against his warm body.

"We spread some space blankets over us as we hunkered down on our luggage and supplies." He checked me over as he said, "We managed to keep everything fairly dry."

"Is everyone okay? Any injuries?" I scanned the group.

"They're fine, but Lisa's upset we weren't able to save her special guitar. Her Walther PPK was hidden inside." Lance shook his head. "Funny what people focus on in a life-threatening situation."

"Speaking of that, did you bring the duffel with the weapons?" I asked, still shivering.

"Hell yeah, we're equipped to fight off a small army." Lance pointed at the canvas duffel.

"Thank God for Jeff's secret weapons compartment. I hope we won't need the fire power, but I'm sure glad we have it."

"You're shakin' like a vibrator, Sam." Lance rubbed my back.

I snuggled my face into his broad shoulder. "If you'll hold me tight for a few more minutes, your body heat will warm me up."

He planted a kiss on the nape of my neck. "I'll hold you as long as you want, but I know a faster way to stoke your feminine fireplace," he joked.

The old Lance was back, at least for a moment.

Then we were surrounded by the passengers and crew.

Perfect timing.

"Is Sam okay?" Tiesha asked.

"She's good, just real cold from the heavy rain." Lance kept me pressed against him.

Loud whirring accompanied warm air blasting my wet head, and a hairbrush tugged on my long, tangled hair.

"Hold still, Sam, and I'll have your hair dry in a jiffy. I've got this handy battery-powered hairdryer," Carlene said. "It'd be easier if you bent down a little."

Between Lance's body and Carlene's hairdryer, I warmed up in no time.

A lightning bolt flashed on the eastern cliff, followed almost instantly by a deafening crack of thunder. I ducked involuntarily and noticed my hands were shaking. My nerves were shot, so I'd have to fake it.

I stepped over puddles and paused on some flat rocks. "If Barbi and Tiesha will hold this blanket in front of me, I can change into dry clothes."

I found my aluminum suitcase and pulled out warm clothing and leather boots. Good thing I'd packed for cool nights in Rio. Their fall weather in the southern hemisphere was the opposite of our spring.

With dry hair and fresh clothes, I was ready to take command again. A brisk breeze swirled my hair around my head as the sun descended toward the western cliff.

"Everyone did a fabulous job gathering survival supplies from the aircraft." I looked over the pile of luggage, bedding, seat cushions, food, beverages, and ocean rafts.

Renaldo nudged an orange uninflated ocean raft with his foot. "Why do we need rafts? I don't see any lakes nearby."

"This will provide a comfortable, round shelter for us. We need to find a low spot on the mesa so it won't blow away in a storm," I said.

"Round? But it's rectangular." Renaldo looked confused.

"It's rectangular so it'll take up less space in storage. When the inflation handle is pulled, it'll open into a round raft big enough to hold thirty people comfortably. And it has a roof and sides like a tent. You'll see. Let's scout around for a depression."

Lance was the tallest member of our group. "There's a low area over there. See the crystals in the rock?" He strode to a place where large embedded crystals sparkled in the intermittent late afternoon sun.

We walked around it. The stone floor was smooth, circular, and about four feet lower than the surrounding ground—the perfect size and shape.

"Huh, it kinda looks like this spot was manmade," I said, surveying the area. "The crystals are evenly spaced around it, and the floor seems unnaturally smooth."

"Well, if it was manmade, there's no sign of them. It looks like it could be hundreds of years old. Maybe it was used for some kind of weird religious ceremony."

"Let's not speculate about creepy stuff like that in front of the flight attendants and passengers." I glanced back at them. "They've had enough stress for one day."

More lightning flashed, and the ground shook with thunder.

"I know one thing." He stood, hands on hips, staring at a crystal. "Based on past experiences, it might be best if you don't touch the crystals."

I half-smiled. "I couldn't agree more."

As we headed back to the group to retrieve the rafts and our stash of supplies, a deep growl reverberated across the plateau.

"Jaguar!" Lance said, glancing around.

I heaved a big sigh.

Haven't we had enough trouble for one day?

The Scorpions

"Firing ballistic netting now!" Scooter called out as an enemy torpedo streaked toward them in the clear ocean water.

Their netting closed tightly around it, but the powerful torpedo's protected metal-encircled propeller yanked their small sub all the way around, towing them toward *Texas*.

Jane selected full reverse thrust as her boat bucked like a bronco, struggling to overcome the weapon's forward momentum.

"Woo hoo! Ride 'em cowboy," Scooter exclaimed.

Jane texted Fred: Netted enemy torpedo. Blast commie subs.

The captured torpedo dragged them toward the nuclear-powered American submarine, which looked like a behemoth hovering over the colorful coral reef.

"Another fish is headed for *Texas*!" Jane yelled. "*Scorpion Two* had better destroy those commie subs."

With only seconds to spare, she switched to forward thrust and dove into the second torpedo, slamming it into the ocean floor before it reached arming range.

Their forward movement had allowed the harnessed torpedo to tow them closer to *Texas* and arm itself. The American submarine seemed to increase in size, filling their clear canopy's front view.

Jane selected maximum reverse thrust again and prayed she could stop the torpedo in time. Shock waves from a massive explosion behind them slammed into their little vessel when their friends in *Scorpion Two* destroyed an enemy sub.

An invisible force from the blast shoved her boat forward, momentarily overcoming her engine's reverse thrust.

"Look out!" Scooter yelled. "*Texas* just fired another torpedo."

Close to the bottom and in line with an enemy target, Jane pulled up and dodged the American weapon before it armed on its way to a North Korean sub.

Silent seconds ticked by, followed by a massive explosion.

Texas had hit its target. Another shock wave slammed into *Scorpion One* as Jane wrestled with the harnessed torpedo. Disaster loomed a mere thirty feet ahead, the giant American submarine dominating the view.

SEVENTEEN

The Mesa

The deep rumble of distant growls changed my priorities. "Lance, help me arm the crew. Give weapons to Carlene and Lisa too."

I handed Glocks and thigh holsters to Tiesha and Barbi.

All Luxury International Airlines pilots and flight attendants had received extensive weapons training after a deadly incident during my round-the-world charter flight last fall. Lance and Carlene had been with me when one of our flight attendants and a passenger were killed during a tour of Petra.

Never again.

Our chief pilot, Captain Jeff Rowlin, intended to ensure that—hence, the weapons and self-defense training and the secret weapons lockers on board all of our airplanes. The lockers were specially lined so nothing inside would show up on X-rays or scans.

Lance gave Carlene a loaded Glock with a holster. Then he handed another one to Lisa. He also gave the MI6 agent an H&K MP7 submachine gun.

"What about me?" Renaldo asked. "Why does a musician get weapons and I don't?" He thumbed at Lisa, still unaware she was an MI6 agent.

"Lisa was a pistol champion in Great Britain, like Carlene was in Texas. I'll need to get to know you better before I decide if I can trust you with a weapon." I slung an MP7 across my back. "Help Lance carry the life raft over there."

Renaldo scowled and picked up one end of the raft. Once they had it in the center of the depression, Lance pulled the inflation cord and stepped back. Almost instantly, we had a huge, circular chamber with a roof and side flaps.

Lightning flashed and thunder boomed nearby as the wind increased and the temperature dropped a few degrees.

Lance cocked his head. "More rain is headed this way."

"Put the extra raft and all our supplies inside in the center. That will anchor the raft and leave enough room for us to sleep in the outer sections." I grabbed two suitcases. "Hurry and finish before that thunderstorm hits us."

Everyone pitched in and hauled our stuff into

the raft. Once all seven of us were inside, we closed and secured the side flaps seconds before the squall hit.

The heavy downpour on the waterproof roof drowned out any attempts at conversation. While the storm raged outside, Lisa, the redhead singer/secret agent, seemed calm, but she kept one eye on Renaldo. He sat with his arm around Carlene.

Barbi and Tiesha looked relaxed as they snuggled against either side of Lance—no surprise there. Women were drawn to him. His confident demeanor made them feel safe, and they knew they could always count on him to protect them. Sweet.

I caught Lance's attention and grinned.

He shrugged and smiled.

The downpour slowed to a light patter as the sun dropped to the edge of the plateau. When the rain stopped, the setting sun highlighted a dark, four-legged shadow that passed by silently on the west side of the raft.

Uh oh.

The Scorpions

Scorpion One was twenty feet from the American nuclear submarine when Jane succeeded in overpowering the launched torpedo trapped in the netting. She backed away with the straining torpedo in tow.

"Look out! *Texas* just fired another torpedo,"

Scooter shouted as *Scorpion Two* fired at the same North Korean sub.

Jane pulled up, narrowly avoiding being hit by friendly fire.

The enemy subs couldn't target the little attack subs, invisible on passive sonar, especially amidst all the exploding torpedoes.

The resulting shock waves slammed into the Scorpions, rolling and jostling them.

Fred texted: Three down, one to go.

Jane texted: Dibs. Our harnessed fish is hot. I'm tired of wrestling with it.

She maneuvered through the turbulent water, dragging the weapon behind the last Sang-O Shark. She needed to get close to avoid the possibility of the torpedo missing the target and maybe hitting an American ship.

"Release the fish, Scooter," Jane commanded.

He released the harnessed weapon, and she pulled up and accelerated away.

Despite the netting, the torpedo's propeller pushed it into the enemy sub, resulting in a close-range detonation. The blast caught *Scorpion One* and sent them tumbling end over end.

Jane allowed three rotations to dissipate their forward momentum before she recovered control and circled back.

Looming over her like a monstrous megalodon, the lethal American submarine was still on the hunt. She tapped out a text to *Texas*: All enemy subs destroyed. Cease fire.

Jane and Fred pulled up and did victory rolls while they waited for the ocean current to clear away the silt.

Rowlin's voice filled their speakers. *"Scorpions One* and *Two*, report."

"Scorpion One reporting all enemy subs destroyed. No damage to our submarines," Jane said.

"Scorpion Two reporting the same, Captain. Total destruction of enemy subs," Fred said. "The detonations were at about a hundred-foot depth, so there's bound to be a lot of flotsam. Somebody had better make sure no body parts wash up on shore."

"Understood," Rowlin said. "Good work, Scorpions. The Navy has clean-up crews on the way."

"Is *Wolverine* all right?" Jane asked, feeling guilty about the missed torpedo.

"They suffered a hit in their bow, but the damage has been contained," Rowlin said. "Take turns re-arming."

After acknowledging Rowlin's command, Jane called Fred in *Scorpion Two*. "We still have all our fish, so we'll remain on point while you re-arm."

"Copy that, Jane," Fred said. "Stay sharp. There's no telling what might be waiting for you up ahead."

The Mesa

"Looks like it'll be dark soon, Sam," Barbi said, peeking out under a side flap. "Shouldn't we gather wood and brush to make a signal fire?"

I scanned the darkening plateau as a cold wind from the east sent goosebumps over me. "No fires. In fact, no signals of any kind. The same people who tried to blow us up might be looking for us."

"But then how'll we be rescued?" Tiesha asked, her tone telegraphing concern.

I tapped my left wrist. "The discrete GPS locator on my DARPA watch is still working. It'll broadcast our location to the good guys."

"That's a relief," Tiesha said, leaning back.

"But we might have a problem." I glanced around at the people in the raft. "We need to figure out who tried to kill us because the emergency locator transmitter in the tail could still be transmitting. If it is, the bad guys can track it, and there's a chance they might get here before the U.S. military."

Lance nodded. "Yeah, we need to know who we're up against."

"How do you know our military will come?" Barbi asked.

"Because they still need my help." I smiled. "Believe me, they'll come."

A gust rippled the flaps on our raft tent, and everyone flinched.

"Sam, do you think Lord Sweetwater tried to kill us?" Carlene asked.

"No, not his style. Sweetwater likes his revenge up close and personal. He enjoys torturing his enemies. I'm number one on his list, but he's not about to come to a place like this."

"Could it be the Chinese?" Lance asked.

"I doubt it. They want to interrogate me, so they need me alive."

Lisa focused on Carlene's boyfriend. "Who do *you* think it might be, Renaldo? A rival drug cartel?"

"I'm no drug dealer!" Renaldo stiffened and shifted his eyes to Carlene and back to Lisa. "Why would you suggest such a thing?"

"You control one of the biggest drug cartels in South America," Lisa said. "Or maybe an African war lord is unhappy with the weapons you sold him."

"This is not the time to play games, Renaldo," I said. "Not if you want to live."

"You've put all our lives in danger." Lance glared at him. "We need to know who's coming to kill us."

Carlene scooted backward, her face reddening. She scowled at Renaldo like he'd just admitted to murdering the Dallas Cowboys. Then she racked the slide on her pistol and pointed it at his head. "Start talking, you lying sack of—"

"Carlene, put away the Glock. We wouldn't

want to damage our shelter." I glared at Renaldo. "Well?"

"Alright, it's probably the Colombian cartel," Renaldo admitted. "I've expanded my territory in the past eight months, and they're not happy about it. They said they'd kill me if I didn't hand over half my business."

"Then why didn't they blow us up after take-off?" Lance asked, crossing his arms.

"How should I know?" Renaldo shrugged, his nostrils flaring.

"Downing a U.S. jumbo jet would bring a lot of heat on them," Lisa said. "But if they orchestrated it so that we lost radio contact over a vast jungle, lost both engines thirty minutes later, and then exploded while descending in the middle of nowhere, we'd never be found, and they'd never be blamed."

"Makes sense," I said. "Problem is they might find us, finish the job, and destroy the evidence."

"So, give me a weapon." Renaldo held out his hand. "You'll need all the fire power you can get if we're going to survive long enough for your military to rescue us."

I shook my head. "Any chance *your* people will rescue us?"

"When we don't land in Rio, they'll find out our flight vanished and think we're dead." Renaldo thrust his hand at me. "Give me a weapon."

"I can't trust an international criminal with a

weapon," I said. "If the rival cartel comes, maybe I'll reconsider."

Lance peeked outside. "It's getting dark. I'd better go and scout a good spot for our latrine."

"Watch out for jaguars," I said.

"I know." Lance shoved an extra magazine in his pocket. "Those varmints are the most aggressive of all the big cats."

I nodded. "We'll sort through the food and plan our rations."

Another deep growl echoed across the mesa.

Lance checked his MP7 and racked the slide on his Glock.

EIGHTEEN

The Scorpions

Fred accelerated away from *Leviathan's* moon pool, searching for Jane in the crystal-clear ocean water off Florida's east coast. He zoomed over colorful reefs, scattering tropical fish. The dark shadow of the big destroyer loomed ahead above them.

"There she is!" Bull called out. "Eleven o'clock."

Fred pulled up beside *Scorpion One* and called them. "How's it going?"

"So far, so good," Jane answered. "*Texas* is guarding *Leviathan's* six, and *Wolverine* is limping along on point. No enemy subs in sight."

"Where do you want us?" Fred asked.

"We'll take the port side forward of *Wolverine's*

course, and you take the starboard side," Jane said. "If the DPRK has more submarines lying in wait, we'll find them."

"They lost one near Atlantis and four near Palm Beach," Fred said. "If we take out a couple more, that might decimate their entire submarine fleet."

"I wish. Last I heard, the DPRK had seventy subs," Jane said. "At best we're only reducing their fleet by ten percent."

"Geez, maybe their nut-job leader sent thirty or forty of them after *Leviathan*," Fred said.

"All the more reason to cripple their navy," Jane said. "Switch to silent comms now and happy hunting."

The Scorpions cruised up the Florida coast as their silent propulsion systems kept them invisible to the enemy. Their thick plexiglass canopies afforded them excellent views in the flowing current of the Gulf Stream.

At almost the same moment, both Scorpions texted: Unknown targets.

Jane texted: We've got one dead ahead.

Fred replied: Same on our side. Have rules of engagement changed since last attack?

Jane texted: I'll check.

She contacted CIC: Rules of engagement?

Rowlin replied: Give me a sitrep.

Jane texted: 2 enemy subs ahead. Permission for preemptive strike?

Rowlin answered: Are their torpedo doors open?

Jane texted: Affirmative. All torpedo doors open.

Rowlin replied: Take them out. If anyone asks, they fired first. Total destruction, no survivors.

Jane texted: Copy that. Destroy targets, no survivors.

She texted *Scorpion Two*: Say they fired first and destroy them. Acknowledge.

Fred answered: Understood. Scorpion Two is responding to attack from enemy sub on our side.

Before Fred's sub fired, the North Korean sub ahead of him fired a torpedo at *Wolverine*. He was close to the enemy sub when the torpedo shot out.

Bull, his weapons specialist, shouted, "Enemy torpedo away!"

Taking a big chance, Fred dove into the torpedo before it armed, slamming it into the sea bed. "Got it!"

He pulled up as Jane and Scooter blew up the sub on their side.

The explosion alerted the enemy sub on Fred's side as a shock wave rocked them.

He banked right and dived toward the Sang-O Shark. "Bull, target the tube door that hasn't fired yet."

He fired, and their torpedo impacted just as an enemy torpedo was exiting the door.

Fred pulled up as the massive explosion pummeled them with another shock wave.

Rowlin texted: Scorpions One and Two, report.

"Both enemy subs destroyed," Jane said over the comm.

"Total destruction with no survivors after they fired on *Wolverine*," Fred said.

"Good work, Scorpions. Re-arm one at a time and then take point. Current rules of engagement apply."

"Aye, Captain, we'll re-arm and then scout ahead and keep our ships safe," Jane replied, and Fred confirmed.

"Woo hoo!" Fred did a victory roll and called Jane. "Your turn to re-arm first."

"Good shooting, you guys!" Jane replied. "We'll return ASAP."

Bull tapped Fred's shoulder. "Think the North Koreans have any more subs waiting for us?"

He shrugged. "We'll find out soon enough."

The Mesa

Lance returned from scouting a latrine site. "I'll be happy to escort anyone who needs a potty break. I didn't see a jaguar, but I heard one out there."

"What about privacy?" Barbi asked.

"I'll take a space blanket and hold it up to block the view," Lance said.

"Let's go in small groups and get this over with." I nodded to the flight attendants. "Barbi and Tiesha, you go with Lance while I stay with the passengers. Then I'll go with Lisa, Carlene, and Renaldo."

Thirty minutes later, everyone was back in the raft.

"Alright, Barbi will pass around our dinners, and Tiesha will hand out the beverages. Thanks to everyone's hard work, we have enough to last several days." I smiled at the group.

"Hopefully, we'll be rescued tomorrow, but it would be smart to plan for a long stay just in case."

"This day has been really traumatic," Carlene said. "Let's open a bottle of wine. My nerves could sure use some."

"Good idea, Carlene." I pulled a corkscrew out of a bag and handed it to Tiesha. "But somebody has to stay sharp, so Lance and I will abstain in case a jaguar crashes the party."

We settled in and enjoyed meals that had already been cooked but had now cooled to air temperature.

Lisa sat beside Renaldo to keep a close eye on him, and Carlene sat on the opposite side of the raft to keep from killing him. Tiesha and Barbi snuggled against Lance, and I sat near an entrance flap.

Tiesha nudged me. "Sam, you think there's a chance the Colombian cartel will come looking for Renaldo?"

Before I could answer, the thundering blades of a helicopter echoed across the mesa.

"Douse the flashlights! They might not be here to rescue us." I peeked out from the side flap to get a glimpse of the chopper. It didn't sound like a Chinook or a Blackhawk from our military. "I can only see the position lights in the dark, but it sounds like a civilian helicopter."

Sharp clicks from slides racking on pistols filled the raft.

The helicopter flew to where our airplane had slid off the cliff and exploded on a high ledge.

A few tense seconds ticked by. Then rounds from a high-caliber machine gun echoed off the cliff wall.

"What are they doing?" Tiesha asked, peeking out.

"They're probably destroying the emergency locator transmitter that was mounted in the aircraft's tail," Lance said.

"Think they spotted our raft?" Barbi asked.

A bright spotlight shined on us, lighting up our interior from the outside as the helicopter flew overhead. The downwash rocked our shelter.

"What should we do?" Barbi asked, glancing from me to Lance.

"Sit tight." I pulled extra magazines out of the duffel and handed some to Lance and Lisa. We pulled out our MP7s and checked that they were ready to fire.

The helicopter landed about thirty yards from us. With the engines at idle RPM, the rotors made the ground vibrate. A spotlight remained fixed on us.

"Our exit flaps are in view of the helicopter," Lance shouted above the whine of the helicopter's engines. "They'll see us if we try to sneak away."

"Why don't we send Renaldo out?" Carlene asked. "They can take him and leave us alone."

"It's worth a try." I poked Renaldo. "You're responsible for this. Get your butt out there and convince them to leave the rest of us unharmed."

He turned pale and trembled. "Please, don't make me go."

"You brought this on yourself. Be brave for once and do the right thing." I prodded him with my MP7 barrel. "Get out!"

Tiesha and Lance helped me shove him through the tent flap.

"Don't be a coward!" I shouted, giving him one last push.

During the struggle, my hand accidentally brushed one of the crystals embedded in the ancient stone circle.

It instantly lit up, beaming brilliant light out in all directions. In seconds, all the crystals blazed with blinding beams.

Disoriented by the sudden illumination, Renaldo stumbled forward and stood with his hands on his head. I ducked back inside the shelter.

The helicopter's engines increased in RPM, and the ground shook harder. Our raft rocked in the swirling air from the rotor blades.

The crystals' combined light blazed almost as brightly as the sun, probably blinding the pilot. The chopper must've tilted sideways because the rotors impacted the ground, breaking into sharp blades. Screeching metal preceded an explosion that spun our raft around and showered it with metal fragments. At least the spinning motion helped repel some of the shrapnel.

The blast must've flung one of the broken rotor blades into Renaldo's neck, decapitating him. At least, that's what I surmised when his bloody head bounced through an entrance flap into our raft and landed in Tiesha's lap.

"Arggh!" she shrieked and jumped up, sending Renaldo's head rolling onto Barbi's feet.

Not one to scare easily, Barbi snatched up the head and tossed it outside like it was a huge hand grenade. "Good riddance!" She wiped her bloody hands on her navy uniform slacks.

Everyone else sat frozen, shocked by the gore.

I coughed as puffs of acrid smoke from the helicopter fire invaded our shelter.

Lance cleared his throat. "You ladies okay?"

We nodded.

Then something even more unexpected happened.

The stone floor beneath our shelter suddenly

slanted downward at a sharp angle, and the opening in the ground swallowed us. Everyone and everything inside the raft became pinned against the lower sidewall.

"Hold onto the handrails!" I yelled as we plunged into a dark void.

The stone trapdoor above us closed, blocking the bright light from the crystals and the burning helicopter.

We slid downward in total darkness, our raft accelerating.

Cold water splashed through tears in the side flaps as I gripped the bucking raft. The high-pitched screaming from some of the women made it difficult to discern what we were sliding on, but I guessed it might be an underground stream.

I prayed it wouldn't spit us out one of the high waterfalls I'd seen shooting out of the mesa before I landed.

NINETEEN

Mayport Navy Base

Rowlin stood in the balmy northern Florida air on the port bridge wing as bright floodlights illuminated his crew unloading the gold vaults. A forward crane placed one into a specially-made wooden crate. After the cover was nailed shut, the crane lifted it off the ship and onto a military flatbed truck. The statue of Poseidon, wrapped in blankets, was also crated.

Seven of the vaults were loaded on the first truck, and the other four were loaded on a second truck with the statue.

As the trucks drove away into the night, Rowlin smiled and glanced at his XO. "Now they're someone else's problem."

"Think they really contain all of Atlantis's scientific knowledge?" Lowes asked.

"I hope so. We sure went through hell to deliver them here." Rowlin reached into his pocket when he felt his cell vibrate. He looked at the phone. "It's my dad."

"Max, bad news," Jeff said, his voice tense. "Sam's flight went down over a remote part of the Amazon basin."

"Dad, I'm so sorry." Max's gut twisted into a knot. "Did she call in a Mayday?"

"No, their radios and transponder had quit transmitting, but I know where they went down because Ross called me."

"Are you talking about SAS Captain Ross Sinclair?" Max had never met Ross in person, but they'd had several phone conversations in the recent past.

"Yeah, Sam's boyfriend. The military has a GPS tracker in her watch. Our military and the UK's SAS keep track of it. It stopped moving about an hour before sunset. That's how Ross knows where she crashed."

"Are they sending an SAS team or SEALs to look for her?"

"Both. It turns out there was a British citizen on board with our American crew, along with an American passenger and one from Brazil."

Max sucked in his breath. "Who was her copilot?"

"You know him. It was Lance Bowie."

"He's one brave sonofabitch." Max remembered his recent adventures with Lance and the dangerous mission his father and Lance had flown to save millions of people. "If he survived, he'll save Sam—especially since he's in love with her."

"Yep, he's smitten for sure," Jeff said. "I'm counting on him to remember his military survival training and help keep everyone alive. He was a fighter pilot in the Air Force."

"Has anyone checked satellite footage along her planned route?"

"Both the Brits and our military checked—nothing," Jeff said. "There were a lot of big thunderstorms along her route. The airplane's ELT showed them far off course at the crash site, which agreed with her GPS watch."

"Good thing they have the ELT signal and her GPS tracker."

"About that—the ELT stopped transmitting fifteen minutes ago, and her GPS signal vanished a few minutes later."

The Mesa

Our trip down nature's waterslide took only a few minutes, but every second was terrifying. The steep downward angle lessened right before our raft shot out onto an underground lake. We skipped across the water like a flat stone and bumped up against the opposite shore. The roar of waterfalls emptying into the lake echoed off the rock walls.

On top of the heap of bodies and supplies, I crawled off to an exit and peeked out. Large, bioluminescent plants grew along the shoreline, emitting eerie pink, blue, and pearl-colored light. Beyond the lakeshore, similar trees and plants dimly illuminated strange buildings carved into the rock. Waterfalls splashed down into stone aqueducts that weaved through what appeared to be an ancient city. The conduits emptied water into the lake.

The glow from the various colored plants gave the shadowy city an otherworldly appearance. I slipped outside and pulled the raft up on shore a foot or so. It was too heavy to pull it any farther.

I couldn't hear anything over the water noise, but a primal warning bell rang in my head. I looked around. Nothing moved.

"Okay, everyone out so we can check for injuries." I held the flap open.

"Whoa, where the heck are we?" Tiesha asked as she climbed out.

Barbi stepped out and stroked long leaves on a pale-blue bush. "It looks like we went through a wormhole into another dimension." When she wiped her hands on her pants, glowing blue smudges covered her thighs.

"Better not touch the weird plants in case they're poisonous." I offered my hand and helped Carlene out of the raft.

Wide-eyed, she glanced around. "This don't look like our planet. Maybe Barbi's right about a wormhole."

Lisa and Lance climbed out last.

Lisa held her hand close to the nearest blue plant. "This feels warmer than the surrounding air. Interesting. Brazil is known for having unusual plants and wildlife, but I've never heard of any that were bioluminescent."

Once everyone was on shore, we pulled our raft onto the beach and checked each other for injuries. Luckily, there were just a few small cuts from the metal fragments that had pierced our raft roof.

Lance pointed at the lake. "It's filled with luminous fish! Look at the bright streaks they leave as they swim."

"We're lucky there are plenty of glowing plants and fish." Lisa squinted at the massive underground cavern. "Otherwise, it'd be pitch black down here."

"All the water noise makes it difficult to hear if anyone's sneaking up on us." Lance scanned the dark city. "But this place looks deserted."

I faced my crew and passengers. "The good news is we're safe from the cartel. The bad news is we don't know how big this place is or if there's an exit to the jungle."

"The cartel destroyed our jet's ELT," Lance said, "and the military won't be able to receive Sam's GPS signal while we're underground."

Tiesha bit her lip. "So then, how will they find us?"

"Don't worry." I smiled reassuringly. "My GPS signal vanished when I entered the mountain in Petra, but Ross figured out where I went and followed me."

"We should talk about what happened topside." Lance faced me. "Did you touch one of the crystals?"

"Yes, but it was an accident. My hand brushed against one when we shoved Renaldo out of the raft."

Lisa stepped closer. "What does that have to do with what happened?"

"It's a long story. My body carries a unique frequency of electromagnetic energy that triggers some ancient mechanisms. Turns out I'm descended from a race whose women were worshipped as goddesses by the people of Atlantis."

"So, when you touched the crystal, you activated the blinding light and the trapdoor?" Lisa raised a brow.

"It's a reasonable assumption based on my past experiences." I paused. "Unless you have a better theory?"

She shrugged. "Maybe the strong vibrations from the helicopter triggered the lights and trapdoor. I mean, that mechanism could be a thousand years old. No telling what might set it off after all those years."

I glanced at Lance.

He nodded. "I've seen Sam open all sorts of ancient portals. She's even activated 3-D holographic images from thousands of years ago. If there's a door out of here, her touch will open it."

Lisa stared at me like I'd just arrived from Mars.

"If the cartel sends another team, they'll find what's left of Renaldo and assume the rest of us died in the airliner when it exploded. They won't come looking for us," I said.

"Good. Let's explore the city." Barbi flicked on her mini magnesium-light. "We might find a stairway up to the mesa or a door into the jungle."

"Alright, but I'd like someone to stay with the raft." I glanced around the group.

Carlene raised her hand. "I've had enough excitement for one day. I'll stay and guard the wine."

"And you can tidy up the raft supplies while you're at it. Arrange everything in the center again, so we can sleep along the perimeter." I checked my watch. "It's almost morning. We'll be back soon."

Lance, Lisa, and I slung H&K MP7s over our shoulders and carried flashlights. Barbi and Tiesha were armed with Glocks and mag-lights.

"Let's turn off our lights to conserve the batteries." I stuck my flashlight in my jacket pocket.

Sounds of rushing water echoing off the hard walls and cavernous ceiling drowned out our footsteps as we strode down the smooth-hewn path into the dark city. Dwellings were carved into the rock on several levels, creating a terraced community. Large crystals were embedded in the stone at regular intervals.

I elbowed Lance. "Maybe if I touch a crystal, the city will light up."

"Or maybe it'll explode. Better not chance it."

The stone underworld was cloaked in darkness with just the dim lights of bioluminescent plants to light our way. I couldn't see anyone lurking nearby, but I had the uneasy feeling we were being watched —probably my imagination playing tricks on me. I glanced up and spotted an enormous snake carved into the rock. Its huge head arched above us with its gaping mouth looking like it intended to swallow us.

Welcome to Hell.

We had traveled the length of a football field when I tripped on something. Recognition triggered a primal fear suffered by every woman since the Garden of Eden. My heartrate soared as I sucked in my breath and used every ounce of self-control to stop myself from screaming and running away. I had to remain calm.

My crew and passengers are depending on me. God help us!

A snakeskin over forty feet long had been shed on the city's main walkway. I'm no fan of snakes— especially big ones. I don't care if they have an important role in the ecology of our planet. If they want to live, they'd better stay the hell away from me. Spiders too.

Tiesha took one look at the massive snakeskin, spun around, and face-planted into Lance's chest. She pulled back. "We've got to get outta here!"

He wrapped his arms around her. "Calm down and stay with the group. The snake's probably long gone by now."

"I'm not staying in no city with giant snakes!" Tiesha's wide eyes radiated panic. "We should get in the raft and sleep out on the lake." She jerked away from Lance and sprinted back toward the beach.

Barbi, who was working on a Ph.D. in zoology, called out, "I hate to tell you this, but that skin is from an anaconda, and they can swim!"

TWENTY

C-17 Globemaster III

SAS Captain Ross Sinclair—tall, dark-haired, and square-jawed, with deep-blue eyes—stood beside his lieutenant and best friend, Derek Dunbar, who shared similar features, except for his eyes, which were emerald-green. They checked their gear and weapons.

Ross glanced across the broad interior of the C-17 where Sam's brother, SEAL Lieutenant Mike Starr, was doing the same thing with his fellow SEAL, Sergeant John Ozman, whom everyone called Oz. Mike was blond, blue-eyed, and six feet of toned muscle, and Oz was medium height and barrel-chested, with brown hair and hazel eyes.

Ross glanced at his watch and yelled to Mike,

"We jump in ten minutes. Ready for the final mission brief?"

Mike nodded and tapped Oz to follow him. The men were decked out in combat gear with special tactical parachutes strapped to their backs.

When the three men gathered in front of him, Ross said, "We aren't expecting any hostiles, but be ready for anything. And make damn sure you land on the mesa. It's a helluva long climb up. After we land, I'll contact the pilot, and he'll make a low pass over us and drop the supplies and equipment. Questions?"

"Do you have anti-venom kits?" Mike asked. "If not, I brought extras."

"You Yanks have everything." Derek extended his hand. "I'll take one."

Mike pulled two kits from his pack and handed one to Derek and one to Ross. "Don't be surprised if we run across jaguars and anacondas too."

"Huh, sounds like a fun vacation spot." Oz checked his watch.

"Five minutes." Ross tightened his parachute. "Move to the aft door and do a final check."

The UK and US had agreed to combine men from the Special Air Service and SEALs for a joint search and rescue mission. They chose two men from each team because time was critical and they weren't expecting armed interference from anyone. Ross and Derek had worked successfully with Mike in the past on missions involving Sam, so he was an obvious choice from the SEALs.

A horn blared and a red light blinked, warning the soldiers the jump was imminent.

The aft loading door opened and the jump light turned green. Ross yelled, "Jump!" as he ran down the ramp and dove into the colorful dawn sky. Derek, Mike, and Oz followed him.

Noting wind from the east, Ross dove toward the east side of the mesa. On the way down, he spotted the aircraft wreckage on a ledge shrouded in shadows under a cliff on the west side. He popped his chute and landed in the middle of the long, narrow mesa.

Derek and Mike landed beside him. Oz was about to touch down when a gust caught his chute and blew him toward the western cliff. He released his harness, dropped, and rolled to a stop inches from the edge. His chute blew over the cliff and floated all the way down to the dense jungle, catching in the trees.

Ross pulled out his radio and contacted the C-17 pilot. "Four good landings in the LZ. Cleared to drop the pallets. Favor the east side."

"Roger, four down safe, prepare to receive pallets, east side," the C-17 pilot replied.

Mike and Derek jogged over to where Oz had landed, and Ross joined them a minute later.

"You good to go?" Ross asked Oz.

"Hell yeah. I saved myself the walk." Oz pointed down. "The wreck is below us."

Mike already had his binoculars out, scanning the wreckage. "Looks like multiple explosions after the landing." He hesitated. "No evidence of bodies."

Ross squeezed Mike's shoulder. "Relax. No way she could've been in there when it blew. Her DARPA watch was still transmitting several minutes after the ELT stopped."

"Think they're up here somewhere, or did they climb down?" Mike asked.

"Uh, guys? Check this out." Oz reached down and picked up two .50-caliber shell casings.

Mike focused his binoculars on what was left of the tail cone. "Looks like somebody peppered the tail with .50-cal rounds. Probably destroyed the ELT. Who the hell did this?"

Derek tapped Mike's shoulder. "I suggest we look over there." He pointed at a spot in the middle of the mesa where vultures circled overhead.

Just then, the massive C-17 roared past and dropped several pallets near the spot where the birds had been circling.

"Alright, let's get to it." Ross jogged toward the pallets as the sun edged above the mesa.

Underground City

Ear shattering screams jolted me. They seemed to come from the lakeshore. Lance and I raced to the beach with Lisa and Barbi. We found Tiesha standing beside an empty raft.

I glanced around. "Carlene!"

No answer.

Tiesha sputtered and pointed, "It…it swallowed her!"

"What swallowed her? Where is it?" I asked, scanning the lake.

She pointed at a track in the sand—one that could only have been left by a massive snake. It led to the water. "A…a giant snake…ate her and disappeared in there!"

Lisa shook her head. "How could this happen? She was armed."

"It snuck up behind her when she stepped out of the raft. It all happened so fast." Tiesha sobbed. "Carlene is so tiny, it swallowed her in an instant."

I scanned the lake as Dragon Master's words replayed in my head. *"All sea creatures are yours to command."*

The lake was like an underground sea, and the snake swam in it. Did that make the snake a sea creature? Or could it be that all creatures, land and sea, were susceptible to my commands? I stared at the water and concentrated on contacting the anaconda telepathically.

Would my fear of snakes prevent me from saving Carlene?

Was the anaconda's brain big enough to understand me?

And could I really face that monster?

I racked the slide on my Glock and released the safety on my MP7.

Seconds ticked by.

Barbi screamed. An enormous snake raised its head above the water like a mythical sea serpent. A large bulge protruded in the neck area below its head.

"Don't shoot!" I yelled. "You'll hit Carlene!"

The monster reared up in front of Tiesha, who stood there, stunned, with her feet glued to the shore.

The anaconda had to be at least forty-five feet long. It opened its mouth, unhinged its jaw, and vomited its prey onto the sand at Tiesha's feet.

Everyone froze at the sight of Carlene covered in slime. The snake dived into the dark lake and vanished in a circle of ripples.

"Quick, rinse her off in the water and start CPR!" I leaped into the raft and grabbed the first-aid kit.

Lance scooped her up and dunked her in the lake to rinse off the corrosive digestive acid. He laid her on the beach and breathed air into her lungs between Barbi's chest compressions. Thirty seconds into the CPR, Carlene gasped and opened her eyes.

Lance helped her sit up. "Can you breathe okay now?"

"My chest hurts." She gasped. "My whole body feels like it's been crushed."

"You were crushed." I checked her for broken bones. "Do you remember being swallowed?"

Her eyes widened and she glanced around. "The snake! Where is it?"

"It dove back into the lake after it spit you up." I looked at her delicate, fine-boned body. Her face and exposed skin were inflamed similar to a bad sunburn. "I guess you were too big for it."

Barbi held a can of Coke to her lips. "Drink this. The sugar and caffeine will help revive you."

Carlene took a drink and moaned. "Swallowing hurts too."

I glanced at Lance. "Get her inside the raft and cover her with a blanket."

"I'll put moisturizer on her skin." Barbi followed Lance into the raft.

While I waited for them to come out, I wondered if the snake had followed my commands or if Carlene really had been too big for it. This was all new to me. My only personal experience with animal telepathy had been commanding an enormous kraken. I'd seen the triplets command orcas, but killer whales were known to be intelligent.

Lance and Barbi emerged from the raft.

"She's resting now," Barbi said. "Probably has some cracked ribs."

Tiesha regained her voice, albeit in a higher pitch. "What are we going to do about the snake?"

I paused. "There's six of us, but Carlene's in no condition to help. That leaves five people for now. We can group together and take turns standing guard."

Barbi and Tiesha each grabbed one of Lance's arms. "We're with Lance," they said in unison.

"Okay, Lisa and I'll take the first watch." I grabbed a raft strap. "Let's drag this raft a little farther from the lake."

Where's the monster now? Will it glow in the dark if it eats a big bioluminescent fish?

Just thinking about it made me shiver. Goosebumps creeped over my skin. Then an even worse thought invaded my brain.

I whispered a private prayer, "Please, God—no giant spiders."

We had to find a way out of this nightmare.

Special Ops Team

Ross circled the helicopter wreckage and paused. "Looks like the pilot lost control, and the rotor blades hit the ground, causing the chopper to crash and explode."

"That's not the only thing the blades hit." Mike held up Renaldo's gory, severed head. Birds had already eaten the eyes.

"Five charred bodies in a helicopter with a five-person capacity." Derek toed Renaldo's headless corpse. "He must've been the Brazilian passenger from Flight 515. I wonder where the other passengers and crew went."

Oz picked through the debris. "The chopper had a .50-cal machine gun mounted in the nose, and the men inside were armed with automatic weapons. No room to take on passengers. This wasn't a rescue mission."

Mike touched the wreckage. "None of it feels warm. The crash and fire must've happened last night."

"Aye, Sam's crew and passengers probably ran and hid from the hit team. We'd best find them before more shooters arrive. We'll take the ATVs." Ross disconnected a crate housing one of the all-terrain vehicles.

Mike uncrated the other one. "Oz and I'll search the east side. You guys start at the north end on the west side, and then we'll meet in the middle about five miles south."

Ross glanced at his watch. "We have plenty of daylight. Should be easy to spot them." He started the engine and Derek climbed aboard, his binoculars ready.

The men roared away, searching the mesa. After four hours, they met halfway across the southern end of the plateau.

Ross jumped out and approached Mike.

"I think we must've missed something back

where the helicopter crashed," Ross said. "What if this is another Petra situation?"

Mike stiffened his stance. "Are you thinking they may have found a way inside?"

"It's worth considering. Sam led her people into the mountain in Petra to escape armed killers. Your sister is full of surprises."

Mike pulled out a satellite phone. "She was on Max Rowlin's ship a few days ago. Some top-secret mission. Then Chinese secret agents targeted her in Palm Beach. Could be connected. I think we should call Max."

Ross nodded. "Make the call."

Mike dialed Max's cell. He answered on the first ring.

"Rowlin here, who's calling?"

"Max, it's Mike Starr. I'm in South America looking for Sam and her people. They seem to have vanished on top of an isolated mesa after a hit team in a helicopter tried to take them out."

"A hit team? What the hell's going on down there?"

"We're not sure. Do you know anything that could help us find Sam?"

"There's a Chinese guy named Dragon Master who might be able to help you. He advised Sam how to use one of her abilities to save my Hardsuit divers. He's still here. I can send him with one of my SEALs if you like."

"I'm sending you our coordinates. How fast can you get them here?"

Max paused a moment. "I can have them on a C-17 out of NAS JAX in thirty minutes. My SEAL, Banger, can do a tandem jump with the old Chinese guy. Expect them in about five hours."

"Thanks, Max. We're pretty sure Sam's alive. We just have to find her before another hit team arrives. This Dragon Master guy may be the key."

"Happy to help. Of course, you understand our military needs her in Atlantis, which is how I'm able to do this. Keep me in the loop, Mike."

"I'll call as soon as we know something." Mike switched off the SATCOM and told Ross about the men Max was sending. "They'll arrive by parachute in five hours."

"We'll pitch the tent and set up a defensive perimeter in case another hit team flies in. Everything will be ready by the time Max's men arrive." Ross strode back to his ATV.

They returned to where vultures circled overhead.

TWENTY-ONE

Underground City

Carlene slept curled up in Lance's lap. She'd insisted she needed him to hold her or she'd be too scared to sleep. He took the first rest period with Tiesha and Barbi. That left Lisa and me on guard duty outside the raft. We sat back-to-back on the beach with our submachine guns on our laps.

"This may sound weird, but ever since we landed inside here, I've felt like we were being watched." I glanced around. "And I don't mean the anaconda. Do you feel it?"

"After plenty of close calls during missions with MI6, I've developed a sort of inner radar," Lisa said. "My alarm bells haven't stopped ringing since that helicopter landed. I'm not sure what to think now."

"My inner voice is telling me the snake is the least of our worries." I glanced around. "Hard to imagine something worse than that monster."

"How often is your inner voice right?"

"So far, it's batting a thousand."

"You Yanks and your baseball references—does that mean it's never wrong?"

"One hundred percent accuracy, always."

"Bugger! Can you ask your inner voice to be more specific about the danger?"

"I wish. All I know is something is lurking out there in the shadows, and it's way worse than the anaconda." I rechecked the magazine on my MP7.

"That does it," Lisa said. "No danger of me falling asleep on guard duty."

"I've heard that singing can tame a savage beast. Do you know any soothing songs?"

"I guess it's worth a go." Lisa began singing "Somewhere Over the Rainbow." Her voice had a lovely, lilting tone that echoed off the granite.

The ominous sense of dread that had been hanging over me lifted and floated away.

After six hours of listening to the sounds of rushing water, I could barely keep my eyes open. It was time for us to be relieved from guard duty.

Lisa and I walked to the raft, and I lifted the entrance flap. I said over my shoulder, "I guess they weren't too scared. They're all sound asleep."

"See if you can wake them without rousing Carlene." Lisa stood watch while I tried to gently wake Tiesha, Barbi, and Lance.

I whispered their names and held my finger to my mouth when they opened their eyes. "Wake up. It's your turn for guard duty. Try not to wake Carlene."

Barbi yawned and stretched. "I need caffeine." She grabbed a can of cola.

Tiesha squeezed my arm and whispered, "Did you see the snake?"

"No, it never came back. Maybe it's out in the jungle now." I gave her a reassuring smile.

"Give me a minute," Tiesha said. "As soon as Lance leaves, I'll change into my comfortable jeans."

I gave Lance a soft kiss on his cheek. "Wake up, handsome."

He opened his eyes and whispered, "How do I get up without waking Carlene?"

"Lay her down beside you, and I'll snuggle against her. She just needs a warm body next to her to feel safe."

He did as I instructed, and Carlene continued sleeping. When he stepped out, Lisa entered and settled on the other side of Carlene.

Tiesha opened her suitcase and pulled out her jeans. I closed my eyes and was almost asleep when

I heard Lance yell, "Everyone come outside nice and slow. Do it now!"

Lisa and I sprang awake and woke Carlene. We crawled through the door flap while Tiesha finished changing clothes.

I stood still while my eyes adjusted to the dim light. It took a moment to realize we were surrounded by muscular, half-naked people with pitch-black skin. They were armed with spears and blowguns.

The weapons were aimed at us.

USS LEVIATHAN

Max finished briefing Banger and Dragon Master about their mission to South America. He squeezed the old man's shoulder and toed a duffel bag. "We scrounged some extra clothes from one of our crewmen. Should have everything you need in here."

Dragon Master bowed his head. "Many thanks, Captain. May I use toilet before we depart?"

"There's one down that corridor to the right." Max pointed. "We'll wait for you here by the helipad."

The elderly Chinese man strode briskly down the dim corridor and ducked into the head. He pressed a button on his watch. Moments later, the call connected.

"Queen stranded in South America. It five-hour flight in C-17 from NAS JAX. You depart now. I'll send signal over crash site. Bring enough men to defeat five Special Operators." He waited for confirmation and ended the call.

Max looked up from his phone when Dragon Master returned. "The Seahawk will fly you to a nearby Naval Air Station where you'll take a C-17 to the crash site and parachute in like we briefed. Any questions?"

"I am ready." The old man gave a quick bow.

"Thanks for helping out." Max shook his hand.

Dragon Master climbed aboard the helicopter with Banger.

A little over five hours later, Dragon Master pressed a signal button on his watch seconds before he made the tandem jump with Banger. They landed near a large tent in the center of the mesa.

The Chinese elder was surprisingly fit for his age. With Banger's help, he released his harness and helped roll up the billowing chute.

Mike offered his hand. "Gentlemen, welcome to the jungle. Good to see you again, Banger."

Banger grinned and slapped Mike's back as the rest of the men gathered around them.

"Allow me to introduce Dragon Master, and that's Banger. He's on the SEAL team assigned to *Leviathan*," Mike said.

Ross, Derek, and Oz greeted them.

"Thanks for coming on short notice," Ross said. "Dragon Master, we're hoping you can help us find the crew and passengers from LIA flight 515. The woman you refer to as Golden Twin was the pilot."

"She *was* Golden Twin. Now she Queen of Atlantis." Dragon Master bowed. "I will find her."

"Great." Mike rolled his eyes at the "queen" comment. "Where should we look?"

The elder cocked his head, turned, and scanned the area. His eyes focused on a large pallet of supplies. "Search under there." He pointed at the pallet.

"Under *that*? Really?" Mike shook his head. "He makes no sense."

"Powerful dragon currents intersect here." The old man put his hand on the pallet.

Underground City

"Drop your weapons," I said to my people. "We don't want to provoke them. Looks like they outnumber us by about fifty to one."

We laid our weapons on the sand and placed our hands on our heads. The natives gathered the Glocks and MP7s and tossed them into the lake. They bound our hands behind us with strong narrow vines and lined us up single-file facing the city.

Then something unexpected happened.

Our captors gasped, dropped to their knees, and bowed their heads.

I turned, expecting to see the giant snake. Instead, Tiesha stood on the beach wearing fancy jeans embellished with gold snakes curling around the pant legs and a matching T-shirt with two gold snakes forming a wide heart shape on her ample chest.

She took in the scene and glanced at me. "What the hell?"

"They seem to think you're a goddess or something. Maybe they saw the snake spit Carlene at your feet. Play along." I nodded to my right. "That one seems to be their chief. Give him your best smile and offer him your gold bracelet."

Tiesha's bracelet was an eighteen-carat gold snake with ruby eyes and its tail in its mouth. I had no idea just how appropriate that gift was.

The tribal chief looked at Tiesha with awestruck eyes when she presented him with the bracelet. She raised her hands, motioning his people to stand.

He shouted instructions in their tribal language.

Our bonds were cut, but they kept us surrounded by guards.

Tiesha's Glock remained strapped to her thigh as the tribe led us into their city.

I glanced sideways at Lance as we passed a crystal embedded in the rock.

He mouthed, "No."

The city was enormous. We weaved through narrow stone pathways bordered by terraced structures carved into the mesa. After an hour of steady walking, we reached the central square. An elaborate throne adorned with snake carvings dominated the open courtyard. It faced an altar encircled with an open-topped cage with nine-foot-high wooden side bars.

The sound of water rushing through open aqueducts echoed in the square, masking murmurs from the crowd and the noise of anything that might be sneaking up on us.

Opposite the throne on the far side of the altar stood a partially coiled stone snake with its upper body reared up as if ready to strike. The statue's head loomed thirty feet above the courtyard.

Could this be where the tribe sacrificed animals or people to the giant anaconda?

Tiesha was led to the throne. Once she was seated, a native arrived carrying a sack made from jaguar skin. He handed it to the chief, who pulled out a spectacular gold crown adorned with gold snakes and too many emeralds to count. He handed the jaguar skin and the crown to Tiesha.

She smiled, nodded, and placed the emerald-adorned crown on her head. It fit perfectly.

The natives cheered, bowed, and then offered her food and drink.

The chief sized up Lance and me. He said two words I understood: "Alpha mates."

He ordered the guards to place us in a window-less holding cell that bordered the square. Barbi, Carlene, and Lisa were locked in one beside ours.

Alone in our prison, Lance checked the door lock. "Any chance you can find another way out of here like you did in Petra?"

I glanced around the stone prison cell and saw something move in a dark corner. Edging closer, I realized it was a giant spider. I shrieked and climbed onto Lance.

Not one of my finer moments.

"Sam? What's wrong?"

I pointed behind me. "Monster spider!"

He peered over my shoulder. "Hey, that's a Goliath birdeater—world's largest spider. I saw one on the Discovery Channel."

"Oh God, is it poisonous?" I had my arms wrapped around Lance's neck and my legs wrapped around his waist.

"It has inch-long fangs, and its bite hurts like a bastard, but it won't kill you."

"Screw that! Kill it before it bites us!" I bit my lip and tightened my hold on him.

"Darlin', I can't maneuver with you clinging to me." He pushed my legs down. "Get behind me and I'll deal with it."

I scanned the cell, hoping there was only one enormous spider, and hid behind Lance. He eased toward the giant arachnid, and it froze in place.

He tried to stomp it, but it was a fast bugger.

Each time he missed, I screamed like a little girl. Couldn't help it. The beast was really big—its body was at least a foot long. I mean the thing ate *birds*! And I hadn't slept, and my nerves were shot from everything that had happened. Maybe I would've handled it better if I'd been rested. *Maybe.*

Lance finally succeeded in his battle with Goliath and scraped his shoe off on the stone floor. "You can stop screaming. The big bad spider is dead." He turned and looked at me. "Seriously, are you okay now?"

I eyed the somewhat flattened giant arachnid and sucked in a deep breath. "Sorry, Lance, I feel like such a wimp. I guess all the stress finally got to me, and I've never been good around big spiders. Thank you for protecting me." I hugged him and kissed his cheek.

He gave me a quick squeeze. "Okay, but now I need my captain back because we have much bigger problems to deal with."

I glanced around. "What do you mean?"

"The serpent must be hungry after it puked out Carlene. And I haven't seen any animals down here. The natives need to do something to appease it. Face it. We're destined to be snake food. Better find a way out of here fast."

TWENTY-TWO

Special Ops Team

"What the hell's a dragon current?" Oz asked.

Banger raised his hand. "I can take this one. Dragon currents, also known as ley lines, are rivers of electromagnetic energy that flow through the earth and crisscross the globe. Our Chinese friend here is an expert on them."

Ross was the highest-ranking man on the makeshift team. All eyes turned to him.

"Right, let's get to it. Move everything off that spot." Ross began pulling things out of the pallet and stacking them nearby.

The team joined in and had the pallet's contents emptied and the wooden crate moved in about thirty minutes.

They stood around the perimeter of a strange

circle with crystals embedded in the stone. The smooth floor was recessed about four feet below ground level.

Ross and Derek stared at the site and shook their heads.

"Looks a lot like what we encountered in Petra." Ross glanced at Dragon Master. "Is this an ancient portal?"

The old man nodded. "Atlantis once ruled the world. They had colonies everywhere."

"What can you tell us about this site?" Mike asked.

"Atlantean Queen activated crystals that made helicopter crash. Also opened portal. I cannot activate crystals to open it."

"No problem. That's what this is for." Derek held up blocks of C-4 explosives. "We'll have that portal open in a few minutes."

"Place the charges in the center so we don't damage the crystals," Ross said.

The men worked together and had the device rigged in about fifteen minutes. Ross held the remote detonator and waited until everyone had taken cover behind the ATVs.

"Fire in the hole!" Ross pressed the detonator.

A loud boom echoed off the mesa, followed by a cloud of smoke rising from the explosion site. When the smoke cleared, the team looked into the hole.

"Too dark." Mike pulled out a magnesium light

and shined it into the pit. "Looks like running water. Probably a fast-moving stream."

"Let's hope it doesn't end up in one of those waterfalls shooting out the sides of the mesa." Ross glanced at the elder. "What do you think?"

"Stream is fast pathway to secret place where Queen went with her people. It would not send them over cliff. We need raft."

Derek glanced at Ross. "We've seen this movie before. We didn't need a raft in Petra."

"Sam's people couldn't have had a raft here, right Mike?" Oz asked.

"Actually, all their airliners carry survival rafts. They inflate into round rafts with sides and roofs— just the right size to fit on that stone circle." Mike turned and stared at the ATVs. "We can use the inner tubes from the balloon tires. Could be a long water journey—let's be prepared."

"I agree," Ross said. "Let's get to it."

The men worked steadily for an hour. They lashed the inner tubes together in a rectangular raft two tubes wide and four tubes long and secured weapons, ammo, rations, and first-aid supplies to it. The final task was a makeshift rope harness to keep them tethered on it.

"The initial drop may be a bit steep," Ross said. "We'll position the raft so we can all jump in together as it falls."

The team placed the raft beside the gaping hole and rechecked everything.

"Fasten your tether straps." Ross scanned the team. "Ready?"

Everyone nodded.

"Jump!"

A true leader, Ross jumped in at the head of the raft, followed by Derek, Banger, Dragon Master, Oz, and Mike. They wanted the old man in the center where they could protect him.

"Hold tight!" Ross yelled as the white water swept them downward into a pitch-black night-mare. Their waterproof night-vision goggles provided a limited view.

He glanced over his shoulder past Derek. Banger and Oz each had one hand on Dragon Master's combat vest, holding him on the pitching raft. Their bodies flopped up and down with the rushing water on the steep, curving stream. Mike was half on, half off the raft, clinging to the tether as they raced downward.

After a few minutes on the turbulent stream, they were ejected onto an underground lake. Their momentum carried them across to the opposite shore.

Ross jumped off and began pulling the raft onshore as Derek did the same from the opposite side. Banger and Oz helped Dragon Master out of the raft, and Mike lifted the aft end of the raft onto the beach.

Bioluminescent plants shined brightly through their NV-goggles.

"What the hell is this place?" Derek asked.

"Never heard of plants like these, and look at the lake," Mike said. "The fish are lit up too."

Banger lifted a flap on the airliner's survival raft. "It's full of luggage and stuff from the airplane, but nobody's here."

"Check out that stone city carved inside the mesa. It looks a lot like Petra," Ross said.

"Holy shit!" Oz said. "Is that what I think it is?" He pointed at a broad track through the sand that looked like it could've been made by a giant snake.

"Uh oh, look at all the footprints. Way more people than were on Sam's flight," Mike said.

"No telling who those people are. Could be hostiles. Bring all the ammo we can carry." Ross shoved magazines into his cargo pockets.

"And that snake track is fresh, heading inland over the footprints." Banger pointed at the city.

"Bugger!" Ross checked his MP7. "Gear up for combat. Best hurry!"

Dragon Master stood calmly beside the snake trail. "No worry. All creatures under Queen's command."

Mike rolled his eyes. "Yeah, right, my sister commands giant snakes. Let's roll."

Banger elbowed Mike and whispered, "He's telling the truth. Sam saved my ass from a sea monster that's way bigger than that snake."

"Of course, she did." Mike shook his head.

251

"When will I learn not to be surprised by anything she does?"

The men checked their gear and jogged into the dark city. It wasn't long before they reached the point on the path where an enormous snakeskin covered the trail.

"Sonofabitch! This has to be over forty feet—which means the snake is even bigger now." Oz held up a portion of the shed skin.

"We'd best find it before it finds Sam and her people." Ross rushed up the path.

City Center

Lance's suggestion about us becoming snake food made me forget about the spider. I searched for a way out. There was a six-inch opening running along the tops of the walls letting in air and light, but it wasn't wide enough to crawl through.

Lance lifted me up. "See anything out there?"

Before I could answer, natives rushed in and dragged us out. They put us in a viewing box over-looking the altar. It was similar to box seats in a the-atre. We were above and to the side of the throne, facing the altar. Guards flanked us. Barbi and Car-lene were dragged in and seated in front of us.

I nudged Carlene. "Where's Lisa?"

She shivered and pointed downward. Guards were shoving Lisa into the altar cage. They barred the door and bound it with twine.

Lance gasped. "Why'd they put Lisa in there?"

"She's a redhead. They probably assumed the snake doesn't like blondes since it spit out Carlene. That rules out Barbi and me."

"I wonder how they signal the snake," Barbi said.

"Uh oh, it looks like they expect Tiesha to place her hands on the throne's crystals and make them light up." I glanced around and spotted a crystal in the rock behind our seats. "If she touches them and they don't light up, we're toast."

Lance leaned into me. "What's your plan?"

"Distract the guards. I'll reach back and touch the one behind us at the same instant Tiesha touches the ones on the throne and hope it works."

"Are you crazy? There's no telling what will happen!" Lance gripped my shoulders.

"If I do nothing, we're dead meat. Get ready. She's about to touch the crystals."

Lance yelled and pointed at a dark area leading to the square. The guards stepped forward and looked in that direction.

I turned and touched a crystal the moment Tiesha placed her hands on the ones embedded in the throne. I prayed they were all interconnected to the city's electromagnetic power grid.

Instantly, the center square was bathed in the brilliant light of thousands of crystals throughout the stone city. The inhabitants settled in upper seats behind the throne.

Silence covered the gathering like a shroud. Distant waterfalls provided a soothing backdrop, concealing the approaching horror.

Minutes ticked by in silence.

Loud gasps from the crowd heralded the arrival of the monster.

It slithered up to the cage and sniffed Lisa through the wood bars. It must've liked her scent because it reared up above her.

I yelled, "Lisa, sing!" I wasn't sure I had time to connect telepathically with the snake—or if I ever could.

Her secret-agent nerves of steel kicked in, and the lovely rhythmic tones of her voice singing "Somewhere Over the Rainbow" reverberated off the stone walls.

The snake swayed back and forth, mesmerized by her song—apparently too mesmerized to hear my commands in its head.

As she sang the lyrics, "and the dreams that you dare to dream really do come true," I struggled to connect with the monster.

Nothing.

What would it do if she reached the end of the song, and I failed to take command?

Tiesha, like most women, was terrified of snakes. At first, she froze in place like she was welded to the throne. Then she looked around at all her frightened subjects, and her sense of regal responsibility took over.

She stood, drew her Glock, took aim, and emptied the entire magazine into the anaconda's massive head.

Lisa stopped singing.

The monster crumpled into a heap beside the altar.

The square became deathly silent. Would the natives be angry or happy?

Loud cheering filled the square. Guards released Lisa from the altar cage.

The populace surrounded Tiesha's throne and bowed before her.

"Release my people!" She pointed at us.

Guards led us down to her.

"Lead us up!" Tiesha pointed at the ceiling.

The chief nodded to a guard, and he led us to partially hidden stone steps carved into the rock.

The guard's wide eyes telegraphed fear as he slowly started up the dark steps with Tiesha and the rest of us following him.

I wanted to believe fate had taken a turn in our favor, but I couldn't help wondering if something even more terrifying than the giant anaconda might be lurking in the shadows up ahead.

Had the native chief rewarded us or tricked us?

Special Ops Team

Ross led his men down the main path into the city. Normally, he would've moved with caution,

255

checking every hiding place for hostiles. He feared time was running out as he rushed forward, doing his best to spot potential enemies lurking in the stone structures.

His team had covered about a mile when they were blinded with bright light shining into their night-vision goggles. They stopped, flipped up their goggles, and crouched behind a stone wall while they waited for their vision to recover.

After several minutes of silence, distant gunfire echoed off the rock walls.

"Rapid fire!" Derek said. "Hard to tell where the shooters are. This place is like an echo chamber."

"It just stopped," Mike said. "Couldn't have been much of a battle."

"Maybe they shot the damn snake," Oz said.

"We should be so lucky," Banger said in his usual sarcastic tone.

"If everyone's good to go, let's move." Ross noted their nods and set off in a jog.

Loud cheering echoed throughout the stone city.

Ross held up a fist, and the team stopped.

"They're celebrating something. Could be their guard is down. Hurry, but don't shoot unless fired upon." Ross rushed forward.

The team moved through the ancient city with efficient speed and stealth, slowing at curves in the path and speeding up where the view was clear.

They swept their infrared scopes at surrounding plants and buildings, checking for hidden attackers.

All the while, the cheering grew louder, masking their approach.

Ross signaled a pause at a small rise in the path. He peeked over a low stone wall. "There's a huge gathering of natives in the center square." He pulled out his binoculars for a closer look.

"Well, I'll be damned! Somebody shot the snake." He pointed at a huge heap of flesh coiled beside what looked like a cage-enclosed altar.

Mike raised his binoculars. "Yep, the snake's head is full of holes, but there aren't any spears or knives stuck in it. Must've been killed by the gunfire we heard."

Derek scanned the crowd. "I don't see any firearms."

"Where are Sam and her people?" Ross focused his binoculars. "Maybe they're locked inside one of the stone buildings."

"Looks like the buggers outnumber us," Derek said. "But we've faced worse. How do you want to handle this?"

Dragon Master stepped forward. "Queen killed snake to win natives' trust. Do you have photo of her?"

Ross pulled out photos of everyone on LIA flight 515. He shoved the picture of Renaldo into a pant pocket and handed the rest to Dragon Master.

"With your permission, Captain, I will hold

Queen's picture." He handed Tiesha's picture to Banger. "Perfect mate for you." He held out the remaining photos. "Each man should hold one picture."

Mike took Lance's picture. "I know him."

Derek said, "I'll take the redhead. FYI, she's undercover for MI6."

Ross raised a brow at Derek, then took Barbi's picture, leaving Carlene's for Oz. He asked the old man, "What's your plan?"

"Approach leader respectfully, bow in greeting, and show him pictures. Behave as though we come in peace, and he will help us."

"It's worth a try, but keep your weapons within easy reach," Ross said.

"I look harmless," Dragon Master said. "Allow me to lead."

Ross waved him forward. "Let's go. Slow and steady."

When they stepped into view of the natives, the cheering stopped and the people froze.

"Hold pictures in front of you so they can see them," the old man instructed.

The team fanned out and waited as the chief approached. He stopped in front of Banger, recognized Tiesha's picture, and fell to his knees.

"Mighty warrior king...your queen...up." The chief pointed at distant stone steps.

TWENTY-THREE

Stairway to Heaven

We struggled up what seemed like endless stone steps carved into the mesa. Steep and slippery with moisture, the steps were dark and curving. A handrail would've been nice. Small crystals every hundred feet provided dim light between the long shadows.

Lance stayed behind Carlene. With his strong hands firmly holding her waist, he did his best to help her up.

Everyone gasped for breath after about an hour of climbing.

"How much farther?" Carlene asked. "My dogs are howlin'."

"Each step is about a foot high, and I've been counting them." Out of breath, I sat on a dank step. "Assuming the underground city isn't all the way at the bottom of the mesa, we're about two-thirds of the way up."

"That means we have five hundred more steps!" Barbi said, breathing hard.

"You always were good at math," Tiesha said, adjusting her crown. "Seems like the natives should've carried *me* up, seeing as how I'm their queen and all."

"The main thing is you got us the hell out of there." Lance bowed. "Well done, my queen."

"Your queen needs rest." Tiesha glanced down at me. "I decree a ten-minute break if that's okay with you, Captain."

I paused and listened. "Good idea. I don't hear anyone coming after us."

Lisa was one step below me. "What or who do you think we'll find at the top?"

I glanced at my watch. "A military rescue team should be here by now."

"Good! I'm ready to get out of this hellhole." She took a deep breath. "Maybe MI6 will give me a little vacation now that Renaldo is out of the picture."

"The Colombian cartel might be eliminating Renaldo's underlings right now." I rubbed my calves. "Let's hope they've given up on sending hit teams to the mesa."

Ten minutes passed too quickly.

"Time to find our way into the sunshine," I said.

We trudged up the steps for almost another hour, pausing several times to catch our breath.

No monsters waiting to pounce on us.

And finally, we reached the top.

The exit was blocked by a stone door. Beside it, a gold handprint was recessed into the rock, and a lever protruded next to the handprint.

Uh oh.

I yelled, "Tiesha, play dumb and don't touch the gold hand. Pull the lever instead." I knew she didn't have the right electromagnetic frequency in her body to activate the hand trigger.

Our native guide directed her to place her hand on the gold handprint.

She smiled, nodded, and pulled the lever.

Smart queen.

The door sprang open, and sunlight filtered into the stairwell.

Our guide shrugged and led us up through a big rock formation that hid the entrance and outside steps.

I peeked out between the boulders. There were four helicopters on the ground near the center of the mesa where our ride to the underworld had begun.

"The rescue teams are here!" Tiesha pushed past me, her crown sparkling in the sun.

I grabbed her shirt and yanked her back. "Keep out of sight."

Lisa and Lance peeked over my shoulders.

"I doubt the cartel would send four helicopters," Lisa said.

"They're not military birds, but they're armed with external weapons," Lance said.

As we watched, the pilots fired up their engines. When the choppers were warmed up and ready to fly, they lifted off.

Relief flooded me.

They're leaving.

Instead, the helicopters turned and headed straight for us.

"Shit!" I ducked. "Are they tracking the GPS signal on my DARPA watch? How'd they get the frequency?"

"I don't know, but they're definitely coming this way," Lance said.

I yelled, "Quick, hide in the stairwell!"

We rushed down to the door.

Our guide was gone, the door was closed, and there was no way to open it from the outside.

Damn.

Special Ops Team

Ross's team followed the native chief to the partially hidden stone steps carved into the mesa. The chief pointed at the pictures the men held and then pointed up the dark steps. He backed away.

"He must've showed them the way out after they killed the snake," Mike said.

"Best climb the steps slowly so we don't startle them. Remember, they're armed." Ross led his men up the steep stairs.

"Where'd they get the firearms?" Oz ran his hand along the dank wall.

"Like I said, Lisa is undercover with MI6." Derek glanced at Ross and shrugged. "We dated a bit." He then grinned at Mike. "Mike shares my preference for redheads."

Oz broke in. "So, you're assuming she smuggled a weapon on board?"

He nodded. "Just for her. The others probably aren't armed."

Last in line, Mike paused on a step behind Oz and Dragon Master. "Everyone, stop." He waited while they ceased climbing and turned. "I swore to my sister I'd keep this a secret, but you guys need to know. I'm counting on you not to betray her trust."

"Sam and I don't have any secrets," Ross said. "What's this about?"

"It's not about Sam. It's about her employer, Luxury International Airlines. They installed secret weapons compartments in all their custom jets after one of their flight attendants and a passenger were shot and killed in Petra. Their crewmembers received extensive weapons and self-defense training.

Obviously, they had to keep it all a secret. Expect the entire crew to be armed with Glocks, and the pilots will also have MP7s."

"If that's the case, you'd think they would've unleashed all their fire power on that monster snake," Banger said. "Sounded like a quick burst from one weapon."

"Maybe the crew didn't get a chance to access the weapons after the forced landing," Oz said.

"Why did she tell you and not me?" Ross asked Mike.

"Her boss asked her to get my advice on how to cloak the compartments so the weapons wouldn't show up on a scan. He didn't want to involve foreign nationals, which is why he didn't want her to ask you." Mike shrugged. "It wasn't personal. Jeff likes you."

"Right, then, we'll discover their weapons status soon enough. Just don't sneak up on them." Ross turned and resumed climbing the steep steps.

Every few minutes, he'd halt the team and listen for sounds of Sam's people up ahead.

The stairwell remained silent.

Thirty minutes later, Ross signaled a halt and whispered, "Footsteps."

A native on his way down froze when he reached them.

Ross showed him the pictures, and he pointed up.

"Let him pass," Ross said.

The native slid past them and continued down.

Another thirty minutes brought the team closer to the top.

Ross signaled a halt and cocked his head. "Hear that?"

Faint knocking sounds echoed off the stairwell.

"Huh, sounds like someone's trying to signal something," Oz said.

"Slow and steady," Ross said. "We can't be sure it's Sam's people until we see them."

"And I'd be really pissed if my sister shot my ass," Mike said.

"Go." Ross led his men up the curving steps.

The Mesa

I grabbed Tiesha's Glock and checked the magazine. Empty. "Any extra mags in the holster?"

"Sorry, I used all my ammo on the snake," Tiesha said. "The extra mags were in my bag."

I handed Lance the Glock. "Everyone, stay by the door in case it opens. Try knocking on it to signal the native who led us up here. I'll check if those choppers were sent by the cartel or Sweetwater." I climbed up the outer steps and peeked between boulders.

Four helicopters had landed nearby. The men wore short-sleeved camouflage shirts, which revealed dragon tattoos on their forearms. Their tattoos matched the one Dragon Master had.

Could this be a rescue mission?

A man with a bullhorn said, "Samantha Starr, come out now and no one will be harmed. Dragon Master sent us."

Lance grabbed my arm. "Don't go. They're lying. Probably Chinese Special Ops here to take you prisoner. I told you they wouldn't give up."

"It doesn't matter who they are. They want me, and if I don't go out there, they'll kill my crew and passengers and take me anyway. I have to go."

"Wait! Maybe we can stall long enough for our military to get here." He gripped me tighter.

I tried to read what was printed on a pallet in the center of the mesa. It was too far away, but a large American flag was stenciled on the side. No American soldiers were visible anywhere on the mesa.

"I hate to tell you this, Lance, but our military has already arrived. They must've followed us down that underground stream."

"How could they open the portal?"

"Explosives, just like Ross used to follow us inside the mountain in Petra. They're probably in the underground city looking for us."

"They must be heavily armed, like always. We should wait for them to burst through the stone door. They'll take out the Chinese operatives." Lance's liquid-green eyes were filled with desperation.

The bullhorn blared, "Last chance. Come out

now or Way of the Dragon will kill your crew and passengers."

Pulling Lance to me, I met his eyes. "Take care of our people."

I pushed past him and stepped into the open with my hands on my head.

A man who was obviously their leader waved me forward. I stopped in front of him and stood still while he frisked me for weapons and handcuffed me. Then he removed my DARPA watch with the GPS locator and stomped on it.

I glared at him. "Why do you want me?"

"Dragon Master is leader of Way of the Dragon. He sent us. You Queen of Atlantis and only person who can help us achieve goal." He bowed his head briefly.

"What is your goal?" I asked, stunned that Dragon Master had sent them.

"Destroy communist regime in China and return China to traditional rule by divine emperor."

The awful truth hit me like a sucker punch. "Dragon Master is descended from the royal blood of emperors. He's next in line for the throne, isn't he?"

"And now, Queen will serve him and fire Atlantean weapon." He waved at the waiting helicopter.

Dragon Master wasn't on it. Was he waiting for me on *Leviathan*?

I faced the team leader. "Your future emperor

knows I have many unique abilities. If you harm my people or allow anyone else to harm them, I'll know, and your mission will fail. Ask Dragon Master. He'll confirm it."

A brief look of surprise crossed his face. He nodded. "I will keep promise."

"I wouldn't want to be you if you don't. Remember, *I'll know*." I turned and boarded the helicopter.

As soon as I was buckled into a seat, the chopper lifted off and flew northeast. The other three helicopters and most of the men remained behind.

Special Ops Team

Ross signaled a halt when he reached the stone door. Someone was tapping on the other side with a heavy object.

"Who do you think it is?" Derek asked.

"Sam and Lance know Morse code," Mike said. "Let's ask."

Ross drew his pistol and tapped the butt against the stone a few times to get the attention of whoever was on the other side. The tapping stopped. He then tapped the code sequence for, "Who are you?"

He repeated it twice and waited.

After a pause, someone on the other side tapped, "LIA 515 crew and pax."

"Pax?" Derek asked.

"That's airline code for passengers," Mike said. "Ask if they're alone."

Ross tapped in the question, and moments later he received the response, "We're trapped by armed helicopters and fourteen Chinese operatives. Pull lever to open door and let us in."

Ross scanned his men. They were ready.

Dragon Master said, "Open door and I will negotiate for you with Chinese."

"I need to assess the situation." Ross glanced back. "We'll get Sam's people in here first. Banger, don't let this door close until I say so." He turned and pulled the lever.

The door swung inward, letting in the sunlight. Ross spotted Lance standing behind the women. "Come in, ladies." He moved aside and waved them in as his men slipped past them.

Banger leaned his six-foot-four muscled body against the door, holding it open. When Tiesha entered wearing her crown, he said, "Welcome, my queen."

She paused and smiled at his handsome face.

Lisa's eyes widened. "Derek, thank God!" She hugged him.

"You're safe now, lass," Derek said.

Carlene shoved past them saying, "Flirt later!"

Ross peeked out at the helicopters and armed men. He turned to Lance, "Where the hell is Sam, and who are those men?" Then he noticed the anguished look in Lance's eyes.

"There were four helicopters when we first came through the stone door. Their leader announced Dragon Master had sent them to take Sam and said they'd kill everyone and take her anyway if she didn't go willingly." He swallowed hard. "Sorry, Ross, we only have one pistol, and we're out of ammo."

Ross grabbed Dragon Master by the collar. "Did you send those helicopters to take Sam?"

"No, I came to help rescue her. Those men must be Chinese Special Forces."

Ross turned to Lance. "How long has it been?"

"She left almost an hour ago. Not sure why the rest of them stayed."

While Ross and Lance were talking, Dragon Master acted like he was trying to see what was going on and slipped past them.

He jogged to the nearest helicopter, climbed inside, and was joined by two soldiers.

Moments later, the chopper lifted off and dropped out of sight beneath the eastern cliff.

"What the hell?" Ross said.

Before he had time to react to Dragon Master's hasty departure, a rocket-propelled grenade slammed into one of the two remaining helicopters, transforming it into a fireball.

"Lance, get your ass in the stairwell!" Ross shoved him.

The scent of burning jet fuel filled the air.

Mike jabbed him. "Incoming!" He pointed at two civilian helicopters approaching fast from the west.

The RPG had been fired from one of those birds.

"Who the hell are they?" Ross asked.

"I recognize the logo on the choppers," Mike said. Two assault rifles formed a cross on a skull over a red background. "It's the symbol for Predator International, Sweetwater's company."

"Which side do we fire at?" Derek asked.

Before Ross could answer, a Chinese soldier fired an RPG into one of Sweetwater's helicopters and blew it out of the sky.

The air was filled with swirling smoke and the sounds of automatic weapons firing.

The second helicopter landed and Sweetwater's mercenaries leaped out. One of them fired an RPG into the last Chinese helicopter, destroying it.

A heat wave from the explosion rolled over Ross as he signaled his men to take positions behind the boulders. "Take out both sides while they're aiming at each other." He turned and yelled down to Banger, "Close the door and protect the civilians."

Ross and Derek fired at Sweetwater's men while Mike and Oz fired at the Chinese team. All four Special Operators were proficient in the one-shot-one-kill method.

It took several losses on both sides before the enemy teams realized a third force was in the mix.

Sweetwater's helicopter pilot fired an RPG at the boulders shielding Ross's team.

Ross yelled, "RPG! Get to the steps!"

All four men dived into the stairwell leading to the stone door. A fraction of a second after they hit the stairs, the RPG exploded against the boulders.

When the dust settled, it was obvious the rubble had sealed their escape. Only a small opening remained.

"We'd best get behind the stone door in case they toss a grenade through that hole," Ross said as he tapped out Morse code for, "Ross says open door."

The door swung inward, and the men crawled inside.

The door closed, muting the outside gunfire.

Ross glanced at his men. "Everyone good?"

Derek, Mike, and Oz nodded.

Ross noticed Carlene and Barbi stood glued to Lance, Lisa calmly leaned against a stone wall, and Tiesha clutched Banger like he was her lifeline.

Banger ran his eyes over the team's dirt-covered, scuffed-up uniforms. He couldn't resist a little of his usual sarcasm. "So, how'd it go out there?"

Ross filled him in while the group listened.

"Are you sayin' we're trapped under a pile of rocks?" Carlene asked.

Derek grinned at Carlene. "Lassie, have you forgotten we followed you into that mountain in Petra? How do you think we got through all those stone doors?" He held up a block of C-4.

"Why aren't you out there setting the explosives?" Barbi asked.

"We're waiting until the bad guys finish killing each other. Then we'll blast our way out of here," Mike said.

"In the meantime," Ross said, "I hope Lance and Banger can shed some light on who the hell Dragon Master really is."

TWENTY-FOUR

CMS Sun Dragon

We circled a Chinese freighter equipped with a small helipad on the forward deck. It wasn't long before we were idling on board.

Armed crewmen pulled me from the helicopter. As they led me across the broad deck, the helicopter took off and flew toward Cuba. I knew that because the first helicopter had taken me from the mesa to an airport in South America, where a private jet had flown me north. That jet landed in Cuba, where I transferred to the helicopter that flew me to this ship.

Close to Atlantis, no doubt.

I glanced around, but all I could see was the Atlantic Ocean. My view ended when I was led belowdecks and locked inside a small cabin with no windows. The first thing I did was use my metal handcuffs to scratch a message into the sidewall beside the bunk's mattress.

I stretched out on the narrow bunk and closed my eyes, trying to relax and plan my next move. Why did Way of the Dragon want me to fire the weapon inside the pyramid in Atlantis? How would that help them take control of China?

I ran scenarios through my head. If I fired the weapon, it would send a massive energy blast into the seabed under Atlantis, causing an earthquake that would push the tectonic plates together and raise Atlantis to the surface. A landmass that large would displace a tremendous amount of water and send thousand-foot tsunamis in every direction, moving at a speed of approximately 600 mph. I learned all that the last time I narrowly averted this disaster.

The entire eastern seaboard of the United States, all of Florida, many island nations, and key coastal cities in Europe, England, Ireland, and portions of eastern South America and Western Africa would be destroyed, and millions of lives would be lost.

China, safely on the other side of the world, would be unaffected. How could the tsunamis help Way of the Dragon take control of their homeland? It made no sense.

A man rushed into my cabin and stabbed me in the arm with a hypodermic needle.

Everything went black.

When I awoke, which could've been hours later, Dragon Master stood beside my bunk.

"Sorry for drugs. Not want you contact mother telepathically."

"Your plan won't work." I tried to sit up, but my body was tied down with straps.

"Ah, but it will." He sat in a chair beside my bunk. "Great change requires great sacrifice."

"The destruction caused by the Atlantean weapon could trigger a power grab by China, Russia, and Middle-Eastern nations undamaged by the tsunamis. And North Korea will seize the opportunity to nuke what's left of the US, resulting in World War Three. Your plan could make Communist China stronger than ever. Or you'll cause a nuclear winter that will destroy the world. Either way, you'll never be the next emperor of China if I fire that weapon."

"Washington and London will be destroyed by tsunamis, leaving US and UK in chaos with no functioning governments. We have loyal followers in North Korea who are in positions to implement Phase Two."

"Phase Two?"

"Crazy leader of DPRK will seize opportunity to fire nukes at US. But we have set his missiles to hit Beijing instead. Communist leaders will be killed and government destroyed. Millions of Way of Dragon members in Chinese military will step forward and seize control for their emperor. Rest of world will be too busy with own problems to care."

"What about the millions of innocent people who will die? There has to be a better way." I felt sick thinking about the worldwide carnage.

"World population crisis, food and water shortages, all solved by tsunamis."

"You can't expect me to help you murder my family, friends, and countrymen."

"Your mother safe in Scotland, fighter pilot brother safe on ship in Mediterranean, other brother and boyfriend safe looking for you in middle of South America. I will allow you to send text message to Chief Pilot Jeff Rowlin, advising him to move all his people and airplanes to an airport in Midwest."

"What about everyone else?" My gut twisted into a knot.

"Sorry. No time. All we need is your touch, which we can force. Soon, you will reign over risen Atlantis, and the world will benefit from Atlantean technology."

"How will you get me inside the pyramid?" I asked, stalling for time.

"Way of Dragon has control of nearby Chinese nuclear-powered submarine. They have American-made Hardsuits like one you used to help recover gold vaults. Divers will escort you into pyramid. After you fire weapon, you will ride pyramid to surface and rule your island nation."

"And I suppose you'll take the long way home in the submarine?"

"All will be ready by the time I arrive at port in China. If you cooperate, I will receive you as honored guest." He stood and bowed.

I played along. "Alright, when will I be transferred to the submarine?"

He glanced at his watch. "Soon. Will you behave?"

I nodded. "No point in resisting. May I send the text message to Jeff now? He'll need time to organize moving the airline's assets."

He pulled out a cell phone. "Our ship has WI-FI. You dictate text and I type. Say only what I authorized."

"Emergency message from Sam. Move Rosa, Romeo, and all LIA assets and people to Midwest immediately. Time is short. Hurry!" I watched him type. "Was that acceptable?"

He nodded, showed me the text, and hit SEND. "Once you get settled in Atlantis, come and visit me." He bowed and left.

I concentrated hard to send a telepathic message to Mom. *"Sam is near Atlantis on Chinese freighter CMS Sun Dragon. Will soon transfer to Chinese submarine and be forced by Way of the Dragon to fire weapon in pyramid."* Before I could send more, another needle was plunged into my arm.

My world went black again.

The Mesa

Ross pulled the lever and stood with his weapon ready as the stone door swung inward. He cocked his head. "It's quiet out there. May as well set the charges." He glanced at Banger. "Hold the door open."

Derek, Mike, and Oz helped Ross rig the explosives to blast an opening in the rocks that were blocking their escape. When they finished, they ducked inside the stairwell and closed the stone door as Ross pressed the detonator. The door sealed shut at the same instant the charges exploded.

"Best wait a few minutes for the dust to settle and see if we attracted the attention of any survivors out there." Ross leaned against the door.

"Do you think there'll be men waiting to shoot us?" Barbi asked.

Mike gently squeezed her shoulders. "If they try, they won't live long. You're safe with us."

She stroked his handsome face. "Thank you."

Lisa nudged Derek. "Everyone here knows I'm with MI6. Give me a weapon."

Derek glanced at Ross and raised his brows.

"Give her a pistol and extra mags." Ross checked his watch. "I'll open the door in two minutes. Banger and Lisa will stay and protect the civilians until we give the all-clear."

"Got any mags that'll fit this Glock?" Lance held up Tiesha's handgun.

Mike reached into a cargo pocket and handed Lance two full magazines.

"Thanks." Lance ejected the empty mag, inserted a full one, and racked the slide.

Ross grasped the door lever. "Ready?"

The group nodded, and he opened the door.

Sunlight and smoke filtered in. The boulders had been blown clear.

The team moved stealthily up the debris-littered steps to the surface and peered out from behind the rock pile.

Nothing moved except the vultures circling above.

They pulled out binoculars and surveyed the scene. The ground was littered with bodies and wrecked helicopters.

"Check the bodies. See if any are alive. I'd like a chance to interrogate one of the Chinese operatives." Ross slipped onto the mesa and checked the nearest body.

Dead.

He found Sam's smashed watch nearby. He held it up. "We can forget about tracking Sam's watch."

After several minutes of picking through the carnage, Oz called out, "I've got a live one over here."

Ross jogged over to him. Oz held the man up in a sitting position and gave him water.

"Who are you, and why did your men take the woman and Dragon Master?" Ross asked.

The man had lost a lot of blood. In a weak voice, he said, "You too late. Way of Dragon cannot be stopped. Mission will succeed." He gasped his final breath and collapsed, dead.

Ross took pictures of him and then said to his men, "I want pictures of every combatant—faces, tattoos, anything that might help reveal their identities."

The men photographed the widespread battlefield and all the fallen soldiers. They checked for IDs and insignias. None of the bodies carried IDs or personal items, but the Chinese men all had the same dragon tattoos, and Sweetwater's mercenaries had Predator International logos on their clothes and company tattoos on their shoulders.

Ross pulled out his SATCOM and called Mission Command. "I need transport for five operators and five civilians. Time is critical."

"Understood, Captain Sinclair. You have an emergency call from Loren Starr. Shall I put her through?"

"Aye, do it now." Ross waited a moment. Soon, Loren's voice filled his satellite phone.

"Ross, Sam sent me a telepathic message, but I couldn't answer her. Everything suddenly went blank."

"They probably drugged her like they did in the Himalayas. What was the message?"

"She's near Atlantis on a Chinese freighter, CMS *Sun Dragon*. She said a group called Way of the Dragon plans to force her to fire the Atlantean weapon in the pyramid. They'll transfer her to a Chinese submarine soon to complete the task. Is Mike with you?"

"Aye, he's here, and he's fine. You stay with Duncan in Scotland and tell him to increase security until this crisis is over. Thanks for the call, Loren."

"Ross, please, save my daughter!"

"You know I will. We have to go now." He ended the call and turned to Mike. "That was your mother." He told him what she'd said. "You'd best call your SECNAV and relay the message." He handed Mike the SATCOM.

Once the necessary calls were made, the men returned to the stairwell and led the group to the landing zone where a Chinook would pick them up and ferry them to an airport.

Lance grabbed Mike's arm. "Any news about Sam?"

"Yeah, and it's not good." He filled him in.

"I thought we prevented the whole tsunami disaster a couple months ago," Lance said. "Any chance she can fire that weapon?"

"She *can*, but she won't. I know my sister. She'll die rather than kill millions."

Ross broke in. "Not if I can help it."

Mike shook his head. "We need to get to Atlantis fast."

The others had been listening.

"What's going to happen now?" Tiesha asked Banger.

"You're going to give me your number so I can call you and take you to a nice dinner after this crisis has been dealt with." He pulled out a pen and wrote her number on the inside of his sleeve.

She grinned. 'The natives thought you were my king. Those people have excellent judgment."

"They certainly do. They chose you for their queen." He pulled her close and planted a kiss on the nape of her neck. "Better hide that crown before the chopper picks us up."

Tiesha slipped the crown into the jaguar sack she'd tied to her belt.

"Where the hell is *my* king?" Barbi asked.

Mike said, "My sister is Queen of Atlantis, so I guess that makes me royalty. Will I do?"

"I'll gladly take a handsome prince like you." Barbi hugged him.

"Banger," Tiesha whispered in his ear, "am I allowed to know your real name?"

"Ben Johnson. I grew up in Alabama and played football for the Crimson Tide before I joined the Navy. I've been with the SEALs six years." He paused and looked into Tiesha's eyes. "You're the best thing that's ever happened to me." He pressed his lips against her ear, sending shivers down her spine.

Tiesha slid her hands up his chest of molded

steel. "You know, you look a lot like The Rock, only better. Any relation to Dwayne Johnson?"

"No, but thanks for the compliment." He grinned.

"Time to kiss my king." She tilted her head up.

Banger leaned down and kissed her with the passion of a man who'd found the woman of his dreams.

The thundering blades of a Chinook interrupted their embrace.

Tiesha put her mouth close to his ear. "How'd you get the name Banger?"

"Uh, I don't remember why the guys on my team call me that. We use nicknames to protect our identity. Time to go." He took her hand and led her to the helicopter.

Everyone climbed aboard. The big chopper lifted off and headed northeast.

As soon as they landed, a military C-17 fired up its engines. The group transferred to the big jet and were airborne in minutes.

A crewman approached Banger with a message from Max. Banger read, "Return to *Leviathan* ASAP. We're en route to Atlantis. Sam sent text to my dad to move all the airplanes because weapon in pyramid will be fired soon. Must avert disaster. Invite Spec Ops team to join us." Banger passed the message to Mike, who read it and passed it to Ross.

Tiesha snuggled into Banger's arms in the sidewall troop seats, and they fell asleep. Barbi did the same with Mike, Lisa with Derek, and Carlene with Lance.

Oz nudged Ross. "I guess we're the odd men out."

"They can have them," Ross said. "Sam is my woman. I hope to God I can save her."

"She's also Mike's sister. You can count on us to help." Oz leaned his head back.

Ross closed his eyes. *I'd like to get Sam back and an-nihilate Atlantis. Put an end to this.*

TWENTY-FIVE

CMS Sun Dragon

I woke feeling weak and groggy. My restraints had been removed, but four guards stood beside my bunk in the tiny cabin. It seemed like a lot of time had passed, but that could've just been the effect of the drugs.

"You come now," one of the guards said.

They pulled me up and walked me into a passageway. I feigned weakness and collapsed, and they lifted me and dragged me forward.

Dragon Master waited at the end of the passage.

"Ready, Queen?" he asked.

"No. I haven't had anything to eat or drink since I left Florida on the flight to Rio, and I'm shaky and dehydrated. The drugs have weakened me. I'll need my full inner strength to fire the weapon. Give me a good meal and plenty of water before I leave."

He studied me a moment. "As you wish, Queen." He led me into a stateroom.

My guards plunked me down at a table across from Dragon Master. He barked orders in Chinese.

It wasn't long before a large bottle of water and a glass were set before me. I drank as much water as I could manage, not knowing when I'd get more.

A waiter carried in a tray and served me a steaming plate of chicken and rice. I was given a plastic fork. Dragon Master wasn't taking any chances.

I dragged the meal out as long as possible. When I'd swallowed the last bite, he said, "Time to go."

"Fine, but first I need a toilet." I patted my mouth with a napkin and smiled.

"Quickly." He stood and led me to the nearest head.

I used the facilities and took my time washing my hands and face. The door opened.

"Ready?" Dragon Master seemed impatient.

I gave him my best fake smile. "Yes, thank you. I'm eager to complete the mission. Has enough time passed for my employer to move their jets to the Midwest?"

"Several hours have passed. If they heeded your warning, they should be fine." He led me up the steps to the outer deck.

I was surprised to step out into darkness. I'd lost track of time, and it seemed to be late at night now. Starlight revealed a submarine on the surface a few yards away on the port side. A wicker chair hung from what looked like a zip line connected to the submarine. Rolling waves broke against the freighter's hull and splashed the submarine's deck.

"You go first." He motioned for my guards to help me into the chair.

I was hoping for a chance to fall into the water and maybe get my kraken buddy to whisk me away if it was nearby. Dragon Master must've read my mind. His men lashed me to the chair and bound my hands. So much for trust.

The chair slid down to the submarine's deck, where more guards waited to catch me. As they pulled me from the chair, I heard rotor blades thumping in the distance, but the helicopters were too far away to see them in the dark. Was my rescue imminent?

The sailors heard the choppers too. They sent the chair back for Dragon Master. He landed on the deck just as thundering blades echoed off the ocean. I couldn't see what kind of helicopters they were from such a distance. Before they got close enough to identify, the crew dragged me below.

In moments, the submarine submerged and dived into the depths.

Damn.

Earlier on the USS LEVIATHAN

Captain Max Rowlin waited by the lighted helipad as the Seahawk landed. Five men leaped out as the helicopter shut down.

As soon as the noise abated, Ross saluted. "Captain Ross Sinclair of Her Majesty's Special Air Service reporting for duty, and this is Lieutenant Derek Dunbar."

Max grinned and held out his hand. "Good to finally meet you, Ross."

"Aye, it's good to put a face with the voice after that tense situation in March." Ross nodded to Derek. "He was with me on the Himalayan mission."

Max smiled and shook Derek's hand. "You must be a very brave man."

"You have no idea." Derek grinned. "The missions involving his girlfriend are always high risk, bordering on bizarre."

"If we had more time, I'd tell you about what happened the last time she was here." He waved the SEALs forward. "Welcome home, Banger. Good to see you again, Mike."

Mike and Oz saluted. "This is Oz. He's from my team," Mike said.

"Welcome," Max said. "Now let's get to it. Commander Bern will brief you in the conference room. You'll be joining his SEALs for the rescue mission."

The men followed Max through the ship and into a large conference room. Max made the introductions.

"Glad to have you join us," Bern said. "We now have thirty Special Operators on board. The platoon from Virginia and two of my SEALs will remain here to defend *Leviathan*. Ross, Derek, Mike, and Oz will join the strike team. We'll send five Spec Ops and two crew on each Seahawk for the assault on the Chinese freighter."

"What are the rules of engagement?" Mike asked.

"No rules. Your sister is an extremely high-value asset. Do whatever it takes to get her back," Bern said. "*Texas* is standing by to assist us while the UK's nuclear sub, *Audacious*, guards the pyramid."

"May I make a suggestion?" Ross asked.

Bern nodded.

"Derek and I just completed a mission with Mike, Oz, and Banger," Ross said. "I suggest keeping us together on the same helicopter team."

"Good idea," Bern said. "My team will be designated Striker One, and your team will be Striker Two."

Mike raised his hand. "Are you expecting the Chinese to attack this ship?"

"No, but the North Koreans have already attacked us three times," Max said. "No reason to think they won't try again, especially now that we're back over Atlantis."

Ross's team from the mesa exchanged surprised glances.

Bern glanced at his watch. "Gear up. Wheels up in five. Samantha Starr's safe return is priority one."

Five minutes later, the men climbed aboard two Seahawks—the U.S. Navy's version of Blackhawk helicopters—and sped toward the Chinese freighter, which was about thirty miles south of *Leviathan*.

As they closed in on *Sun Dragon*, Ross's team received a message from Bern. "*Texas* reported a Chinese submarine in close proximity to the freighter. We have to secure the package before that sub gets a chance to take her aboard."

"Understood," Ross said. "We're ready."

As soon as the helicopters were in position, Bern said into his helmet mike, "Execute! Execute! Execute!"

Ten Special Operators dropped down from ropes onto the Chinese cargo ship, the teams boarding near the bow and stern with their weapons ready. As they descended, crewmen fired at them, and they returned fire.

Ross's team managed to reach cover on board without being hit by any of the bullets being sprayed from Chinese machine pistols. His men took aim with their infrared sights and green lasers and decimated the men defending the afterdeck.

Ross said, "Striker Two is clear."

"Copy that. Check lower decks and Striker One will cover the upper decks," Bern said.

Ross led his men belowdecks as Bern's team annihilated the forward crew and then moved aft to check the bridge and crew quarters.

Striker Two moved methodically, tossing flash-bang grenades ahead in passages to stun defenders, then rushing in and shooting them before they could regain their senses.

The team checked every cabin, expecting to be met with gunfire behind every door. Many areas were empty, and some had defenders in small groups. The stun grenades did their job—casualties were avoided on Ross's team as they continued downward.

Halfway through the next deck, Mike yelled, "Ross! In here!"

Ross ducked into a small cabin where restraints were still fastened to a bunk's side rails. Mike pointed at a spot on the sidewall that was even with the right bedrail.

"Looks like *SAM-SUB-PYR*," Ross said. "They must've transferred her to their submarine. That means they'll drag her into the pyramid soon. Bugger!"

Derek nudged Ross. "Best advise *Texas* our package is on that sub so they don't sink it."

Ross called Bern. "Striker One, package may already be on the sub. We found a message scratched on a wall where it looks like she was held."

Mike held up a long blond hair.

"Correction—Sam was definitely in this room. Mike found a strand of her hair."

"Copy that, Striker Two. We searched the bridge tower. No package. Check the cargo holds just in case," Bern said. "Start in the bow and we'll meet you in the middle. I'll notify CIC the package may be in that submarine."

"Understood," Ross said. "Striker Two will meet you in the middle."

The holds were empty, which expedited the search.

Bern assembled his teams on the central deck as the Seahawks hovered above them. They hooked themselves onto lines dangling from their helicopters.

"Time to bug out." Bern signaled the pilot.

The Seahawks climbed and cleared the ship, towing the teams under them.

Ross glanced back and spotted two crewman who had emerged from a hidden compartment on the deck. Each held a shoulder-fired rocket launcher.

He yelled into his mike, "RPGs!" as rocket-propelled grenades streaked toward both helicopters.

The Seahawks had been too close to the shooters. There was no time to evade the rockets.

It was obvious the Seahawks would be hit, so Bern commanded, "Release and drop!"

All ten Special Operators dropped into the sea seconds before their helicopters spun out of control from direct hits to their tail rotors.

The choppers crashed into the sea just a few feet from Ross's team.

Chinese Submarine

My guards locked me in a small cabin. This time they left me untethered. No drugs, either. My Hardsuit dive into the 2000-foot depths of ancient Atlantis must be imminent. They'd need me sharp to fire the weapon inside the obsidian pyramid. They were assuming it worked the same way as the one the US had bombed in the Himalayas.

I closed my eyes, and a vision flashed into my head. Ross, my brother Mike, and several soldiers with them in two helicopters were shot down by RPGs. I saw the SEALs drop into the water moments before their choppers crashed with the air crews inside. The birds sank in seconds.

Worse, two Chinese men were firing at the soldiers from the deck of the freighter.

I contacted the kraken telepathically and prayed it would do my bidding again. Time was critical. I had to make certain assumptions about the teams from the helicopters and command accordingly. *Dear God, I hope this works!*

The door to my cabin opened just as I finished sending my instructions to the kraken. Dragon Master stepped in.

"Queen, we almost ready for historic mission. Ironic, ancient city will change modern history. Your electromagnetic energy will pass through metal claspers in Hardsuit when you fire the Atlantis half of Poseidon's Sword." He motioned for me to follow him.

Two guards waited in the passageway. They took positions behind me as I followed the future emperor of China to their dive center. Four Hardsuits connected to cables stood ready for divers.

"You go with two divers. Other suit is for backup." Dragon Master pointed.

"No, I need three divers to help me fire the weapon. It's not like the one on the Himalayan pyramid." I didn't want them to have any backup divers once I was out of this submarine.

The Chinese elder crossed his arms. "What different?"

"There are four energy stations, the triplet goddesses and Poseidon, all of which must be operated in a specific order. That's why we need four divers."

"But only Queen can fire weapon. Other divers cannot help you."

"I will fire the weapon from Poseidon's throne, but I'll need divers at the three goddess's thrones to disarm the safety features in the proper sequence first. It's rigged so I can't fire it until after the final safety is released."

"How do you know this?" he asked. "You've never been there."

I took a big chance and told him the truth for a change. "The triplet goddesses transferred all their knowledge to me seconds before they died."

"And you still intend to help us by firing the weapon?" His tone was tinged with suspicion.

"I've had time to consider everything you said, and I realized you were right. It may be harsh, but the monumental loss of life will solve many world-wide problems. Also, it'll be easier for me to take my place as ruler of risen Atlantis without interference from the US. They'll be too busy dealing with the total destruction of their eastern seaboard."

Dragon Master stared at me for a long moment. Finally, he said, "I am glad you agree with my plan, but if you double-cross me, my divers will shoot you."

"You can trust me. There's just one problem you seem to have missed."

He straightened. "What problem?"

"You said I'll ride the pyramid to the surface, which is fine with me, but first I'd need to cut the cable tethering me to your submarine, and I'm not certain how soon Atlantis will rise after the weapon is fired."

He nodded to the divers. "Cut her cable after she fires weapon."

"Thank you." I smiled at the divers. "Now, how do you intend to get us past the British nuclear sub that's guarding the pyramid's entrance?"

TWENTY-SIX

Strike Teams

Mike and Oz swam toward the choppers to rescue the air crews while Banger, Ross, and Derek struggled to tread water and fire at the snipers on the ship. Bern's team had been partially pinned by one of the floundering birds. His free men struggled to rescue the rest.

The main rotor blades had hit the water when the choppers tilted sideways in the swells, churning the water and flinging metal shards from the broken blades. In moments, sea water had rushed into the open side doors, and the Seahawks had slipped beneath the inky surface.

The crewmen who'd fired the RPGs stood at the railing, firing rifles at the teams in the water.

Then something unexpected happened.

A huge tentacle rose up out of the water in front of the ship and swept the shooters off the deck as if it were swatting flies.

Ross, Derek, Mike, and Oz aimed their weapons at the sea monster.

Banger yelled, "Don't shoot the kraken!"

Bern shouted the same thing.

Ross turned to Banger. "Are you crazy?"

"Sam's commanding it to save us. Look at the helicopters." Banger pointed.

Ross turned and spotted huge tentacles holding up the wrecked choppers.

"Attention, Seahawk crews, don't shoot the squid! Deploy life rafts," Bern said.

As massive tentacles supported the wrecked choppers, the air crews dragged the rafts out and inflated them.

An enormous head surfaced, and giant eyes watched the activity.

After the teams climbed into the rafts with their air crews, the kraken pushed them toward *Leviathan*.

Mike glanced at Ross and Derek. "Holy shit! My sister really is Queen of Atlantis!"

"Too bad the kraken can't get her out of that big-ass Chinese submarine," Banger said.

"She'll have to leave it to enter the pyramid," Ross said. "That'll be our one opportunity to save her."

"Maybe she won't be the one who needs saving." Oz focused on the enormous tentacles pushing them.

Chinese Submarine

I watched a Way of the Dragon diver enter the air lock in a Hardsuit. He was soon released outside the sub. A video screen in Dive Ops displayed his progress as he used his thrusters to approach the stern of the UK's nuclear-powered sub, *Audacious*.

The diver had a satchel clipped to his metal suit. When he reached the submarine guarding the pyramid, he pulled a device from the satchel and secured it to the hull close to the idling propeller. He placed another device on the opposite side. Then he thrusted himself about a hundred yards away from it.

I watched the video screen as he pressed the detonator. The devices fired metal rods into the massive propeller, destroying it. The diver remained stationary with his video camera pointed at *Audacious*.

It wasn't long before the crew of the huge British submarine realized they'd been sabotaged. Dead in the water, their only option was to blow their ballast, surface, and get towed to port for repairs.

I watched as the sub rose rapidly and soon disappeared from view. I wasn't happy about what Way of the Dragon had done, but at least they hadn't sunk them. No one had been injured or killed on the British sub—not yet anyway. If a tsunami were to hit their sub on the surface, I doubted it would survive.

The Chinese submarine glided into position beside the entrance to the massive 500-foot black pyramid.

I knew that each side of the ancient structure was approximately 786 feet long at the base, and that the entrance door was halfway across the base near the bottom. That meant the circular chamber housing the weapon in the center of the base was about 300 feet in from the outer door.

The entrance door and corridor to the central chamber weren't big enough for my kraken buddy, and even his longest tentacles couldn't reach that far anyway. Besides, right now the beast was busy saving Ross, Mike, and their teammates—at least I hoped it was.

It was up to me to outsmart my dive partners and figure out a way to destroy that weapon without causing an underwater earthquake. And it would be nice if I could manage to survive somehow.

Several men carried in a metal-encased rectangular device about four feet long and a foot and a half wide. It had an electronic control console on the top side protected by a six-inch thick plexiglass shield. A bright LED timer was counting down from sixty minutes.

I glanced at Dragon Master. "What's that?"

"Tactical nuclear weapon—insurance in case you fail to fire weapon in pyramid. Bomb will detonate into fault line, causing earthquake and compression of tectonic plates. One way or another, Atlantis will rise and tsunamis will destroy much of the world." He smiled.

"How will we deactivate the bomb after I fire the Atlantean weapon?" I stared at the numbers counting down from one hour.

He held a small device. "This will deactivate bomb. I will send the signal after you fire the weapon."

"You'd better do as you say. If that bomb explodes after the weapon has fired the energy beam into the fault line, it may have the opposite effect and push the tectonic plates apart."

My gut tightened as I watched them place the bomb in the air lock.

"Get into your Hardsuit. Time is running out." Dragon Master pointed at the bomb and gave me a sinister smile.

Checkmate.

USS LEVIATHAN

Max focused his night-vision binoculars on the teams in the life rafts. "Full stop!" he commanded.

Leviathan drifted to a gentle halt a few minutes after its engines shifted to idle. The kraken pushed the rafts about halfway down the five-hundred-foot hull and stopped. It raised its enormous head above the surface and looked up at the ship.

Executive Officer Vance Lowes shook his head. "Dang it, what do we do now? Sam isn't here, and it might not be friendly to our crew."

"It saved our teams and brought them back here. I just wish I knew exactly what she told it to do." Max licked his lower lip. "Let's wait a minute and see what it does."

The giant squid proceeded to use its long feeder tentacles to lift a raft full of men onto the open deck where it had deposited the gold vaults recently. It gently released its grip and then lifted the other raft onto the deck. Once the men were safely on board, the massive beast submerged and vanished into the depths.

Lowes exhaled. "Thank God! Now I can breathe again."

Max shook his head. "None of that is going in my report."

An ensign rushed onto the bridge and handed Max a printout at the same moment *Audacious* breached the surface beside the ship.

Max stared at the sub and then read the message. "Sonofabitch! The Brits suspect a diver from the Chinese sub sabotaged their propeller. Before *Texas* could maneuver around to take their place, the commies parked in front of the pyramid's entrance."

"That means they're in position to drag Sam

into the pyramid and fire the weapon. I don't think our ship can survive a thousand-foot tsunami," the XO said.

"We won't need to survive it because we'll be stranded on top of the risen city of Atlantis. So will the Brits in that submarine." Max clenched his fists.

"You're right, it's our eastern seaboard and a bunch of other places around the Atlantic that won't survive."

Max pounded the console. "Dammit! We can't let them win. XO, you have the conn. I need to talk to Kip and Banger. They're the only ones on board who've been inside that weapon chamber."

"Aye, Captain, I'll maintain status quo until I hear from you."

TWENTY-SEVEN

Obsidian Pyramid, Ancient Atlantis

I exited the air lock into inky black water. It was late at night, but sunlight couldn't have penetrated the 2,000-foot depth if it had been high noon. Headlamps on the Hardsuits provided bright tunnels of light in the clear, cold ocean water. The dark entrance to the black pyramid came into focus when we were about twenty feet away.

I glanced back at the huge submarine Way of the Dragon had commandeered. It rested on the seabed about thirty yards from the enormous structure we were about to enter and shined bright floodlights at us. The guy who'd sabotaged *Audacious* guarded me while the other two divers carried the nuke.

I had a bad feeling that even if my Chinese

nemesis pressed the button, the bomb's deactivation signal wouldn't penetrate the pyramid's thick volcanic blocks. And he probably didn't intend to press it.

I glanced at the timer. The bright numbers read 35:25. Too bad that didn't mean hours and minutes, instead of minutes and seconds. I looked ahead and followed the men with the nuke through the broad entrance door that had been blasted open a couple of months ago by men from *Leviathan*.

We entered a wide corridor flanked by eight-foot statues of Atlantean kings and queens wearing gold crowns. I might've enjoyed the view if I hadn't been so worried about the nuclear bomb.

I spoke into my voice-activated mike, "We'd better hurry. It's a long way down this hallway to the weapon chamber." Everything I said was heard by my three dive companions and the crew listening in Dive Ops on the submarine.

My guard said, "You go first. We follow."

I took the opportunity to use maximum thrust and zoom ahead. It only took a few minutes to reach the arched entrance to a huge circular chamber with a domed ceiling about nine stories high. Brilliant light emanated from inside the round room.

I rushed in. A hundred statues lined the broad perimeter. Four thrones were evenly spaced along the circumference, each throne sitting with twenty-five statues on either side of it, dividing the perimeter into four quadrants.

Four orca statues in the center of the room supported a huge diamond as they stood back-to-back on their tailfins with their heads facing away from the beaming gem pressed between their upper backs. The jewel, cut in the shape of a rhombus, was like a two-foot-high vertical baseball diamond and reflected light in all directions. It also had energy beams that shot straight up and down from the vertical tips of its geometric shape. The weapon couldn't be fired without it.

A fifteen-foot statue of Poseidon on one of the gold thrones dominated the domed chamber. He held a scepter with a lighted crystal pointed at the rhombus. Statues of the Goddesses of Sun, Moon, and Fire sat on the other thrones. The goddesses held lighted crystals that were also pointed at the giant gem.

I turned as the divers carrying the nuke placed it beside the orca sculpture.

The timer read 26:18.

Damn.

"Are you guys ready to help me fire the ancient weapon?" I asked, noting they had dive knives clipped to their utility belts. I'd need one soon.

"Ready," they said in unison.

"I need a diver beside each goddess on a throne. Be ready to grasp her lighted crystal when I tell you." I thrusted over to Poseidon's throne.

This had better work, or I'll be toast, and millions of people will drown.

USS LEVIATHAN

Rowlin entered the conference room where the men from the failed rescue mission waited with marine biologist Kip Peterson.

"Gentlemen, I can't emphasize enough the gravity of the situation." Rowlin ran his hand over his blond buzzcut. "The Chinese sabotaged the UK's submarine and then took its place in front of the pyramid. We know they have Sam, and they intend to force her to fire the Atlantean weapon."

Mike stood. "Put me in a Hardsuit and send me down there."

Banger and Oz stood.

"Oz has Hardsuit experience," Banger said. "Send him down with us."

Ross raised a hand. "I'm not Hardsuit qualified, but I'm a fast learner. Send me too."

Rowlin held up both hands. "I didn't assemble you to get volunteers. I need intel, and fast. First, tell me everything you know about Dragon Master."

"Sam first met him in Hong Kong, where he gave her the key to Poseidon's Sword," Ross said. "At that time, he was working for the Atlantean remnant hiding in the Himalayas."

Max hit a button on a phone speaker positioned

in the center of the long table. "I have my dad and Lance on the phone." He spoke near the central speakers. "Dad, tell me anything you or Lance know about Dragon Master."

Jeff said, "During the flight from Hong Kong to Honolulu, he admitted he'd captained the ship that kidnapped Sam from the Weddell Sea. He claimed he serves Sam now that she's Queen of Atlantis."

Lance interrupted. "The part about serving her is a lie. He leads a group called Way of the Dragon. His soldiers told us that before they took Sam from the mesa."

"Is it possible his group is working against the Chinese government?" Max asked.

"Yeah," Lance said. "Dragon Master isn't a communist. His people said something about returning to when China was ruled by divine emperors."

"Any chance his soldiers could be in control of that Chinese nuclear-powered submarine that took Sam and parked in front of the pyramid?" Max asked.

"The Chinese are known for playing the long game," Jeff said. "Way of the Dragon could've been working toward this goal ever since the communists took over China."

"How does wiping out a large portion of the world's population help them take control of their homeland?" Kip asked.

"Maybe they're counting on world powers to

help them overthrow the government after they blame the disaster on Communist China," Jeff said.

"This could be our excuse to destroy their sub without starting World War Three." Max grabbed the ship's phone. "Get me SECNAV and hurry!"

Weapon Chamber

I waited until Dragon Master's divers were positioned in front of the statues of Solraya, Luna, and Blaze, the Goddesses of Sun, Moon, and Fire. I trusted the ancient defense system to read my electromagnetic energy signature and accept me as the queen. I also counted on that system to attack my dive companions who had the wrong body energy.

Nothing would happen until they touched the crystals. If I was wrong about the system sparing me, the Atlantean weapon would never be fired, but there'd be no one left to deal with the nuke.

I glanced at the divers. "Place your graspers on the lighted crystals held by the goddesses."

The moment they touched the crystals, a loud ping reverberated inside the chamber.

"Good, that means the system is working," I said. "The next step is for you to remove the crystals with one quick pull. Now!" I knew the crystals couldn't be removed.

When the divers yanked on the crystals, more loud pings reverberated in the chamber as long, deadly spears dropped from the domed ceiling and pierced their Hardsuits. Their deaths were instantaneous as the immense water pressure imploded their suits and compressed their bodies into bloody mush.

I rushed through a cloud of gory gel to the nearest diver and grabbed the knife from his belt. I needed to saw through the cable that connected my Hardsuit to the submarine. Oxygen wasn't an issue —each suit had a self-contained system that provided forty-eight hours of air. I was worried about surviving the next nineteen minutes and thirty-six seconds that kept ticking down on the bomb's timer.

For the benefit of the men listening to me in the Chinese sub's Dive Ops, I said, "It worked! The safety mechanism has been deactivated. Now I can fire the weapon. I suggest disarming the nuke first so your submarine can move a safe distance from the pyramid before I trigger the weapon."

Dragon Master's voice filled my helmet speaker. "We have time. Fire weapon first. Then I will disarm bomb."

Something in his tone told me he'd never disarm the bomb.

"Stand by and brace for impact," I said, bluffing.

I sawed through my cable and thrusted over to the orca sculpture. The bomb's timer read 17:22.

I grabbed a ballistic spear gun that a diver had dropped on the floor.

Maybe a spear can penetrate the electronic casing that houses the bomb's controls.

I aimed a spear at the thick plexiglass housing and fired at close range. The spear bounced off the clear cover, making only a tiny scratch.

Before I could plan my next move, an explosion from somewhere outside the pyramid sent a shock-wave into the chamber. The powerful current had a bathtub-effect inside the circular room, tossing me back and forth.

I had a sick feeling the explosion had come from the Chinese submarine, which meant the remote disarming device had been destroyed.

As I floated from side to side above the nuke, which was now wedged between two of the orca statues, the timer read 15:42.

Damn.

TWENTY-EIGHT

Earlier on the USS LEVIATHAN

Max spoke to SECNAV on the satellite phone while the men in the conference room waited. Jeff and Lance were still connected to the table phone.

"Understood, Admiral, I'll hold." Max turned to his men. "We're at DEFCON 1 now. SECNAV is conferring with the President and the Joint Chiefs. The UK raised hell with China after *Audacious* was sabotaged. Add that to the three attacks on our ships by North Korea, and we're dangerously close to World War Three."

Max glanced from Banger to Kip. "While we wait, what can you tell me about the defense mechanisms inside the pyramid?"

"The British archaeologist was killed when he

tried to move the diamond rhombus," Banger said. "The first time he touched it, we heard a loud pinging sound. Then, when he tried to turn it, more of those sounds blasted through the chamber, and spears dropped down from the ceiling and pierced his Hardsuit."

"And after Ace got killed, I went in with shields for Banger and me," Kip said. "The system kept dropping spears on us until we were about halfway down the corridor to the outside exit."

"Was it different when you guys went in there with Solraya and Blaze?" Max asked.

Banger nodded. "I avoided contact with everything, and nothing bad happened when Solraya touched the same diamond rhombus the Brit had handled. It just lit up and activated all the crystals held by the chamber's perimeter statues."

"It was the same for me with Blaze," Kip said. "I didn't touch anything. When she touched the Goddess of Fire's crystal, it lit up and sent a light beam into the diamond. That brilliant gem sent out light beams that activated the crystals held by the other three deity statues, and then it blazed like a miniature sun. The defense system never activated. I'm not sure if the goddesses' presence protected us, or if we were left unharmed because we didn't touch anything."

"If the security system recognizes Sam as Queen of Atlantis, she'll be safe no matter what she touches. That means they might be able to make her trigger the weapon." Max clenched his jaw.

"Maybe not," Banger said. "Unless Dragon Master knows something we don't, I didn't see anything in that chamber that looked like a trigger. The system was energized a month ago, but it hasn't done anything except produce brilliant light."

"I agree with Banger," Kip said. "There probably isn't just one thing that has to be touched to fire the weapon. That chamber has the most complex system of electromagnetic energy fields I've ever seen."

Jeff's voice filled the speakers. "I know Sam. She wouldn't have warned me to move the airline's people and assets if she knew they couldn't force her to fire the weapon."

"Maybe she didn't know for sure," Mike said. "Remember, she'd never seen that chamber. She didn't know it was radically different from the weapon in the Himalayas."

"Or she learned something from Dragon Master that convinced her the weapon would be fired, and that's why she warned my dad," Max said. "She knew he'd tell me."

The Secretary of the Navy's voice blasted from the satellite phone's speaker. "China just confirmed they lost control of their nuclear-powered submarine two hours ago. They suspect Way of the Dragon infiltrated their navy. I just ordered *Texas* to blow them out of the water. Have you heard any-thing from our civilian asset inside the pyramid?"

"No, sir, our only means of communication with her is if she contacts her mother telepathically and then Loren relays the message via phone from Scotland," Max said.

"You have ten minutes. If we don't get confir-mation that the weapon is secure, we have to de-stroy that pyramid. Call Loren Starr."

"Aye, sir, I'll call her now." Max hit disconnect and immediately dialed Sam's mother.

He explained the situation to Loren. "Sam's life depends on you contacting her right away and get-ting back to me with an answer."

"I understand, Max. I'll do my best. Please help her any way you can from your end."

"Believe me, Mrs. Starr, we don't want to lose her either, but millions of lives are at stake. Please hurry!" He set down the phone and informed his men.

Weapon Chamber

I racked my brain for a solution as the minutes ticked down. Of course, I'd heard the stories about the megalodons *Leviathan's* crew had destroyed re-cently in these waters. Too bad there wasn't a baby megalodon left to swim in here and swallow the nuke.

I stared at the blazing diamond held in place by

the orca statues. It held tremendous electromagnetic energy, fed by a hundred and four crystals blasting their light beams into it.

Hmmm.

I tried to move the nuke. It was wedged between two orca statues and was probably too heavy for one person to lift.

Then a thought hit me.

I wonder if the kraken has a baby, and if that baby is small enough to fit in here but big enough to do what I need done?

I sent the monster a command and waited. Time was running out fast.

The timer read 9:11.

Not a good number.

My mother's voice filled my head. *"Sam! Tell me what's happening. If the Navy doesn't hear from you right away, they'll torpedo the pyramid."*

I answered telepathically, *"Tell them not to destroy the pyramid. Way of the Dragon placed a nuclear bomb on a timer next to the Atlantean weapon as backup. I have a plan to disarm it. Call them now—hurry!"*

"How much time do you have before the bomb explodes?"

I glanced at the timer. *"Eight minutes."*

"Oh my God, Sam!"

"Call now and tell them not to torpedo the pyramid!" I cut our connection.

Water swirled around me as a dark form blocked the light on the entrance side of the chamber.

I moved behind the orca sculpture and held my breath.

A giant squid about thirty or forty feet long had slithered into the chamber.

7:22 counted down on the timer.

The baby kraken paused and then reached for me.

The saying "Be careful what you wish for" popped into my head as I struggled to connect telepathically with the monster.

USS LEVIATHAN

Max took a deep breath. "Based on the assumption that the pyramid's defense system won't attack unless you touch something, I'd like to send Kip, Banger, Mike, and Oz in there to help Sam—but there's no guarantee the giant squid won't kill you. It's up to you guys."

All four men stood.

Banger said, "Send us in, Captain."

Max glanced at SEAL Commander George Bern. "Go with them to Dive Ops and supervise the preparations. Get them geared up and ready. Then wait for my order to deploy."

"Aye, Captain," Bern said and led the men down to Dive Ops.

Right after they left, the satellite phone rang.

Max answered and recognized Loren's voice.

He listened as she explained about the nuclear weapon and the short time left.

"Thank you, Loren. I'll do my best." He ended the call, punched in the number for SECNAV, and engaged the speaker.

When the Secretary of the Navy answered, Max said, "I just got a message from Sam, sir. She said the Chinese dissidents planted a nuclear bomb next to the weapon in the pyramid. It's set to go off in eight minutes, but she's working on disarming it."

"Considering the time lag since you received her message, we probably have about five minutes. I'll warn *Texas* to move back to maximum firing range before they destroy the pyramid. We can't risk having that nuke explode into the fault line."

"Sir, if you bury the bomb in rubble, won't it still explode?" Max asked.

"We have to take that chance. It's our only option."

"Sam's also an option, sir. My money is on her. Give her two minutes."

"It'll take at least that long to reposition *Texas* to a safe firing range. If our girl isn't out of there by then, there's nothing we can do. That pyramid has to be destroyed."

The men at the table had been listening to Max's conversation on speaker.

"Understood, sir." Max pocketed the satellite phone. "Sorry, Ross, I tried." He snatched up the interphone and punched in the number for Dive Ops. "Bern, cancel the dive mission. There's a nuke in the pyramid, and *Texas* has been ordered to destroy it."

Max called the bridge. "XO, sound general quarters and steam east at flank speed. Order the crew to secure the ship. A nuke may explode two thousand feet beneath us in the next few minutes."

As the klaxon horn blared, the Special Ops soldiers rushed from the conference room to help the crew.

TWENTY-NINE

Weapon Chamber

I exhaled a sigh of relief after a tense few seconds during which I finally managed to establish communication with the baby kraken. I knew I'd succeeded when it wrapped its tentacles around the two orca statues that were pinning down the bomb.

The rhombus blazed above the side of the nuke.

I had to time this just right.

I stood close to the brilliant jewel and waited. The squid yanked two orca statues off their mounts, up and away from the bomb. All four orca statues had been holding the massive diamond in place. When two statues were removed, the gem fell.

I caught it and instantly felt its power surge through me.

One hundred and four crystals ceased sending

their light beams. The room darkened, the rhombus and the bomb timer providing the only light. Although the ancient weapon was no longer armed, the diamond retained a massive energy charge.

The timer read 0:07.

I rammed the bottom tip of the energized jewel into the bomb's control panel as hard as I could. Sparks flew but extinguished quickly in the water.

The panel light blinked, and the plexiglass cover popped open. I spotted a red covered switch and flipped it to the OFF position. The timer stopped at 0:01.

I called Mom telepathically. *"Hurry and tell the military I disarmed both weapons!"*

"Good, now get the hell out of there!"

Assuming our military followed the when-in-doubt-blow-something-up mode of operation, I commanded the monster to carry me outside as fast as possible.

We were almost out of the pyramid when multiple torpedoes slammed into it.

USS LEVIATHAN

Max stood on the bridge, clutching the satellite phone as his ship sliced through the water at flank speed. The SATCOM rang, and he answered.

"Max, it's Loren. Sam disarmed the nuke and the ancient weapon. Tell your people not to destroy the pyramid!"

"Thank you!" He grabbed the interphone and called CIC. "Call *Texas* and tell them to hold fire. The weapons in the pyramid have been disarmed."

"Sorry, Captain, it's too late. They just fired six torpedoes into the pyramid."

"Understood. Tell *Texas* we're turning back to search for survivors." Max hung up the interphone and pounded the console.

He turned to his Executive Officer. "Turn us around and proceed at flank speed back to Atlantis. I'm not ready to give up on Sam."

"Aye, Captain, returning to Atlantis at flank speed."

Max called Mike and Ross to the bridge. They rushed in with worried looks on their faces.

"The good news is Sam disarmed both weapons —no idea how she did it. The bad news is *Texas* didn't get the message in time and torpedoed the pyramid."

Ross swallowed hard. "Was Sam inside when it blew?"

"I don't know," Max said. "The only communication we had was through her mother."

Mike picked up the SATCOM and handed it to Max. "Call my mother."

Max nodded. He punched in the number.

Loren answered on the first ring. "Is Sam safe?"

Max put the phone on SPEAKER. "We don't know. We need you to contact her and ask where she is."

"Hold on."

The men waited several minutes in silence.

Loren's voice filled the speaker. "I can't reach her. Maybe she's unconscious or…"

Mike grabbed the phone. "Mom, it's Mike. Don't even think that. Keep trying. Call us when you hear from her. In the meantime, we'll start looking."

"Okay, please find her."

Mike tapped END and handed the phone to Max. "Step one will be lots of men with night-vision binoculars scanning the sea. Don't forget the damn kraken is still out there. She can't command it if she's…unconscious."

The return trip didn't take long. Max stopped the ship over the pyramid and ordered his crew to scan the water on all sides.

The Krakens

My suited arms were wrapped around the rhombus, and a tentacle from the baby squid was wrapped around me. It managed to zoom through the exit a nanosecond before the pyramid collapsed into a massive pile of obsidian rubble.

The kid was headed straight for its mommy, and she'd be protective of her baby. I'd need all my mental focus to survive a commanded transfer from child to parent.

My mother's voice invaded my head at the

worst possible moment. I had to block her and concentrate on the giant squid.

The water was pitch black. I couldn't see the monster, but I was pretty sure she could see me. The jewel was still glowing, but it was no longer filled with blinding light.

The big kraken was my ticket to the ship. The crew would never find me at 2,000 feet in so many square miles of ocean.

And they wouldn't dare enter the depths to look for me with a dangerous sea monster cruising around.

The youngster held me out to its mommy like it was offering her a gift.

I took a deep breath and concentrated on the adult, illuminated by the big diamond and now my suit's floodlight. Her head was about forty feet high. She reached out with one of her long feeder tentacles and reeled me in close to her smart-car-sized right eye. It was the scariest thing I'd ever seen, but I couldn't afford to lose my nerve.

My steadfast mental commands must've worked because she began swimming toward the surface—or maybe she was just eager to be rid of me and my pesky orders. I glanced at my Hardsuit's digital depth gauge as the numbers grew smaller.

We breached the surface beside *Leviathan*, and the kraken lifted me to the top deck over the open area where it had deposited the vaults. It gently set me down on my side and released me. Then it vanished into the dark ocean.

In moments, I was surrounded by crewmembers. Commander Bern pulled me from the suit. I stood on shaky legs and yanked the diamond away from the Hardsuit.

"Thank you, George. That's the second time you've pulled me out of one of these metal prisons. I really hope there won't be a third time."

"Are you all right?" he asked.

"I need to sit down a minute." I sat cross-legged, clutching the two-foot-long glowing gem. The energy in it was slowly fading away. "Did the teams make it back from those downed helicopters?"

"Thanks to your kraken buddy, we all survived. Ross and Mike will be here any second. They were scanning the sea for you at the other end of the ship."

"Sam!" Ross yelled as he hurried toward me.

Max, Mike, and Derek rushed up, smiling.

"Lass, are you all right?" Ross kneeled beside me.

"I'm fine, I think." I tilted my head up as he leaned in and gave me a passionate kiss. It felt wonderful to have his strong arms around me.

But when he tried to lift the rhombus from me, I turned defiant. I wasn't sure what was driving me. Jewels had never been important to me, and I didn't need money, but I felt a strong connection to the stone I held. Maybe all the trauma had finally caught up with me.

I tightened my hold and said through clenched teeth, "I'm *keeping* the diamond!"

Mike laughed. "It's not like you can wear it, Sis."

"Doesn't matter. I'm keeping it."

Ross took my chin in his hand and turned my face toward him. "Why do you want it, lass?"

"Because diamonds are a girl's best friend—especially this one. It saved me from being vaporized by a nuke." I hugged the jewel and glared.

Ross sighed and glanced up. "Well, Captain Rowlin, it's up to you. What do you want to do about the diamond?"

"What diamond?" Max grinned. "There are no diamonds on my ship."

A crewman handed Ross a blanket.

"Right, I'll wrap Sam and her *rock* in this blanket." Ross helped me up.

Mike hugged me. "We're dying to know how you disarmed a nuke underwater."

Vicky Edwards, the marine engineer I'd saved in the Hall of Records, pushed through the men crowding around me. She held a chocolate bar in her outstretched hand. "This will make you feel better, Sam."

I shifted the full weight of the giant gem to my left arm and accepted her gift with my right hand.

A Godiva morsel melted in my mouth, soothing my jangled nerves.

"Thank you, Vicky." I savored another bite of the divine chocolate.

"I'd like to debrief you in the conference room if you're feeling well enough, Sam," Max said. "You can enjoy a glass of red wine from the bottle of Opus One I smuggled aboard in Jacksonville."

I kissed his cheek. "Anything for you, Captain."

THIRTY

Palm Beach, Florida, Two Weeks Later

Mom and Duncan flew into town and threw a lavish party at her oceanfront mansion. They wanted to celebrate my safe return and thank the key people who had helped me.

Master chef Niko Bujaj catered the party. He and his lovely wife Meliodora owned my favorite restaurant on Singer Island, The Islander Grill. I'd snuck into the ballroom earlier and admired his magnificent ice sculpture on the long buffet table. It was a pyramid with a kraken draped over it. It must've taken him hours to complete. Now it was nestled amidst an array of his gourmet delicacies, sure to please the most discerning palates.

My twin brothers, Mike and Matt, attended the

festivities along with my boyfriend, Ross, and his SAS sidekick, Derek.

Since Banger and Oz had been on the Special Ops team sent to the mesa, they were invited, along with the passengers and crew who'd shared that adventure with me.

My boss at LIA, Chief Pilot Jeff Rowlin, and his son, *Leviathan's* captain, Commander Max Rowlin, also attended. Invited with Max were his Executive Officer, Lt. Commander Vance Lowes, SEAL Commander George Bern, Scorpion pilots Jane Hoebich and Fred Lichten, Scorpion weapons specialists Scooter McCoy and Bull Simmons, marine biologist Kip Peterson, and marine engineer Vicky Edwards.

LIA flight attendants Tiesha Starkes, Barbi Leonard, Cindy Weeks, Sonia Díaz, Debbie Saari, and Patti Roth, all in their mid-twenties, were invited, and they balanced the ratio of men to women.

Carlene gripped Lance's arm and strode toward me as Ross and I strolled down the marble hall on a Persian carpet runner woven in vibrant blue hues. We entered the magnificent ballroom together as live performers at the other end of the basketball-court sized room filled the loudspeakers singing "Beyond the Sea," an oldie by Bobby Darin.

Floor-to-ceiling windows showcased the ocean view, and a polished white-marble floor reflected sparkling crystal chandeliers hanging over what was now party central.

"Have you recovered from your brief trip inside the anaconda?" I asked Carlene.

"My cracked ribs are still sore, but the bruises are gone," Carlene said, smoothing her snug, low-cut, rose satin gown. "The doc said I'll be back to ropin' cowboys in a few weeks."

I laughed. "Looks like you already roped one." I shifted my gaze to Lance. "I'm glad you both made it back safely from the mesa."

Lance, wearing a custom-fitted tux, nodded at Ross. "We survived thanks to your boyfriend and his team. After you left, Sweetwater's mercenaries flew in and attacked the Chinese dissidents."

I nudged Ross, who always looked sexy in his dress uniform. "You never told me about that."

He shrugged. "We waited while they fought each other and then finished them off."

I sighed. "I don't think Sweetwater will ever stop trying to kill me."

Duncan and Mom walked up just as I'd made the comment about my arch enemy. Duncan wore a formal kilt ensemble, and Mom sported a dazzling gown in champagne silk.

"We got so caught up in the party preparations we forgot to tell you about what happened to Lord Sweetwater last night," Mom said.

"What did he do now?"

She turned to Duncan. "Tell her, dear."

"Sweetwater was flying alone in his helicopter when he met with an unfortunate accident," Duncan said in his upper-crust Scottish baritone. "He crashed into the North Sea and is presumed drowned."

"I won't believe he's dead until they find his short, chubby cadaver." I leaned into Ross. "Remember when he vanished into the water in that underground submarine port and escaped through a secret tunnel? How do we know he didn't stage his death again?"

"We'll know soon enough." Ross tightened his arm around me. "MI6 won't be fooled twice."

Mom said, "We have a nice surprise for you. We were able to book your favorite performers from the Islander Grill, Angela Buzzeo and Mario Rodriguez, for tonight's festivities."

"They were a big hit at Mar-a-Lago last night," Duncan said.

I grinned. "Thank you! They're a big hit everywhere they perform. Seems like they know about a thousand songs."

Mario began singing "Only the Good Die Young" by Billy Joel.

Mike and Matt strolled up with Barbi and Cindy at their sides, all of them smiling.

"The four of you with your blond hair, blue eyes, and awesome good looks should be models for a Scandinavian tourist poster." I raised my glass to them.

My brothers looked handsome in their Navy dress uniforms, Barbi wore a sexy black formal with black stilettos, and Cindy shimmered in an ice-blue gown and silver spikes.

"Mike's taking me scuba diving tomorrow on that reef three miles out from The Breakers in Palm Beach," Barbi said, beaming.

"Great! I'm pretty sure there aren't any krakens out there." I laughed. "Have fun."

"Krakens?" Barbi asked.

"An inside joke." Mike raised a brow. "Not funny, Sam."

Cindy broke in, "Matt's taking me horseback riding."

"Better watch out for anacondas," Barbi said and winked at Mike.

"Now *that's* funny," Mike said when Matt and Cindy looked confused.

Angela and Mario must've noticed all the Navy uniforms because their next song was Kenny Loggins' "Danger Zone" from the movie *Top Gun*.

Changing the subject, I asked Cindy, "Did Matt tell you his fighter-pilot call sign is Rodeo?"

She looked up at him. "How'd you get that name?"

"I used to compete in rodeos—mostly in Texas, riding wild broncos." Matt nodded at me. "Sam was a barrel racer, and Mike was a bull rider."

"So, what you're saying is, crazy runs in the family." Cindy laughed.

"Yep, that about covers it." Matt winked at Mom. "Our mother has her moments too, especially when she's in Scotland."

Banger, decked out in a perfectly fitted tuxedo, sauntered up with Tiesha on his arm. "Isn't my queen looking lovely this evening?"

I admired her sleek, pearl satin gown with matching stilettos. "She certainly is, even without her emerald crown. Thanks again for saving us from that giant anaconda, Tiesha."

"It was worth it to meet my king." Tiesha gave Banger a soft kiss. "I just hope his family likes me. We're going up to Alabama tomorrow."

"They always worry women are only after me for the family fortune." He squeezed her. "But I know they'll see that her feelings are real."

"Especially since her rare emerald crown just sold for thirty million dollars at the Christie's auction in New York." I gave her a high five.

His jaw dropped. "Wow...I hope I'm not too poor for you. My share of the family trust is only worth about ten million."

She squeezed his muscular arm. "You're worth the world to me, darling."

I glanced around the spacious ballroom, staged with a few large round tables along the sides covered in white linen and flanked by blue-damask dining chairs.

Derek and Lisa were alone in a dark corner,

rekindling their relationship over a bottle of fine wine.

SEAL George Bern strode in with a gorgeous redhead on his arm. "Hello, Sam, Ross. I'd like you to meet my wife, Dolores."

Ross smiled and kissed her hand.

"Thank you for coming, Dolores," I said. "I appreciate everything your husband has done for me in some scary situations."

"That's George. He thrives in times like that," she said, obviously proud of her man.

Scorpion pilot Fred Lichten glided around the dance floor with his wife, an exotic brunette beauty, and Scorpion pilot Jane Hoebich danced with a handsome SEAL she'd met while the platoon from Virginia had been assigned to *Leviathan*.

Debbie, a stunning new flight attendant with long brown hair and big brown eyes, eased up beside me wearing a simmering red-satin gown with a plunging neckline and matching red stilettos. "Hey, Sam, how about introducing me to the Nordic god? Is he single?"

"Uh, there are a lot of guys here who fit the "Nordic god" description." I glanced from Jeff to Max to Kip to my brothers. "Which one are you interested in?"

"The one in the James Bond tux."

Jeff and Kip were the only Norsemen wearing tuxedoes, and Kip seemed entranced by marine engineer Vicky Edwards, who wore a sleek aquamarine silk gown with cut-outs in the short sleeves, matching aqua stilettos, and her kraken pendant.

I raised my brow. "Are you referring to *that* guy?" I gestured in Jeff's direction.

Debbie nodded.

"I realize you're new to our airline, but I'm surprised you didn't recognize our chief pilot. That's Captain Jeff Rowlin."

"I finished new-hire class right before your flight vanished in South America. He's been busy dealing with that and then moving all our jets to Indianapolis and back. I never got a chance to meet him." Debbie elbowed me. "So, is he single?"

I hooked my arm in hers. "Yep, come on, I'll introduce you."

After introducing Debbie to Jeff, I slipped away and greeted Max. "I'm glad you and some of your crew were able to come. I wasn't sure you'd ever get a break from your ship."

"*Leviathan* is docked in Norfolk where her battle wounds are being repaired. That freed us up for some R and R," Max said. "This is my lovely wife and better half, Jill."

"It's a pleasure to meet you, Jill. I hope your husband will get a less stressful mission next time." I smiled and raised my glass to them.

"Thank you for helping him," she said. "I don't know the details, but I know your help was crucial to his mission, so thank you."

"It was my honor," I said, "and God knows he helped me too."

Max said, "I can pretty much write my own ticket now that we've saved the world, averted World War Three, and recovered enough gold to all but eliminate the national debt. I hear Naples has a nice, relaxing Navy base, and Italy has delicious food."

Lance, who had slipped in beside me, laughed. "It sure wasn't relaxing when Jeff and I were there last fall."

"Didn't that have something to do with Sam?" Max asked.

"Doesn't it always?" Lance joked.

"Not funny." I punched his rock-hard abs.

"Italy, huh? Does that mean you're done with Atlantis?" Lance asked.

"No reason to go back there. We accomplished everything we were ordered to do." Max glanced at me. "Of course, the eggheads in Washington could keep Sam busy for years translating the scientific data stored in the Atlantean vaults."

"Or I could create a modern-day Rosetta Stone and let the techno-geeks translate all those ancient scrolls themselves. I have better things to do." I took a sip of Opus One.

Lance grinned. "Oh, I don't know, maybe sitting alone every day with a bunch of old documents might be just the thing to keep you out of trouble."

"I could develop a mold allergy. Better to get back in the cockpit where I belong."

As if on cue, Ross moved in behind me, placing his hands on my waist. "Better to be back in my arms where you belong."

I spun around and whispered into his ear, "Always."

The high-pitched clinks of a silver knife tapping a crystal glass reverberated across the ballroom.

Duncan's voice filled the speakers. "Everyone, gather 'round. We have an announcement."

Ross and I joined all the partygoers in a semi-circle in front of my mother and Duncan.

"I am pleased to announce my engagement to the most wonderful woman in the world." Duncan kissed Mom's left hand, which now sported a dazzling diamond ring. "She has agreed to become Lady Loren MacLeod on August 15th of this year."

Mom held out her left hand to show off her ring. "The wedding will be at MacLeod Castle, and you're all invited."

Mike raised his glass. "A toast to the happy couple."

Everyone raised their glasses and cheered.

Mom whispered something to Angela, and she started singing "Nobody Does it Better" by Carly Simon from the James Bond movie, *The Spy Who Loved Me*.

I hugged Mom and kissed Duncan's cheek. "I

knew he'd be perfect for you the first day I met him. Hard to believe that was nine months ago."

She nodded. "A lot has happened since then."

"Boy, is that an understatement!" I laughed and glanced around the room at all the smiling faces.

The men and women seemed to be paired up, at least for tonight.

Carlene clutched Lance's arm while Ross congratulated Duncan.

Mom flashed her fabulous engagement ring at me. The stones sparkled, reflecting light from the crystal chandeliers.

I gazed at the glittering gems and suddenly felt like I'd been transported to a distant land. An image of the diamond rhombus I'd taken from the underwater pyramid filled my head, and an invisible force tugged at me.

"Sam?" Mom's voice sounded far away.

Ross squeezed my waist and pressed his lips to my ear. "Sam."

My diamond-induced trance ended as suddenly as it had begun.

"Sorry, I drifted off. I've been under too much stress for too long. It's good to be back with family and friends."

I gave Ross a quick kiss and said, "Mom, your ring is fabulous!"

She grinned and held her hand close to her face, admiring the ring. "You'll be my maid of honor, of course."

"I'll look forward to it, and I'll be happy to help you plan the wedding."

"Thank you, dear." She hugged me and strolled away to show off her ring.

I glanced up at Ross and wondered if we were headed down a path to future matrimony. I'd never meet anyone better than him.

My mind drifted.

The diamond rhombus invaded my head again. Maybe it would lead me to a new adventure.

That'd be fine with me as long as I could fly there safely, and there'd be no caves, spiders, krakens, giant snakes, or nukes at the destination.

I laughed when Angela and Mario sang an oldie hit by Meat Loaf, "I Would Do Anything for Love, But I Won't Do That."

ACKNOWLEDGMENTS

As always, I'd like to thank my Lord and Savior, Jesus Christ for his many blessings.

My favorite destination for nighttime dining with live entertainment is The Islander Grill inside the elegant Palm Beach Shores Resort on Singer Island. Restaurant owner Niko Bujaj is a supremely talented master chef and a fun guy. Ideas for my stories flow into my head as I dine on the delicious food, sip wine, and listen to the fabulous singers and musicians. And the friendly staff always makes me feel welcome.

Favorites Angela Buzzeo and Mario Rodriguez (sometimes with Greg Carroll) sing every Friday night at The Islander Grill, inspiring guests to fill the dance floor and let loose. The Islander Grill provides top-notch live music every night.

Special thanks to my friends at the Singer Island

Hilton for being so supportive of my work. They make the world a far better place, and the covered deck there provides an ideal spot to dine and write my books. The food and service are always superb, and the fresh ocean air stimulates my creativity.

I'd like to express my deep appreciation to my brilliant critique buddies, George A. Bernstein and Fred Lichtenberg, who invest their valuable time and effort in helping me improve my work. Thanks, guys!

AFTERWORD

Dragon currents, or ley lines, are rivers of electro-magnetic energy that flow through our planet and crisscross the globe. Many of them intersect but probably not where I put them in my books.

The ancient underwater city exists, but it's not Atlantis. It's located in about 3,000 feet of water between Cuba and the Yucatan Peninsula. It has a huge pyramid, but it's not made of obsidian, and the city lacks many of the things I put in my imaginary Atlantis.

Hardsuit 2000s are real, and the U.S. Navy uses them to rescue submarines. The dive suits also have many commercial uses. I "imagineered" the USS *Leviathan* and the little Scorpion attack submarines, but similar vessels probably exist in the military.

Although *Stranded* is fiction, many of the characters in the story are based on real people I know, which made writing it a lot of fun for them and for me. The epilogue was written to wrap up the story and include my friends in one last scene. It made them happy, and I hope you enjoyed it too.

VANISHED

A SAMANTHA STARR THRILLER, BOOK 5

June 3, 7:30 a.m.

The 1939 biplane corkscrewed inverted ever closer to the ground as swirling air whipped my long ponytail into my face. The spinning terrain seemed to rush up to meet us. If I didn't do something fast, the airplane would become a dirt dart, and we'd be splattered across the wreckage like an exploded can of tomato sauce.

The student harnessed into the front tandem seat had frozen with his hands gripping the control stick and his feet locked on full left rudder. My windshield and instrument panel separated us. All I could see through the Plexiglas were the back of his head and shoulders.

Shouting into the intercom mike hadn't worked. Adrenaline pumped through my veins as

I tried reaching over my windshield to bonk him on the head. My girly arms were too short. I couldn't unbuckle my seat harness without falling out of the open cockpit, which was upside down and spinning. Reaching through the narrow space along the sidewall and stabbing him in the thigh with a huge hatpin would be my last resort.

I tried belting out dark lyrics from *Phantom of the Opera*. My voice-activated microphone blasted the Phantom's chilling words into his headset.

Kent snapped out of his trance in the nick of time.

"Holy hell, Sam! If that song was supposed to calm my nerves, it didn't work!" He relinquished the controls and wiped his sweaty hands on his pants.

I neutralized the stick, let the nose fall through, and applied rudder opposite to the spin. Once the rotation had stopped, I gently pulled out of the dive and added power to recover our altitude. Our world was right-side up again.

As the roaring engine propelled us higher into the clear morning sky, the South Florida sun warmed me, and the wind caressed my face.

"You said you wanted to learn spin entries and recoveries in my Bücker Jungmann." I throttled back as I leveled off at three thousand feet. "When you froze, I sang gruesome lyrics to jolt you from your death grip on the stick."

"Your singing was scarier than the inverted flat spin."

"*Funny*. The words seemed perfect for the situation."

"Perfect for dying!"

"Don't be so dramatic. I had to do something, and it was better than stabbing you with my great, great-grandmother's giant hatpin."

"So, if plunging into 'darkness deep as hell' wasn't bad enough, I'd also be gushing blood!"

"Geez, Kent, you sound like a drama queen."

"I didn't realize spins would be so terrifying." He sighed. "I'm too young to die."

"I'd never let that happen, especially since I have a hot date tonight."

"Ooh, is Mr. Tall, Dark, and Scottish back in town?"

"He'll arrive late tonight for a five-day visit, and I don't have any airline flights scheduled until two days after he leaves."

"Lucky you. He's hot, but he's not my type—too scary."

"And too straight." I laughed. "Ross is a captain in the UK's Special Air Service. That's why he's so intense."

I banked over sugar-cane fields and turned us back toward the Atlantic Ocean, sparkling like a sea of blue diamonds in the brilliant sunshine.

"Well, girlfriend, I think we're done for today. I need to go home and change my underwear."

"Don't feel bad. Not everyone is comfortable with aerobatics. Next time, we'll focus on approaches to stalls and spins and how to avoid them."

"Avoiding death sounds good to me. Sign me up."

"Good. Now take the controls and fly us home."

The moment he took the stick, the airplane shook.

"Where did that turbulence come from?" he asked.

"The flight controls are so sensitive that if your hands are trembling, the airplane will vibrate. Try to relax."

"Well, that's not going to happen until I've downed half a bottle of chardonnay." He sighed. "Take the airplane, Sam."

"Okay, I've got it."

During our flight to Lantana, steady airline traffic approached and departed Palm Beach International Airport a few miles north of the busy general aviation airport. To the east, the Intracoastal Waterway and Atlantic Ocean added hues of turquoise and deep blue to the panorama of Palm Beach County.

I announced my intentions over the UNICOM radio frequency at the uncontrolled airport and entered the empty traffic pattern for a landing to the east. As I flew the downwind leg parallel to the runway, I spotted a single-engine trainer taking off.

After cutting the power, I side-slipped down the final approach to keep the runway in sight. The soft whisper of air flowing over the wings was music to my ears as I eased the swept-wing biplane onto the pavement and turned off onto the broad ramp. It only took a few minutes to taxi to the rows of hangars along the southern boundary. Soon my baby was safe inside its home.

"Same time next week?" I asked my rattled student.

"If I don't lose my nerve. I'll text you the day before." Kent waved and climbed into his silver Lexus sedan.

Straddling my red Ducati Diavel, I pulled on my full-visor helmet. Wearing it was hot in the blazing sun, but it was better than becoming an organ donor. The Sunshine State wasn't known for safe drivers. I cranked up the almost-silent engine and zipped out of the parking lot.

Ten minutes later, I crossed the Southern Boulevard bridge to Palm Beach, turned left past Trump's Mar-a-Lago estate, and cruised up A1A to my beachfront condo. I'd have plenty of time before picking up my beloved at PBI around midnight.

I breezed into my sixth-floor apartment, stripped, and stepped into the shower stall. Warm water from the nozzle massaged my shoulders and back, relaxing my muscles.

Without warning, the room darkened, and I experienced a vivid vision. Muscular black men were punching and kicking Ross and his SAS team, helpless with their hands and feet tied.

As I watched the brutal beatings, bile rose in my throat, and my heart hammered my chest.

"No!" I screamed.

The vision vanished.

Available in Paperback and eBook From Your Favorite Online Retailer or Bookstore

ALSO BY S.L. MENEAR

The Samantha Starr Thriller Series

Flight to Redemption

Flight to Destiny

Triple Threat

Stranded

Vanished

Life, Love, & Laughter: 50 Short Stories

ABOUT THE AUTHOR

S.L. Menear is a retired airline pilot. US Airways hired Sharon in 1980 as their first female pilot, by-passing the flight engineer position. The men in her new-hire class gave her the nickname Bombshell. She flew Boeing 727s and 737s, DC-9s, and BAC 1-11 jet airliners and was promoted to captain in her seventh year.

Before her pilot career, Sharon traveled the world as a flight attendant with Pan American World Airways.

Sharon also enjoyed flying antique airplanes, experimental aircraft, and Third-World fighter air-planes. Her leisure activities included scuba diving, powered paragliding, snow skiing, surfing, horse-back riding, aerobatic flying, sailing, and driving fast cars and motorcycles.

Her beloved timber-shepherds, Pratt & Whitney, were her faithful companions for almost fourteen years, and she enjoyed riding her beautiful black and white paint stallion, Chief.

Sharon has flown many of the airplanes in her

debut novel, *Flight to Redemption*, *Flight to Destiny*, *Triple Threat*, and *Stranded*, Books One through Four in her *Samantha Starr Series* featuring a woman pilot.

www.slmenear.com

 facebook.com/slmenear

Lightning Source UK Ltd.
Milton Keynes UK
UKHW020842230822
407709UK00006B/518